Jim,

Thank you for always supporting and being there for me. I love you, Nicole and especially David so very much. You guys are truly my extended family.
Your love and friendship means the world to me. Know that — I love you!

Your best friend!

Julie Dennis
"2010"

We're In It For Life

Julie Dennis

AuthorHouse™
1663 Liberty Drive
Bloomington, IN 47403
www.authorhouse.com
Phone: 1-800-839-8640

This book is a book of fiction, names, characters, places and incidents are either a product of the author's imagination or are used fictitiously, and any resemblance to actual persons, living or dead, business establishments, events and locales is entirely coincidental.

© 2009 Julie Dennis. All rights reserved.

Designing layout, and graphic art by Jimmy Dunn,
Andrew Price and Intercity Oz, Inc Employee
All content,Graphic Art, Layout and Scripting Code
Copyright 1999-2003 by InterCity Oz, Inc.

No part of this book may be reproduced, stored in a retrieval system, or transmitted by any means without the written permission of the author.

First published by AuthorHouse   12/18/2009

ISBN: 978-1-4490-5127-3 (e)
ISBN: 978-1-4490-5125-9 (sc)
ISBN: 978-1-4490-5126-6 (hc)

Library of Congress Control Number: 2009912276

Printed in the United States of America
Bloomington, Indiana

This book is printed on acid-free paper.

This book is dedicated to my mother, my angel Mary E. Jones,
Thank you for always watching over me.
"I kept my promise Momma"

And thanks also to my husband, Desmond Dennis
I do love you……Still

Acknowledgements

My most incomparable thanks to: My incredible family, for all of their love and support, Rayel, Breah, Malik, Kiah, Tina, Lena, Jermaine and Ahmad.

This book is my reverie revised, of people who have touched my life, past and present,

Thanks also to my sisters, Lorraine, Elaine, Sharon and Patricia and my brother,
                Garfield Jr.

Thanks to my friend Leslie, my sounding board, and my best friend Phillis, my rock.

A special thank you to my editor; Elaine Porter

My undying thanks…, and prayers to the enduring memories of my father, brother and brothers-in-law.

        Garfield B. Jones Sr.
        Joseph A. Jones
        Clyde Tyler
        Eric Bruce Porter and
        Theodore Mathis
        My world is a lonelier place without you…

It seems ironic that I was brought up in a time when few people, if any, talked about divorce. Now that I think about it, I don't even know if people were married. Either, I was so naive that I didn't know if they were divorced already, or they just couldn't afford to get one. If there wasn't a daddy in the house the kids didn't ask, why; because, there was always someone there who ran the family--it was either a mother, a father, an aunt or uncle, or a grandparent. What I do know is that every home in our neighborhood had an older person--a sort of figurehead--in it. I'm talking about a time when you knew your neighbor and the kids that your kids played with. Back when you addressed an adult as Miss, Mrs. or Mister...when your hero was someone who was local--from your neighborhood, over on the playground shooting a basketball--or right there in your own home, and you knew him...or her.

You knew what folks were made of, because you knew something about their people. That was back when children, where children, who spoke when they were spoken to...didn't get into grown folks' business, and had to leave the room when 'those' kinds of things where talked about. They did not question--or talk back--or act as if they couldn't hear--when you told them to go outside and play. I don't know about you, but I truly miss those days.

Now, here I sit, some years later, thinking about old times... missing them, and contemplating divorce. And wondering what happened to some of the values that--I always believed--were instilled in me.

I am the youngest of seven children; therefore, no matter how old I get, I am still the baby of the family and--in some instances--still treated as such.

I had a wonderful childhood. Now, I wear so many hats, I don't know which one to put on from one day to the next. Let's see--I'm a daughter, sister, aunt, niece, cousin, wife, mother, grandmother, employee, friend and overweight mentor. It seems I get to be everything, except, myself. I'm probably an unprofessionally diagnosed manic-depressive, as well. I say probably, because I haven't had time to find out for sure, and couldn't own the diagnosis if, in fact, I am, because, my plate seems so full that there isn't even room for the fork. You know what that means don't you? Without the fork, nothing gets removed unless the whole plate gets dumped.

I don't think my plight is so different from that of a lot of women, but I know that sometimes it gets to be a bit much for me... So that is why I have decided to write about it. You know, "physician heal thyself." Therapy!....Purge.......write it down and get it out of your system. Take the time to do it! Make the time to do it... no matter how many times you get interrupted in the process. Do It!

Chapter 1

It was 1965, and I was sitting upstairs in the front window, listening to the neighborhood singing group down on the corner, harmonizing. They called themselves, "Truck Jackson and the Bicycles." On my radio, in the background, the Four Tops were singing, "Baby I Need Your Lovin'." I reached over and turned the radio off, so I could hear "Truck" and the boys a little better. They didn't even know I was listening, until they finished, and I started clapping from up in the window. They all looked up at me and after seeing that I wasn't one of my older sisters, blew me off with a get-outta-here kinda wave of the hand. To which, I yelled, "get off our corner with all that noise or I'm gonna tell my momma."

Just then, I heard Red Dog's falsetto, he was singin', "I did you wrong"... I got up and ran to the front porch so that I could hear them better, because he sounded so good singin' anything by Smokey, especially, "Ooh Baby, Baby." Lookin' up the street I spotted nosey Ol'e Miss Connie sitting on her porch and I smiled and waved, cause if I didn't she would tell my momma that I didn't…with her nosey self. Her daughter, Jocelyn came out, said something to her, and ran up the street to my house. We just sat there talking bout how cute Do-ball was lookin' these days, although, all of those guys were least four or five years older than we were….and wouldn't give us the time of day if their faces were clocks.

They were our heroes, though….whether they wanted the job or not. Poodie came up the street, bouncing his basketball right in beat with the finger snappin' of the group, then finally stopped, and held it under his arm while he listened.

Uncle Gilbert came out on the porch and hollered, "You boys go on up the street with that nonsense, makin' all that noise out here in front of my house," They started walkin' on up the street, throwin' him one of them you-make-me-sick kinda stares, while keeping the harmony tight. My Uncle Gilbert, daddy's younger brother, was something else. He and my momma never got along because he told a lie on her to my daddy; back when my daddy was in the service. I guess he thought that he was lookin' out for his brother's welfare when he was gone, by keeping tabs on my momma. I never knew what the lie was, but it must have been a doozie, 'cause it put a permanent wedge between them for years.

He was married to my favorite Aunt...Aunt Lillie; she was the sweetest person in the world next, to my momma, and I love her to death. We all live in a 4-story brownstone in the inner city of Washington, D.C. The brothers bought it together, and raised both of their families in it. We lived in the upper two stories of the house, which I always thought was strange; because, it was more of us than it was of them--and we made more noise--but that is how it was. I remember, when me and several of my girlfriends were sitting on the front porch trying to learn how to curse in Pig Latin--right outside Aunt Lillie's window. Boy, I could speak that stuff....you know, when you take the first part of a word and put it in the back and add the 'ay'--like a long 'a'--sound, but keep the sound of the word, you know--the word 'cat' would end up sounding like, 'at-cay.' We had heard some of the older kids speakin' it. I picked up on it and designated myself the "Pig Latin" teacher to my crew. Little did I know that the adults knew about it, too. I was cussin' up a "Pig Latin" storm--showing off--and explaining to Precious and them that they could do it, too, and their momma wouldn't know what they was sayin'.

Well, Aunt Lillie knew. And she was close enough to that window to hear me when I said, "Iss-may onnie-cay is so osy-nay, I ish-way at-thay itch-bay ould-way ie-day." My Aunt Lillie's voice said "ou-yay etter-bay atch-way our-yay outh-may" Translation: Me, "Miss Connie is so nosy, I wish that bitch would die." Aunt Lillie, "You better watch yo' mouth."

I was so scared that she was gonna tell my momma that I told Precious and them that I had to go in the house, 'cause I forgot to do something. I bet they knew I was goin' in so that my momma wouldn't come outside and beat my tail right in front of God and everybody, which she would have no problem doing. But Aunt Lillie never told, or if she did, she made my momma promise not to get me for it.

My Momma and Daddy were and are the nicest, most respected, and most intelligent people that I have ever known. I could not have asked for better parents, from whom I learned values, responsibility, common sense, and, most of all, love. Oh, did I forget a sense of humor--a great sense of humor to balance all of the above. They could find humor in any just about anything-- maybe not right at that moment--but, eventually, they could find something to lighten the situation ...something in there somewhere was funny. Like years later, when Uncle Gilbert passed. Momma tripped and fell going into the church for his funeral. I said to her, under my breath, "You know he probably wished that would happen." To which she replied, just a little louder than she should have, "Yeah! If I thought he did..., I go'n slap his face right there in that coffin." That turned more than few heads.....That's how we were taught get through the good and the bad times.....with humor.

Chapter 2

It was the summer before my first year in junior high school, and I was not as nervous as some of my friends, because I had an older brother who would be in his last year there. So, it wasn't like I wouldn't know anybody. Not only that, my brother had a reputation as a good ball player...and a good fighter. What folks didn't know was that he got most of his practice fighting me. We fought about everything, from him trying to pull rank and turn the channel on the only TV in the house--while I was watching it, to drinking the soda that I had cooling in the refrigerator that he told Momma and them that he thought it was his...like I said we fought each other about everything; but, nobody else could fight us.

I started junior high on the unvarnished heals of my four sisters before me. If I heard, "I can't believe that you are one of the Garrett girls, or the sister of Gloria, Sherry, Brenda, and Paige" once...I heard it a thousand times. See, I was more of a jokester that they were...being the baby and all.

Hell, that was the year they started letting girls wear pants to school. This new hairstyle called the "Bush" (also called the "Afro"), came out that year, too. We were a new breed, and had something to prove. I remember it well, because Jean Thomas, my best friend in junior high school, and I had just skipped bookkeeping class and decided to make a hall pass, outta one that Jean had from the day before. We figured we could just change the date on the thing; but, what we didn't know was that the school changed the color of the passes every day. And here we were, walking the halls, as big as dick's dog, with a green pass, while passes for today where blue. As we turned the corner and saw Mrs. Hawkins, the bookkeeping class teacher, we nudged each other like we were gonna put one over on her.

"Jackie Garrett!" she stated, loudly, "What are you two doing out of class?" I was the first to speak--since she recognized me, right off the bat--I said, "Oh, Mrs. Hawkins, we have to go to Mr. Sorrel's class for a special project."

"Let me see your pass," she said. At which time, Jean proudly waved it in her direction. We exchanged a quick we-got-her-now look, when she said, "This pass was for yesterday!"

I should have known something was going to happen, because whenever I hung out with Jean--something would happen. Jean piped up and had the nerve to say "What? Let me see that?" To which, Mrs. Hawkins responded, "You girls come with me to the Principals' Office." Well.....what seemed like a dumb idea, turned into an even dumber one, because all of a sudden, Jean broke out running... and, like a dummy....I followed.

We ran out of the school and didn't stop until we were about two blocks away. The only reason Jean slowed down then was because, between deep breaths, I wheezed...."Ok,......ok,.....Jean,.... she's not behind us anymore."--She most likely stopped at the end of the hall, and most definitely at the school door.--We, however, had stopped right in front of the 7-11, and so we decided to split a "*Slurpee,*" to help cool us down, and give us a chance to think. We sat on the wall out in front of the store and I said "My momma gonna kill me, Jean."

"No she ain't, 'cause I got an idea…"

"Jean, you don't know my momma…," I insisted. I couldn't see no way outta this one.

But, according to Jean, if you know one momma, you know 'em all, because she then proceeded to explained how she had worked her momma's nerves so bad 'til, "She just sits in the dark and eats vanilla ice cream now."

I didn't want to do anything to upset my momma like that. "Wow! How'd ya do that … and, ………………why?!"

Jean snapped, impatiently, "Stop worrying, and listen to me".

This was the plan: We would go over to Jean's house and wash and style our hair in that new bush hairstyle; then go back to school like nothing happened, because--this was the big part--Mrs. Hawkins was old, and with our new "do's", we could make the principal believe that she didn't know what she was talking about... that she had actually stopped two other students without a hall pass that morning--so how could the students that she was reporting be us?

The girls she stopped had their hair pressed. They didn't have their hair like ours.

"Girl, you are too smart for your own good," I said, impressed, not only by the simplicity of the idea; but, by it's sheer brilliance. We proceeded to put our plan into action.

Ok, tell me that Mrs. Hawkins did not call my momma and tell her that not only was I skipping class, but, I had forged school documents (the green hall pass), had run away from her, and had left the school grounds without permission. Now any one of these four things was enough to get me killed, but,....oh, no!....Jean, had all the answers, because she was whole year older than me. She got left back in kindergarten.......Now, I know why. So we went back to school, just as cool as we could be. My hair was still damp at the roots, so my bush was kinda droopin'...not like the women we had seen in the magazines at all. But, Jean explained that they had short hair like hers and that mine was suppose to droop, 'cause it was longer--but it looked good. Several of our classmates thought so, too--and had just finished telling us outside of Mr. Gregory's world history class-- when over the loud speaker came, "Will Jackie Garrett and Jean Thomas report to the principal's office, immediately". I could hardly hear my name being called over the collective, "Ooooh....you in trouble," that the passing students were crooning. I decided, then and there, that I would never listen to anything else Jean had to say from then on out, because like I told her earlier ..."my momma's gonna kill me."

After the beatin'...I felt I had learned my lesson, but I guess being grounded for a month was added on for good measure. All phone privileges were taken away. Everyday, the phone would ring, and I wasn't allowed to answer it for fear that I might, accidentally, have contact with anyone other than in school. And no hangin' out 'til the street lights came on, with the kids in the neighborhood. I can't tell you how mad I was at that 'damn' Jean,--not to mention that every other time the phone would ring, I could hear momma saying, "Jean, didn't I tell you that Jackie can't talk on the phone.... So stop calling here."

I coulda killed Jean.

"Your so-called friend is just adding to your punishment by being so hardheaded and calling here when she knows you're on punishment," momma said. I told her that it wasn't my fault that she keeps calling and that she must not be on punishment like, I AM.

"Oh really...? And what is that supposed to mean?"

"Jean's momma didn't punish her. Jean just told her that she was sorry and that it wouldn't happen again," I tried to respectfully clarify.

"Well I'm not her momma and if she don't stop callin' here, you will be on punishment until 'pigs can fly'." *I can't wait 'til I see Jean, so I can tell her to stop callin', 'cause my momma ain't playin', and she ain't gonna go sit and eat vanilla ice cream in the dark like her momma does, ...whatever that means.......*

Daddy had just come home from work and was sitting in the living room in his favorite chair. I walked up to him, and hugged him 'round his neck, from behind the chair, and said in my best, I'm-the-baby voice, "Daddy could you pleeeze talk to momma for me?"

While never looking up from the newspaper, Daddy said, "about what?" My daddy was so cool...he never got worked up like some people....anyway...

"About this punishment thing..., I said I was sorry, and it's been two weeks, since I've been able to go outside." He turned the page of his paper.

"Baby, that's between you and yo momma. You know how she is about y'all cuttin' up in school."

"But it wasn't my fault."

"Oh, really? Then whose fault was it?"

I couldn't say anything. "Ok...Well maybe it was my fault, but no phone or friends for a month is a lotta punishment...don't you think?"

"Not if your mother doesn't think so."

"Well how 'bout if I could just sit on the front porch? I wouldn't even go as far as the steps... just up on the porch."

"Well, I don't see any harm in that."

I kissed him hard on the cheek and ran outside....on the porch.

No sooner had I come out the door, did I see Oopsie and her sister Precious--coming out of Fat Man's store will a bag full of candy. I've known Oopsie, Precious, and their whole family, all my life. They live down the street.

Fat Man's was the neighborhood grocery store, which because of its unique location--smack dab in the middle of the block--made it more like our own personal store than neighborhoods that had their stores on the corner. Also, it was owned and run by a really fat man, his fat wife, and their fat sons, hence, the nickname, 'Fat Man's'."

Stopping right in front of my gate, Precious said, "Hey, Oopsi, have I been out in the sun too long, or did I eat some bad candy from Fat Man's? I could swear I see Jackie outside?"

Oopsie looked up at me, started laughing and said, "If she outside it must be 'cause Ms. Garrett is either sleep or not home."

"Shut up, both of y'all and throw me a piece of candy."

Oopsie started digging the candy outta the bag, but Precious stopped her and said, "Come get it yourself." Sending the obvious message to Oopsie that, yeah....I might be outside, but, I couldn't come off the porch--while I tried hard to remember why I had ever liked Precious in the first place.

Oopsie, the echo, chimed in, "Yeah, Jackie, come get some."

"Forget it," I said, and looked up the street where Five Pound was just turning the corner on his new ten-speed bike, with the radio attached to the under bar. Five had always been sweet on me, even though he was supposed to be going with Precious.

"I sure could use a box of pumpkinseeds and a sour pickle from Fat Man's..." Five, came to an abrupt halt in front of us and said, "I'll go get some for you," and was gone just that fast, which made

Precious so mad, 'cause she knew that if I wanted a boyfriend; heck, if I wanted Five--which I didn't--I could get him in a heartbeat.

Laughing, Oopsie said, "Who does Five go with, anyway?"

Precious slapped her on the head and stomped off saying. "Tell Five he can take those seeds and that pickle and stickem!" Boy, me and Oopsie fell out laughing, 'cause Precious really had no reason to be jealous....I wouldn't have had Five Pound on a bet.

Five used to hang out with my brother, you know, playing ball and stuff, and grinning at me every chance he could get. He would call the house and say "Hey Jackie is your brubber home?' to which I always replied." I don't have a brubber." and hang-up the phone. Five was nice, but he always usta sound so dumb. He was kidda cute, though. Five came back sliding to a screeching halt, I guess, to impress me--bike all to the side, got off it and ran up on the porch with the goods. I said, "You know Precious mad at you..." he just looked stupid and left in a hurry, peddlin' fast, in the direction of Precious' house.

I had just taken the first bite of my pickle when I did a double-take at what I saw coming up the street. I couldn't be sure because it was about half a block away and it looked like a door with hands on either side of it, being carried on someone's back. About that time, the basement door opened and my brother, Garrett, and about eight of his friends, came up the stairs. Bubba said, "Man, look at that nut...carrying a door on his back up the street!" Everybody looked and started laughing. My brother was cracking jokes talkin' 'bout "Man that's yo Momma," everybody was giggling....until the door with legs turned into our yard.

It was my momma, talking' about, "Y'all help me with this door! Some dummy threw this nice door in the trash, just had it laying in the alleyway." All the guys moved forward to help, except my brother, who looked like his face had cracked.

Never slow on the up-take, she immediately addressed the fact that I was outside, and, of course, I put it all on Daddy. She just gave me that you-betta-not-be-lying look and went on in the house. You know, to this day, they still talk about "Ms. Garrett, wit that door on her back."

Just before the street lights came on, I saw Mr. Mac pullin' up in that old Ford that he drove at no more that 10 miles-an-hour, on a good day, and parallel park in front of his house. This in itself was a show, because he would pull that car in and out about 15 times before he felt he was close enough to the curb. I always liked Mr. Mac. Personally, I think he took so long parking his car, because he was married to nosey old Ms Connie, and was in no hurry to go in the house and hear all the neighborhood gossip.

That's when I started giggling to myself and noticed that Ms Connie wasn't out on the stoop this evening. I yelled, "Hello," to Mr. Mac. He just waved his hand and kept his head hanging down and went on in his house.

Chapter 3

The street light on the corner came on and, keeping my promise to my daddy, I got up to go in for the night. As I was closing the front door, I overheard the end of a conversation my momma was havin' with Aunt Lillie. "...Yeah, I heard she was sick, but I didn't think it was serious. You know, a cold could knock Connie offa her feet; she ain't big as a minute."

"I just feel sorry for Mac," Aunt Lillie said. "That poor man work so hard, and now this..."

I was straining to hear more when my big head brother snuck up behind me--talking loud--sayin', "Momma, did you know Jackie was out here just standing in the hall!?" He laughed and I punched him on the arm as he passed, while I tried to explain, stammerin', "I wasn't just standing here....I was waiting 'til y'all stopped talking.... to ask you a question."

"You better take your noisy tail on upstairs...or else." I was glad she didn't ask me what I wanted, 'cause I never could think of a lie that fast.

The next day, Jocelyn, Ms Connie's daughter, wasn't in school. I was worried because she had gotten the perfect attendance award every year since I could remember....I couldn't wait until I got out of school to find out why. When I turned on our street, there were cars everywhere, much more than usual. Folks were going in and out of Ms Connie's house. I turned to go up our steps just as my momma and Aunt Lillie were coming out the door. Momma took my hand, and said sadly, "I know you still got one more week of punishment left, but I want you to come wit me and talk with Jocelyn, because

Ms Connie died last night. She might need someone her age to talk to about it."

I was shocked! I couldn't believe what I was hearing. Nobody in our neighborhood had ever died....at least, that I knew of. "Yes, ma'am, I'll talk to her...but what do I say?"

"You know...stuff like, 'She's in a better place.'...'God has called her home.'....stuff like that."

"Ok," I said, but I knew I would just sit there--looking dumb--and saying how sorry I was that something like this had to happen.

When we went in, people were everywhere, so many that it took me a minute to recognize Jocelyn, sitting in the corner in her momma's favorite chair just rocking back and forth. I went over to her and asked if she wanted to go out on the porch and get some air--and get away from all the people. She said, "Ok," and we made our way through the crowd and out on the porch.

We just stood there for what seemed like a long time before I said, "I sure am gonna miss Ms Connie sittin' up here on this porch all the time."

Jocelyn looked at me, sadly, her eyes real red and said, "Yeah, I know what you mean. She was out here all the time wasn't she?"

"Yep, with that blue dress on...with the little white dots all over it..."

"That was her favorite porch-sittin' dress..." Jocelyn said.

"It must have been, 'cause she always had it on when she was telling my momma 'bout somethin' I did."

Jocelyn kinda gurgled--you know, that sound you make when you cryin' and laughin' at the same time--and the tears ran down her cheeks. I reached over and hugged her. I told her, "I know I'm not your momma, but me and my momma will always be here for you if you need anything." She laid her head on my shoulder and cried harder than I ever heard anybody cry before in my life.

I could hardly sleep that night just thinking about how I would feel if something like that happened to my momma. I felt so sorry for Jocelyn, her older sister Bonnie, and their brother, Poodie.

This would be the first funeral I had ever gone to...and I didn't know what to expect. See, we were Catholic; matter of fact, we were the only Catholic's in the neighborhood. Everybody else was Baptist..., or something. The service was gonna be at the New Hope Baptist Church up on 8th Street. I passed that church everytime I went to Stan's Discount store and there was always some kinda noise..., drums or shoutin'...comin' outta there. In our church everything was always whispered or talked in Latin. Also, in our church, girls had to wear somethin'--a hat or a scarf--over their head...? So, the most noise I ever remember hearin' in church was the whole second row tryin' not to laugh, the day Marie Jackson came tippin' in late, with a Bon-Ton potato chip bag pinned on her head.

The service was very nice; everybody was trying real hard not to cry too loud. Everybody, that is, except Ms Lizabeth. Ms Lizabeth would read the papers to find out who died just so she could go to their funeral and cut up. I remember hearin' my momma and Aunt Lillie laughin' about how one time 'Lizabeth' went to some man's funeral and cried so loud that his wife sent her son over to find out who this woman was, fussin' so and raising cane over her dead husband. Momma and Aunt Lillie cracked up laughing about that one. Aunt Lillie chuckled, "Bet it won't stop her none. Chile, she lives to go to other people's funerals." This funeral was no exception, but I felt kinda sorry for her, 'specially since they had lived next door to each other for over 20 years, and she loved Ms Connie like a sister.

Just as the services were about to end, Ms Lizabeth did her thing, shouting, "Lawdy Jesus, Lawdy Jesus, Why, Why, Why!!! Why Lord, why??! And just as the ushers reached her,...with perfect timing, she fainted. It was a good thing they didn't miss a step or Ms. Lizabeth would have hit the floor. When I said that to my momma, she said, "Yeah right," and winked at my aunt saying, "Lizabeth always did have good timing," but they wished that they had been asked to do the ushering that day 'cause it would have been a different story.

That next day, me, Wanda, Oopsie, Precious, Gail, and Tee all met over to Jocelyn's house. We tried to make it look like a coincidence, but I had called all of them the night before. I thought that if we could keep Jocelyn busy, she might not be so sad. Precious was the only one of us who didn't go to the funeral, and she chose this time to start talking about it. We all tried to give her that wide-eyed could-you-change-the-subject please-look, but, she just ignored us, looked Jocelyn right in the face and said, "I heard your momma looked just like she was sleep, layin' up there in that coffin." Jocelyn burst out crying and ran upstairs.

"Stupid didn't you see us looking at you like you was crazy?" I was upset, too.

"Yeah, but y'all look at me like that all the time. I'm sorry, but I was just tryin' to make conversation. All y'all sittin' up here like y'all dead or something, shoot."

"Forget it!" I said. "I'll go check on her."

Gail said, "Maybe we oughta just go home and let her alone for a while."

"Yeah, maybe you're right, let's go home, y'all," I agreed.

When we got outside, Tee asked, "Has anybody seen Bonnie, since the funeral?"

Bonnie was Jocelyn's older sister. Bonnie was strange....she always had been....."No," I said. I wonder how she's handling all this. Y'all know Bonnie was already crazy."

"Yeah, we know," everybody replied.

"She'll probably just walk around with her hair dyed some weird color and her eyebrows shaved off again," Oopsie said.

"Yeah, she probably will," said Wanda. "Y'all know what we could do? We could have a séance', so Jocelyn could get to say goodbye to her momma........that's probably why she so sad, 'cause she didn't get to say everything she wanted to before Ms Connie died."

"I don't know about that," I said.

"We could try it! It might make her feel a little better," Precious said.

"Ok, but how do you have a séance?" I asked.

"The one I saw on TV..., all they did was turn the lights out.... hold hands and lit some candles," explained Wanda.

"We got some candles at home. I can get'm!" I said. "Let's do it! It's supposed to be at night, right?"

"Yeah!...And on a Saturday," Precious confirmed.

"That's only two days away. By then, we'll have time to get everything together," I planned out loud. We all agreed that the séance was gonna take place Saturday at 7 o'clock, since it would be seven of us there; plus, it had to be at Jocelyn's house because I figured her spirit would be strongest there.

Saturday arrived, and I got the box of candles that my momma kept in the bottom of the linen closet. There were seven of 'em in there. I had always heard that seven was a lucky number. I took that as a sign that what we were gonna do was the right thing. I came out on my front porch and looked up and down the street. I didn't see Wanda, Precious, or anybody. Just then the street lights came on, and I knew it was 6 o'clock, 'cause the street lights always came on at exactly 6 o'clock everyday. I sat down, kinda looking off in space, and having second thoughts about what we were plannin 'to do, when Oopsie's dumb laugh broke my concentration. She and Precious had just come around the corner from Gail's saying that Gail's momma said she couldn't come out right now.

"What do you mean she can't come out right now?" I gasped. "We won't have seven people if she don't come!"

Precious thought for a second, and then said, "Maybe we can get Bonnie to sit in on the séance."

"Are you crazy!?" I said. "Ain't no telling what Bonnie will do if we really do talk to Ms Connie, wit her crazy self." Just then we heard, "Hey y'all here I come!" Gail came running down the street. "I snuck out when my momma got on the phone. It'll take her a while before she even notices I'm gone."

I looked at her and said, "Girl, you crazy, your momma gonna break yo' neck."

"Well c'mon then let's get started." Gail stopped for a second to catch her breath.

"It's too early," I said. "We gotta start at seven or it won't work."

Everyone seemed to say, "Who said?" collectively, and since I didn't have an answer we went on up the street where we were joined by the others.

Jocelyn came down the stairs and walked into the dining room, lookin' a lot better than she had two days ago.

"Hi, Jo,… How ya doin?" I asked.

"Fine," she said. "How y'all doin', and why y'all got all them candles?

"Because…, we got a surprise for you!" I announced.

"Yeah….What?" she asked.

"Well, we were talkin' and we thought that maybe the reason you are so sad is because you didn't get a chance to say some things to your momma that you wanted to say before she…died." Jocelyn's smiled faded a little. "So, we thought that if we had a séance you could talk to her… You know, to say some of the things you wanted to say and maybe you won't be so sad anymore."

Jocelyn, immediately, started smilin' again, "Do you think it could really work? I mean, how you go about doin' something like that?"

"Well, first, we all have to sit down and close all the curtains, so that it's real dark in here, 'cause they won't come if it's not dark."

"Who is 'dey'?" Oopsie piped up. "I thought you was tryin' to contact Ms Connie! 'Dey' seems like more than one person, and I'm not tryin' to call up no whole group of dead people."

"Shut up! Oopsie!" Gail said. "Ain't no 'DEY,' she just tryin' to explain what we tryin' to do to, fool! You so scared of everything."

"Anyway, Jo,….like I was sayin'," as I rolled my eyes at Oopsie, "we need to close the curtains, turn out all da lights, and light these candles. Then we all have ta hold hands and rock from side-to-side sayin', 'Miss Connie…, Miss Connie…., caaaan yooou hear meeee? Miss Connie…., Miss Connie…., caaaan yooou hear meeee? If you heeeaaar meeee, give me a sign.' like that, over and over, 'til she gives us a sign or speaks through one of us."

Oopsie screamed, "WHAT!! 'TIL SHE SPEAKS THOUGH US?!.....SPEAK THROUGH US?.... WHAT YOU MEAN SPEAK THROUGH US?!"

"Sometimes, since they can't talk by themselves they use one of the people in the room to speak through," Precious said.

"Well," stated Oopsie. "I can tell you who she won't be speakin through! ME!... I'm goin' home right now!"

Gail grabbed Oopsie before she could leave, "C'mon, Oopsie, stop actin' so stupid, she ain't gonna speak through you even if she wants to say somethin, 'cause you too scared. She'll probably speak through Jackie or somebody, 'cause they ain't as scared as you. So sit down and hold my hand....and shut up!"

Yeah, but I really don't want Ms. Connie speaking through me either, 'cause I remembered what I said to all of dem that day in pig latin 'bout wishin' her nosey ass would die.

I was getting kinda scared, 'til Jocelyn started to talk, "Ok, let's get started, 'cause I sure would like to say somethin' to my momma, you know,...just tell her not worry about me, and daddy and dem, and to tell her that I love her one more time.

"Ok, then," I said. "Oopsie, you pull down da shades and close da curtains. Wanda, you turn out da lights and light the candles. Let's get started."

Chapter 4

We lit the candles, put all of them in a circle on the table, sat down, and held hands. I started the chantin' in a low, shaky voice--not on purpose, though--'cause I really was gettin' kinda scared. Oopsie, Wanda, and everybody started chimin' in, "Miss Connie,....Miss Connie, caaan yooou hear meeee? Miss Connie... Miss Connie... Caaan yooou hear meeee?" After doin' this for what seemed to me like 10 or 15 minutes, the candles started glowin' a little bit brighter and kinda flickerin'. I looked around to see if I was the only one who was noticin' this, and I could tell by the look on Oopsie's face that I wasn't. To tell the truth, I didn't hear Oopsie chantin' anymore, but her mouth was movin' like she still was. I looked at Jocelyn and she had her eyes shut real tight..., chantin' the Miss Connie chant...over and over. But, Wanda wasn't lookin' as determined as she had before, either.

About that time, we heard what sounded like something was movin'. It wasn't a loud sound...just a sound...like something moved. Just to be sure, in between the chantin', I said, "Ok, let's stop rocking now, but on keep chantin'." I did that because I wanted to make sure it wasn't one of us who made that noise, 'cause of the way we was rockin'. Everybody continued to chant "Miss Connie,... Miss Connie..." All of a sudden, a loud noise--like a thud--made everybody stop with their mouths open. It was so quiet in there that all we could hear was each other breathin'. Everybody was lookin' at everybody else like, "Did y'all hear that?" Nobody moved...or said anything for about two or three minutes--well. it seemed like it, anyway--and then the thud sound came again. But this time it sounded like it was in the hall right offa the dining room. We got quiet so fast....completely silent....nobody moved or made a peep. Finally, Gail whispered, "I know y'all heard that noise."

Oopsie breathed shakily, "I know....I heard it!"

Jocelyn looked around, saying, "Momma is that you? Momma can you hear me? If you can hear me let me know." By this time we were all lookin' at her like, 'Don't call her no more...', 'cause, it sounds like she really tryin' to contact us.' Just then, six of the candles went out! And wouldn't you know it, all of the candles was out except the one in front of Oopsie. She was just sittin' there with her eyes as big as dinner plates, starin' at me like I was suppose to do something. Then another thud came from out in the hallway and we all turned, strainin' our eyes to see what was goin' on--which was hard to do, 'cause the only light we had left to see by was from the candle in front of Oopsie.

Just then, I saw something move in the hall, I gasped and squeezed the hell outta Wanda's hand which made her holler. Jocelyn, speaking in the direction of the hallway said, "Momma is that you?" To which, a soft voice replied, "Nooooooo!"

Well..., that was all we needed to hear! You never heard so much yellin' and screamin', as we were runnin' into each other, trying to bunch up in the corner. I know for a fact that Oopsie peed on herself, 'cause Gail slipped on somethin' wet, tryin' to get past Wanda for a good space. I closed my eyes real tight, so that when I opened them I would be able to focus better in the dark, and when I did...I swear, I saw spots--I don't mean the kind you get from closing your eyes real tight--I mean spots like the ones on the dress that Ms Connie use to wear all the time!

I screamed and took off running towards the hallway, 'cause whatever was out there was between me and the front door, and I was determined to get out of that house as fast as I could, no matter who I had to run over...or kill...to do it! When I broke out runnin', so did everybody else, and boy, we were hollering and screaming! I ran into somebody...or something... in that hall, knocked em' down, stepped over them, and tore that front door up getting out of there.

I could hear Oopsie yellin', "Get offa me, GET OFFA... ME!........ AAAHHHH!.....

I don't know where everybody else went, but I ran home as fast as I could with Oopsie's screams ringin' in my ears. I ran straight in my house, up seventeen stairs--like they was one-- straight in momma and daddy's bedroom--eyes all wide, breathin' all hard--like something crazy. My momma turned 'round from where she was sitting, at her sewing machine, and said, "Girl, what in the world is the matter wit you, you look like you done seen a ghost!

I was too scared to go to sleep and too scared to stay awake. I had to go to the bathroom, but it was all the way down the hall, so I just held it. I wasn't tryin' to go nowhere, unless I could get one of my sisters to go with me. I looked over at Paige, sleeping in the bed on the other side of the room, and wondered what she would say if I woke her up just to go the toilet with me. She would probably knock me out if I woke her up for that. I decided to start makin' noises like I was sick on my stomach and about to throw up, groaning and gaggin' loud enough so she would hear me and get up to take me to the bathroom before I threw up in the bed. It worked, 'cause when she heard me, she jumped up sayin', "Jackie..., you sick? C'mon let me get you to the bathroom before you throw up all over your bed. When we got back to the bedroom, I was wide awake, scared to death, while I listened to her breathing as she fell back to sleep.

The next morning, after church, Momma was tellin' Daddy that she was going to cook some extra chicken, so she could send some over to Mac and them for dinner. Daddy said that would be nice and he was sure Mac would 'preciate it. Momma said that she would get one of the girls to take it over, since Mac would be too proud to take it from her. She said that she would probably send me. I just sat there trying to think about how I was gonna get outta having to make that delivery. I hadn't talked to anyone since the "séance" and I wasn't tryin' to go over there until I knew it was safe. I decided to call Precious and Oopsie.

Oopsie answered the phone on the third ring. "Hey, Oopsie how ya doin?"

"IN TROUBLE…, that's how!"

I was curious, "Trouble…? What for?"

"Well, after you ran over us last night, tryin' to get outta there…, I knocked Precious and Wanda down Jocelyn's steps and Precious got all bruised up and everything. Wanda made out ok, 'cause she landed on toppa Precious, but you know dem wrought iron steps ain't no joke. They alright though; just bruised up a little."

"Man, that's terrible! Oopsie!" I asked, "Was that really Ms Connie out there in that hall?"

Oopsie sighed, "Well if it was, she dead again, 'cause I know I got four or five good licks in, and Gail was still beatin' on her when I ran out.

Shocked, I said, "We need to call Jocelyn."

"No!…YOU need to call Jocelyn…and call me back and tell me what she said."

"Ok," I agreed, "I'll call you back."

Boy, dialing them seven numbers on that telephone took forever. My finger slipped outta them holes twice, and I had to keep startin' over, but I finally dialed it. The line was busy. *Whew,* I thought! *I'll try back later.* I didn't know what I was gonna say to Jocelyn anyway. I decided to go outside for a while.

My sister Sherry was just coming back from the store when we passed each other on the front stairs.

"Jackie," she asked, "have you seen Bonnie today?"

"Naw, Why?"

"She looks like she got hit by a bus…, or something."

"Whaaaat?!?"

"Yeah, I just saw her goin' in the house, and she was lookin' real bad."

I just stood there with my mouth open as Sherry went on in the house.

I ran over to Precious and Oopsie's house and banged on the door. When Precious opened the door, I almost fell in, sayin', "Y'all, my sister said that somebody beat up Bonnie last night! She said look like Bonnie got hit by a bus or… somethin!"

"She must gone out while we was down there havin' the seance." Precious reasoned.

"I know 'cause, she was there when we got there... She let us in." Oopsie said.

"Dag," I said "what else is gonna happen to that family?!"

Chapter 5

Joe Hot Dog came staggering up the street headed for our front steps. That's where he always usta come when he was drunk, so nobody would bother him. He would come there because he was my oldest brother, and he knew I would sneak him a sandwich or two. Joe got the name "Hot Dog" one summer when he was little and went to camp. When all the counselors had gone to bed Joe snuck up to the camp kitchen and got caught after eatin' about 10 raw hot dogs. When all the kids heard about it the next day, they started calling him that, and it stuck. Anyway, that all happened before I was born, because Joe was 20 years older than me. I don't know when, where, or why Joe started drinking. All I know is that ever since I could remember he drank. I often wondered if he started drinking because of the way things were for a young black man when he was growing up, or if he started drinking after he had that accident on that machine that cut off some of his fingers.

I used to think that my momma was so mean to him, sometimes. She would fuss at me for fixing him a sandwich. I just couldn't understand that! I think back on it now, and I realize that she was one of the first people I knew who practiced "tough love" and knowing my momma as I do, it had to be even tougher on her than it was on him. She loves all of us so much!

See..., me not fixing him a sandwich would make him find a job, become responsible and have money enough to buy groceries so he could make his own sandwiches. I guess that's what she prayed for anyway. Joe died in 1968 from over exposure and cirrhosis of the liver.

I was 15 when he was 35; just a little older than Jesus was when he died.

Chapter 6

My daddy worked for a big company and they were sponsoring a ski trip for their employees and their families to Pennsylvania. Each year they did something in a big way. I guess to show everybody how well they treated the people who worked for them. Earlier that year we had gone on another trip to an amusement park and that was in Pennsylvania, too. Anyway..., none of us had ever been skiing before and we were all real excited about going. We left about 4 o'clock in the morning to meet the charter bus up on New York Avenue.

It was cold, so I asked momma to buy me a cup of hot chocolate from the vending machine inside the snack bar. It was interesting to me to put your money a machine, watch that little paper cup with the handles drop down and fill with hot water and cocoa. I was very careful sliding the little glass door back to get my cocoa; because, it was steaming hot and those paper handles were close to the cup. Just then, everybody started loading on the buses. I stood there blowing on my cocoa for a minute or so, and then I took a sip. Well, I experienced my first chartered bus ride with the numbest burnt tongue known to man. It took all I had, not to stick it on the cool glass of the window beside me for the whole trip from DC to Pennsylvania.

Just then, momma mentioned that the Bingham's were coming on the trip, too. Mr. Bingham, worked with my daddy, so I shoulda figured they was comin', but....anyway...maybe this was just the thing to take my mind offa how bad my tongue was burnt--I started chuckling, and Momma said, "Jackie you better not tease Marsha when you see her, either."

"Groovin," was playing on my little transistor radio, and I was doing just that 'til ole Marsha Bingham, with her buck-teeth self, flopped down beside me on the bus. She had two of the best looking brothers in the world. Marsha was the youngest, the only girl, and you could stand under her front teeth in the rain... She did have real pretty hair, though. She also had on a fake leather jacket. I knew it was fake when I saw it, but, I really knew it for sure when she wore it when we went to Hershey Park and she tried to walk through this ride called "The Barrel."

The Barrel was a big drum, made out of wood, that never stopped turnin', and you had to walk all the way through it to the other side and try to keep your balance. I walked through and staggered safely out the other side, but, Marsha started through, and fell with that 'pleather' jacket on and stuck to the barrel like a piece of bazooka bubblegum. They had to stop the drum to get her out of there 'cause as it turned, she just kept stickin' 'til it was half way up and then she would drop back down and get stuck again. They almost had to scape her outta that thing...I couldn't hardly look at her without remembering that. I can still see the roof of her mouth, while she was hollering...I still can't get that picture outta my head.

I looked back at my momma, who was sitting in the seat, right behind me, before I said, "Marsha, I see you're not wearing your *leather* jacket, ...why not?"

"Oh, that old thing," she said. "I gave it away after we came back from Hershey Park." I just grinned.

"How come Gregory didn't come?" Marsha asked, "I sure was expecting to see him."

"He didn't come, 'cause he had football practice..., or something." I really didn't care why he didn't come, but I couldn't wait to tell him that ole buck teeth Marsha had been asking about him; he couldn't stand her.

The snow was so beautiful; the snow didn't seem to feel as cold here as it had back home. We all got off the bus and headed for the ski lodge; Sherry, Paige, Momma, and me.

"How many layers of clothes you got on?" Paige asked Sherry. "Where'd you think we were going?....To Alaska...?"

"Paige, you can act as stuck up as you want to, but I'm going to make sure I stay warm. I'm not tryin' to be lookin' cute for nobody."

"Some of us know how to do both," was Paige's snooty repy.

"All right girls, cut it out!" Momma ordered.

I asked momma if she was going to put on some ski's, she laughed, and said, "Are you crazy? No, I'm going to sit in that lodge, with my feet up, and drink hot cocoa." I wondered if I should warn her about drinkin' that hot cocoa, but..... Momma continued, "If you're looking for me, I'll be right in front of that big window up there watching other folk break DEY legs! So, y'all go on..., and be careful."

We walked over to the ski rack just as Mr. Jack, one of my daddy's co-workers, came out of the lodge, all dressed up in his new ski clothes--they even smelled real new--and talking trash--like he always usta do, saying… "What y'all doin'..? Trying to get up your nerve? Let ole Jack show you young girls how this ski thing suppose to be done!"

We all looked at him, and muttered in long-suffering unison, " 'Hello, Mr. Jack'."

"Mr. Jack? Do you really know how to ski?" I asked him.

"Little girl, I put the 'S' in ski'n!" He bragged, winking and laughin' real loud.

"I just bet you did." Paige replied, under her breath, sarcastically---while me and Sherry rolled our eyes--behind his back--'cause we wasn't supposed to be disrespectful to grown-ups..., not even dumb ole Mr Jack.

"Now, if y'all just beginners...," he instructed, "ya need to go over there to that little slope over there,...but ME!...I gets on the lift! You know the one that takes ya up on top of the big slope. Now, who's gonna go up on the big slope with Mr. Jack?"

Backing away, we all assured him that we would get over there later, but for now, we wanted to warm up on the little slope.

"OK, I'll see y'all later, then." He stomped off--ski's sideways..... showin' off..., as usual.

We got fitted for our ski's and carried them over to the bench so that we could put 'em on. I finished first and stood up. "You can't even bend your ankles in these boots! How you gonna control your feet... if you can't bend your ankles?" I asked. I was starting to rethink this skiin' stuff.

"You have to lift your feet from the knees," Paige said, as she got up to demonstrate.

"Oh...! OK..., I can do that!" I said, impressed by how much she knew about skiin'.

We all started over to the slope giggling and trying not to look like this was our first time, even though it was. At the bottom of the beginner's slope, there was this rope about 3 inches around, attached to a pulley,...or something, up on top of the slope, and folks were suppose to grab on to this rope to be pulled up to the top of the slope. Then you could ski back down. Well, not only did the rope pull, but it also rotated--a kinda slow spin--as it pulled forward. I guess this was so you wouldn't hold on to the rope too tight... just kinda let it glide through your hand and guide you up the slope.

Well, Sherry grabbed the thing with both hands, and she must've been holdin' on for dear life, 'cause the next thing you know, she got some of them layers of clothes all caught up in the rope and was screaming, coming up the hill. With all the twistin' and turnin' she was doin' tryin' to get loose, she was also slowin' everybody up, 'cause her ski's had got turned to the side and she was scrapin' up piles of snow. We couldn't help her 'til she got to the top; 'cause we wasn't gonna risk fallin' back down the hill ourselves. When we finally got her lose and looked back down that hill, the ski lodge looked like it was the size of a 2-cent milk carton. "Wow! This slope must be about 2 miles long!" Paige said.

Sherry wasn't sayin' nothin'... After goin' a couple a rounds with that rope..., she just looked scared.

"Well, I didn't come all this way for nothin'," Paige said, "I'm skiing down!" As she pulled Sherry with her. I just stood there and noticed all these little kids, who looked to be about 8 or 9 years old, just reaching the top of the hill and, immediately, swooshing back down to the bottom. It looked so easy..., like it was so much fun! I looked down, saw two skiers trying to get their footing 'bout half way down, and recognized them as Paige and Sherry; I closed my eyes and pushed off.

I screamed so long that the back of my throat was dry; I finally opened my eyes just as I passed Paige and Sherry walking sideways down the rest of the slope. I had everything under control, 'til I started thinkin' about how I was gonna stop. I couldn't remember what they said about how you was supposed to stop when you reached the bottom! I saw some kids just reaching the bottom, up ahead in front of me, and they just kinda twisted their knees to the side, kicked up a lot of snow, and stopped.

"I can do this! I can do this!" I repeated, as I unlocked my knees and bent them just enough to twist them so I could stop, but when I did that, instead of making me stop--or even slow down-- it just made me change direction and go to the right. I ran straight into the ski rack full of ski's that was outside of the lodge....screaming all the way. Some little boy skied over, picked some of the skis off me, and helped me get those things off my feet....he never said a word. I could hear my momma laughin' before I opened the door to the lodge. She could was laughin' so hard, she could hardly ask me where my sisters were--Like I cared.

We got back on the bus without any frostbite or broken bones, but we probably can't go back there again... It seems Mr. Jack reached the top of his slope and realized that it was higher up than he thought. He asked the ski lift folks to bring him back down, and they told him no...that he would have to ski down just like everybody else. So, a big commotion started and somebody got punched. Momma was telling daddy about it when we got home, and daddy said, laughin', "That damn Jack makes a fool of hisself everywhere he goes!! He did the same thing at that amusement park; got on the roller coaster and when that thing stopped, they had to pry his hands off the bar and carry him off somewhere!" Anyway...., skiing is fun and all..., but, once was enough for me.

When I got home, I went and checked on Jocelyn. She opened the door and let me in, we walked into the dinning room and sat down. "Jo, how ya doing?"

"Fine," she replied. But, since Ms Connie's passin', she just wasn't the old Jo that I knew.

I said, "Guess what?"

She just looked at me without answering; so, I went on to tell her that they were going to start having weekly dances down at Cappers on Wednesday night for 25 cents a person, plus they gave you a membership card.

"No kiddin!?" She said.

"Yep! And the first dance is this Wednesday comin'. You wanna go? You know you wanna slow drag with Bobby," I said. "I seen the way you look at him."

She smiled for the first time in a long time, "Girl, what we gonna wear!"

Chapter 7

How simple things were then. Life threw you an obstacle, you overcame it, and moved on. That's what we all did... We moved on.

It's been years since I've spoken to most of my childhood friends. Those people I could not imagine living one single day of my life without. Tee got married and moved away; Precious got pregnant, early-on, and took that responsibility seriously; Jo and Bobby got married; Wanda moved away and started a career; and Gail--the only one I still keep in touch with--finished college and went into banking.

I tried my hand at singing for a while. Our group, "Crystal Fortress," consisted of me, Ruth Carter; and Janine and Barbara--the infamous Morgan sisters--who had the kind of harmony only sisters can achieve! We were managed by Nathan, a local photographer, who had a few connections. He was a friend of Hank's, the male half of the "Peaches and Cream," singing duo, and a local policeman, who had crossed over onto the recording scene. We knew we had made a connection; plus, Nat also drove for a local funeral home and had access to a limousine. Now I ask you...was that the ticket...or what? We could have pictures taken and be driven to all of our gigs in a limo!

We sang locally at several of the clubs in the D.C. area, for about a year, and eventually got a spot at *Evans Grill*, opening for the recording artist Walter Jackson. I loved Walter Jackson, because he had overcome so many obstacles in his life. Stricken with polio, as a young boy, he never let his disability get in the way of his musical ambitions. He performed on crutches. I remember standing off stage watching him leaning on his crutches and singing his heart out. I don't know if we were on our way up, or if he was on his way down.

We were four talented, attractive, young ladies being mismanaged by a small-time, local entrepreneur who, apparently, struggled with where we were trying to go as a singing group, and with what he could get out of the deal. I continued singing for about another year or so, realized that it was not going to pan out, and moved on. I met and fell in love with a musician, with whom I, eventually, produced the joy of my life; my son. All the while, still embraced by one of the most loving, strong, semi-dysfunctional families to ever exist.

Chapter 8

It was the summer of 1978, and I had gone downstairs, in the building were I worked, to the donut shop. I heard someone say"" Hey!.. How you doin?" I turned to see one of the most handsome faces that I had ever seen.

"Fine, how are you?" I replied, as I paid for my order and prepared to leave.

"I know you. Your name is Judy Garrett," he said.

All of my newly forming expectations were shattered in that one statement. I turned, "No it isn't." I replied, and walked away.

This guy must know my brother. Now, don't get me wrong. I love my brother, but, he is crazy! When I was growing up, because I was the only one of his sisters that happened to be younger than he was; he was my Big Brother--he controlled my life--or tried hard to. I mean he thought it was his duty to tell me to go home from the playground--even before the street lights came on. We fought everyday! I even think I met and became so involved with my son's father because, he didn't know my brother and did not fall into the category of his buddy or his gofer! Those appeared to me to be the only choices to fall under, if you knew my brother.

As I waited for the elevator, to take me back to work, the voice said, again, "It is Judy, isn't it?"

"No." I said, again, as I stepped onto the elevator and the doors began to close.

He placed his hand between the closing doors, causing them to reopen, and stepped in.

Now, I'm thinking. 'What's next? Surely, he's not going to dig up the ole "what's your sign" line,' because I would have thrown up with disappointment. Instead, he said, "We met briefly last year when you came to pick up Terrence."

I stared at him, trying to recall who and what he could be talking about, when he reminded me that we had a mutual friend whom I was dating, and that I had come to pick him up from a friend's house; Terrence had introduced us.

I, vaguely, remembered Terrence, let alone the incident, but when he said he had been playing ball in Europe for the past couple of years and was home on vacation--I remembered. By now, the elevator had reached my floor and I was standing there, literally, holding the door at bay, to keep it from closing.

"Oh, yeah, I remember, now. How are you?" I finally spoke.

He stepped off of the elevator, and said, "I'm fine."

And that he was! As I stood there gazing up into his face,--did you hear me say "gazing UP?"--I mention this, because I stand 6 feet tall, and he looked to be at least 5 inches taller than me, and I had on 4 inch heels. We just kind of stood there, both of us realizing we had made a connection and not knowing where to take it. I suddenly remembered that I was at work and needed to get back, so I stated the obvious, "Well, I gotta get back to work," and turned to walk away, hoping he wouldn't just let me.

"Ok," he said, and turned to push the button for the elevator.

"Take care." I said.

He looked at me and smiled. That did it! I stood there smiling back at him as he said those magic words… "Can I get your number?"

I didn't have anything to write with, or on, so I asked him to wait for a minute or two, then walk into my office and ask for me.

I rushed past our receptionist, Lula, literally, giggling as she stopped me and asked, "What you so giddy about?"

"You'll see," I said and buzzed myself into the office."

I worked for the Department of Finance, and, of course, if you had a problem with your paycheck, insurance, or a deduction, you could call, make an appointment, and come to speak with a finance manager to get your issue resolved. Since discussions concerning your earnings were of a very personal nature, we had several small conference rooms where we could take employees to discuss whatever problems they were having.

I sat down at my desk, just as Lula buzzed my phone. I answered as if I had no idea why she would be calling me and glanced at my appointment calendar, *'why would she be calling me?'* look. I spoke into the phone, "Yes, Lula."

"There is a gentleman up front, requesting to speak to you," she announced importantly.

I informed her that I would be there, shortly, and to show him to one of the conference rooms. When I grabbed my tablet from my desk, Leslie, my coworker asked if we were still on for lunch, I hit my knee on the desk, turning to answer her while still walking.

"Yeah girl, I'll be right back. Somebody's waiting on me to talk about their benefits." I walked through the office, and buzzed out to the Reception Area.

Lula was sitting there grinning, "He's waitin' in Room 2... Have you seen him?" Lula asked.

"Have I seen who?" I asked, feigning professional interest only.

"That fine ass man waiting to speak to you," hissed Lula.

"No. Why?" I pretended.

"Girl, I couldn't even ask him his name... I didn't want to talk too much. You know, I just had all my teeth pulled 'bout a week ago..., and my damn gums still hurt so bad that I have to rub 'Orajel' on 'em to stop 'em from aching--if I'd known they was gonna hurt this bad, I'da kept the goddamn rotten teeth. I used up all my sick leave when I threw my back out, a few months ago, so I cain't not to come to work.... Anyway, I had my teeth wrapped up in a napkin on my desk when he came in, and I tried to put 'em in before he reached me. I snatched the napkin up and slung my damn teeth on the floor and had to kick 'em under my desk. I know he knew I didn't have no teeth when I was talking to him."

"Lula,....I can't talk to you about that right now." I muttered impatiently.

"Find out if he married, girl!" She requested.

I opened the door, laughing to myself at what Lula had just told me. He looked up as I entered the room. Smiling, he asked, "What's so funny?"

I told him what Lula had just told me, and we both laughed. He had the smoothness voice and most beautiful smile that I had ever seen.

We sat there trying to fill every moment with conversation; while we felt the connection becoming stronger. I asked what he was doing here in the building. He said he had just returned from Holland, where he had been playing semi-professional basketball, and that he was looking for a job. He had just come down from putting in an application in personnel. In the middle of his explanation, I blurted, ".....Jackie!"

"Huh?"

"My name.... My name is Jackie.... not Judy."

"Oh,........uh......I was close." He looked chagrined, but slightly amused.

"Apparently, you know my brother, Garrett; that's our last name, but most people call Gregory, Garrett, as if it's his first name," I babbled...get it together, girl.

He smiled, "We've played ball together several times. But I don't really know him."

I was relieved. "Now,... you know my name, but I don't know yours."

"Deon..., Deon Davis."

Deon asked what my job was; I explained, and in doing so reminded him that I had to get back to work because I actually did have several appointments scheduled.

"I understand," he said, and asked for my phone number so that--hopefully, on my part, at least-- we could continue our conversation later. I tore a small piece off the top sheet of the tablet, wrote my number down, escorted him out........, and exhaled...

Lula was sitting there waiting for an update. "No. He's not married... And, yes. He did notice that you didn't have any teeth!" I chuckled as I buzzed myself back into the office.

"Damn!" She said under her breath, as I walked away.

After solving a few more financial dilemmas, Carolyn, Leslie, and I went to lunch.

"Ok. Speak!! Who was the man Lula was drooling about?" Demanded Leslie.

I started laughing as Carolyn looked on, not knowing what we were talking about. "He's a friend of my brother's… He was here looking for a job," I said.

"He is a friend of your brother's? And you had a conversation with him?" Leslie said, incredulous. "I don't think so." Leslie and I have worked together for years….She's heard all of my 'Big Brother' stories.

"Look, not all of his friends are idiots!" I defended.

"Since, when?" She asked, and laughed.

"This one seems to be different."

"Different, how?" Carolyn asked.

"Well, he just got back from Holland, where he said he was playing semi-professional ball, or something."

"Harlem,! Harlem!?" "Girl,… he's worse than the guys that hang out with your brother! Them fools up in Harlem ain't no joke, Jackie!....Hell!..... Maybe dey are jokes…………huh!!"

"Carolyn, Holland! 'H o l l a n d'…… Not Harlem."

"Oh, I was gitt'n ready to say…"

"Anyway, I gave him my number, and I'll let you know what he's about…, when I know what he's about!"

Chapter 9

"Hi baby! How's my little man doin'?" I said, as I scooped him up.

"Hi Mommy, how was work?" Ray-Ja, my son, proudly inquired.

"It was fine, and thank you for asking!" I said, impressed that he knew how to ask about my day at the tender age of three. I went into the kitchen where my momma was just finishing fixing his plate; I leaned over and kissed her on the forehead.

"How was your day?" I asked Momma.

"Same as yesterday; just another day," she said.

Ray-Ja was trying to climb into his highchair that he was getting to big for when momma said, "Uh uh, you gonna start sitting at the table and I'm gonna throw that chair out, you don't need it anymore." Ray-Ja's little face lit up. He thought that he was a big boy now that he didn't have to sit in the highchair anymore. "On second thought," she paused, reflecting, "I'll keep it around for when we have spaghetti."

Looking at me, she said, "He always makes such a mess when he eats spaghetti."

When Ray-Ja finished eating, I took him down from the table, washed him up, and put his pajamas on him. My momma kept him for me during the week, and I took him home to our little apartment on the weekends. It wasn't an arrangement that I wanted, but it was something that I needed to do for the time being. I was a single parent and this arrangement was best for all of us, right now. I stayed a few more hours, tucked Ray-Ja in and read him a story, like

I did every night. When he fell asleep, I went into the living room. Momma had started dozing, I woke her up, told her to go to bed, kissed her goodnight, and drove home.

When I entered my apartment, I turned on the light and saw that the red light was flashing on my answering machine. I threw my purse on the sofa and checked my messages. The first two were from bill collectors, giving me a friendly reminder that they were not in receipt of my payment. I hurriedly erased them, while making a mental note to put the check in the mail. The third was from a guy who had dialed the wrong number but left a message because he liked the sound of my voice, so he left his number in case I wanted to call him back. ERASED!!

The last was from Lula, wanting me to call her back about the "fine ass guy" who was in the office today.... And there were no more messages.

The next morning I did my usual, got up, showered, dressed, and left for work. I drove into D.C. and parked around the corner from my mom's to catch the Metro. Parking in downtown Washington was too expensive; unless I had a Doctors appointment or something to go to after work. I didn't drop by momma's in the morning because it would take her to long to calm Ray-Ja down, if I only stayed for a minute or two, plus, I was usually just in time to catch the Friendship Heights bus that would take me to my job.

I'd just gotten seated on the Metro and started reading my book about a slave named *"Mandingo,"* by Kyle Onstott. I don't know why I chose to read that book on my way to work; it always gave me an attitude, knowing that we have "arrived," but still ain't got there yet! Anyway, as I was reading the description of this 'Mandingo' slave, my mind started wandering a little about Deon because of the descriptive physical similarities. He was described as tall, with skin the color of dark chocolate; with broad shoulders and strong white teeth set in a defined jaw line. Lord, have mercy!

I glanced up from my book, like people knew what I was thinking; cleared my throat, and continued reading until I reached my stop.

When I arrived at my office, Lula was laying in wait. "I called you last night..... Why didn't you call me back?"

"Lula, it was late, and I was tired."

"You could've called me back no matter how late it was.... You know I wanted to know what happened!!"

"What are you talking about?

"Don't play dumb with me. Tell me about that brother that came to see you yesterday,... wit his fine self."

"Oh.., Him."

"Yeah.., Him!"

"Gotta go," I said, and buzzed my way into the office leaving her there with her mouth opened.

I had lunch with Leslie and Carolyn later that day and Leslie said, "Well?"

"Well, what?" I replied.

"Well, did you talk to him last night?

"No, I didn't."

"Well, he'll probably call you tonight" Carolyn's voice was muffled, as she stuffed her face with French fries.

"If he does, he does," I said and took a bite of my sandwich.

"Lula said he was so fine that her teeth fell right out of her mouth when he came in asking for you." Leslie said.

I started laughing, "Lula's teeth were already out of her mouth, when he came in," I said, and proceeded to enlighten them with Lula's story. We all fell out laughing.

"He must really be something if you gave him your number. Half the guys here have asked for it and you give 'em mine to get them off your back. Don't do that shit no more." she said laughing.

"You can handle it....anyway,....he seems nice, and can we change the subject,..good grief!"

Every day, one of them, Carolyn, Leslie, or, especially..., Lula would ask about "him." Lula had told everybody about him, and how fine he was, almost as though he was some kind of superhero. While I, on the other hand--silently agreed about the superhero thing--but was getting pissed that I had not heard from him since that day in the office.

I come from good stock. My mother and father are very attractive people who made a family of very attractive children; myself, included. I didn't think I was cute or anything, but, I knew that I had it going on, and I was very aware that men found me attractive. I was a little perturbed, to say the least, when I chose to give my number to someone, and they take their time about contacting me. This situation was new to me..., and I didn't like it.

Anyway, I continued my daily and weekend routine.....going to work and going past momma's…

Finally, I finished reading "Mandingo" only to pick up the next several books in the series.

I had stopped by Walden Books, for just that reason and planned on going home, coolin' out   and reading a little, when the phone rang. I answered while still reading…

"Hello...? May I speak to Jackie?"

I closed the book with my finger in it to hold my page and responded, "This is she."

"Hey, what's up?"

"Who is this?"

"Deon...."

I didn't say anything for a few seconds…

"Hello,..are you there?" He asked.

"Yeah, I'm here."

"How are you doing?"

"I'm fine,... how are you?"

"Pretty good." He said.

"I was wondering what happened to you. I gave you my number over two weeks ago, and I noticed that you hadn't called." I said, with a little more feeling than I had intended to disclose.

"Yeah, well I was taking care of a few things and didn't want to call you until I got them taken care of."

"Really! What were you taking care of?" I asked, feeling a little put out.

"Do I detect a little attitude?" He asked.

"You're damn right you do! Look, I don't know who you think you are, but I have never given my number to someone and they took two weeks to call me!"

"Hold up! So I guess you want me to think that you just been sittin' around waiting for me to call or something."

I got so mad I said, "Look! Forget it," and slammed the receiver down on the phone. I was so furious that I jumped up off the sofa, and started pacing around my living room, mumbling to myself, *'who does he think he is, calling me weeks,... two weeks, after I gave him my number!'*

Just then, the phone ran again. I answered it not thinking, "Hello!" I yelled.

"Hi, can we start this thing over?"

I calmed down a little and relaxed my bruised ego for a few seconds. "Hi," I said rather sheepishly.

"Look, I was wondering if I could see you?"

"When?"

"How about, this evening?"

I thought to myself for a moment, I didn't want to appear too anxious. "No,.. not tonight..., maybe tomorrow?"

"That's cool, tomorrow will be fine. What time?"

I explained that I had some running around to do, so about 7:30 would be good.

"Ok," he agreed. We continued to talk for a few minutes longer and then reconfirmed our date for the next evening.

After I hung up, I sat there thinking. '...Yeah..., I'll have him come over tomorrow. Thursday..., so he won't disturb my weekend with Ray-Ja'--not to mention the fact that I never brought my dates around my son. I didn't want them trying to get to me through him, and I was very aware of the image that I wanted to project to him. I picked up my book, which was now lying on the floor by the sofa and attempted to read, but I found myself rereading the same paragraph several times....because my mind was, definitely, someplace else.

Chapter 10

The next morning, I made my usual stop at the donut shop to get a cup of coffee, then walked around the corner to where the elevators were. There stood Becket, our part-time drunk security guard. "Hey there, pretty lady, how you doing today?" Becket had the worst breath in the world and would always try to get up in your face with those long-voweled questions like "HOOOWW you DOOIN…?" He mixed his coffee with liquor and it smelled awful, so it was always a race when he was on duty to try to get on the elevators before he could come around his desk to ask you a life-threatening question. You, literally, had to hold your breath when he spoke to you to stop from gagging. I jumped on the elevator, almost spilling my coffee, laughing, because I out-ran him and was spared yet again! It was going to be a good day!!

I told Leslie that Deon had called me last night--omitting the part about the bruised ego--and that we had a date later that evening.

"What took him so long?" She said.

"He said he was taking care of some business and that he had meant to call sooner, but couldn't."

"Well, what time?"

"What time what?"

"Your date.., what time is your date?"

"Oh, 7:30. Why?"

"Duh…? So that I'll know, what time to call you… Ok, I'll call you about eight, and you can give me the sign that everything's cool," Leslie said.

See, Leslie and I had this thing that we would do whenever we had a first date, we would give the date a few minutes and then call, or 'accidentally' stop by; thereby, giving one the option of ending the date…*'friend in trouble'* or to continue.

I finished work and stopped by her desk on my way out. "8:00 o'clock?"

"8:00 o'clock." Leslie replied.

I stopped by Momma's, and I could smell what she was cooking before I reached the door. I scooped my little man up, kissed him a hundred times, and put him down so that he could continue playing. I went into the kitchen and started looking in the pots. Momma had prepared collards, potato salad, and fried chicken!

"What you cookin' a Sunday dinner for, on a Thursday?" I asked.

"Well, I took the chicken out to thaw this morning, and Chester brought me some fresh greens out of his garden--the ones that the rabbits didn't get to--so I just went on and whipped up some potato salad to go with it."

"You know I'm staying for dinner, don't you?"

"Like you don't everyday!" she said, and started laughing.

"Girl, you would eat, if I cooked monkey hips and rice!"

"Ain't that the truth," said Daddy, as he was walking into the kitchen. I shoved him, playfully and then gave him a big hug.

"Are you gonna to watch the fight tonight?" He asked.

I had forgotten that Mohammad Ali was fighting Norton tonight, and I always watched boxing with my daddy.

"No, not tonight Dad, I've had a rough day so after I eat and get Ray-Ja settled for the night, I'm going to call it a night myself."

"Well, we'll talk about it tomorrow, but you know Ali is gonna to win don't you?"

"That's what you think! Norton is going to kick his butt!" I said to get a good rise out of my daddy, because he thought Ali was the greatest fighter in the world.

When I got home, my answering machine was blinking; I checked my messages.

"Jackie! This Lula..., Leslie told me you going on a date with that tall drink of water! Call me girl." MENTAL NOTE: Talk to Leslie and tell her that Lula was not to know my business and for her not to tell her anything. I know Leslie only mentioned it because Lula could be relentless when she was on a gossip-gathering mission... But give me a break, here. The next message was from Deon, at first I thought that he was calling to say something had come up, but he was just calling to say that he was looking forward to our date and wanted to just say hello..that was nice. I smiled as I hit the delete button and remembered that he hadn't asked for my address or for directions when we spoke yesterday. Oh well. He can get it when he calls. I kicked off my shoes and strutted into my bedroom to prepare myself for my date.

At precisely 6:15 the phone rang. "Hello...? Hi, this is Deon, I was just calling to make sure we were still on for this evening."

"Sure."

"Well I'm going to need your address and directions."

I supplied him with both, and he said that he would see me at 7:30.

Chapter 11

I changed into a pair of slacks and a casual, loose-fitting top to achieve a nice, but relaxed, look. I don't drink, so I didn't have any wine or beer, and I wondered, belatedly, if I should have asked him if he would have liked to have any. I figured, he was an athlete..., so probably juice would suffice; I had plenty of that on hand, because that was one of Ray-Ja's favorite things. I opened some chips, placing them beside the small vegetable tray I had prepared, put on some soft jazz, then sat on the sofa and waited. At 7:25 there was knock at my door, I took my time answering it, trying not give the appearance that I was anxious. In my effort to disquise appearances, I failed to look out of the peep hole and opened the door only to find, Al, my next door neighbor, standing there looking stupid. As he stepped across the threshold to enter my apartment, I stopped him by planting my hand, firmly, in the middle of his chest.

"Hi Al," I said, "What do you want?"

He said, "I heard your music playing, so I knew you were home. I just wanted to hang out for a minute or two."

"I'm kind of busy right now....and I'm expecting company any minute. Maybe we can hang out a while this weekend." I promised, trying to rush him along.

"Oh..., ok, I guess, I'll catch you later then," he said with a hang-dog look.

"Ok, then, see ya." I shut the door in his face.

Al appeared to have resigned himself to that arrangement, but still, I knew he would be looking through that peephole..., as if to see what his 'competition' would look like.

At 7:40, he knocked... I checked myself out one last time, in the magnet mirror on the refrigerator, before opening the door. Which I did at the same time as Al opened his, Deon was beginning to speak when Al blurted out, "Oh,.. I thought someone was knocking at my door...! Sorry..."

I said, "Deon, this is my neighbor,.. Al. As Al stepped over to give Deon some dap, I said, "Ok, Al,.. I'll see you later, and pulled Deon into the apartment and closed the door.

"That was strange..." Deon said.

I said, "No, it's not.... You don't know Al,"

"Did he really think I was knocking at his door?"

"No. He was just being nosey! Anyway... HI...," I said, smiling at him. "Come on in and have a seat. Would you like something to drink? I don't have anything stronger that fruit juice, but if you would like something other than that--the store's just up the street and we could run up there and pick something up."

"Naw...., that's ok," he said. "Juice will be fine," as he took a seat. I just stood there for a minute, looking confused.

"Is everything ok?" Deon asked.

I snapped out of my stupor, "Yeah, everything is fine...I'll get you that juice." As I went into the kitchen, I felt so stupid, 'Jackie!' I said to myself. 'What were you thinking? You should have had a bottle of wine, or at least, a cold beer to offer him!'

"APPLE or ORANGE...?" I yelled from the kitchen.

"What?" As I rounded the corner to the living room, I yelled, again, "Juice....Apple or Orange?"

He, however, had moved from the sofa and was standing in the kitchen doorway, just as I walked around the corner--I slammed right into him. He just stood there smiling, while I, embarrassed and flustered, quickly backed up, apologizing for running into him.

"I'll have whatever you are having," he offered.

I placed the dip and crackers on the coffee table and poured him the last of the apple juice.

"I don't want to take the last of it," Deon said.

"No..., it's ok, I have more," but when I went into the kitchen, there was only a half a glass of orange juice left in the carton and an unopened carton of pineapple juice. " *'Dammit!'* " I said under my breath, "I should have checked!"

I'm allergic to pineapple juice…it has a strange affect on me…like drinking liquor. I only buy it because Ray-Ja loves any kind of juice.

I poured myself a glass of pineapple juice–which remained untouched--and went back into the living room. Deon was still seated on the sofa, bobbing his head to the music.

"You like that?" I asked.

"I really prefer old Motown stuff…, but this is nice."

"Are you kidding?!"

"No, I love the Temp's and The Four Tops…."

"You talk like you know your music."

"I know everything that the Temptations ever made!" He bragged, laughing.

"I bet you don't!" I said.

"Try me!" He challenged.

I walked over to the closet and pulled out a big box. Deon got up from the sofa and came over to where I was squatting on the floor.

"Uh, uh,… git back on that sofa…, I don't want you to cheat."

"What's in that box? He questioned, suspiciously."

I put my hand in and pulled out a stack of 45's.

"Oh…My…God!" He said getting up from the sofa again. I stood up, pushed him lightly in his chest, and lead him back to his seat. Returning to the box, I shuffled thru the stack and looked over my shoulder as I wiped the 45 in a slow circular motion on my hip.

"I bet I have something that you don't know by the Temptations," I said, and put the record on the turntable.

"Hummm.., and I bet you don't!" He replied, easily getting into the mood.

After the crackling at the start of the record; Melvin Franklin's deep voice sang, "Don't send me away…, don't send me away…." Deon jumped up from the sofa, singing the next line of the song and grabbed for my hand to dance. I started laughing as I fell in step with him.

"I can't believe you know this song!" Everyone always plays the flip side...I though that I was the only one that knew this one...!"

As he turned me, he laughed, "You have got to be kidding!! This is one of my favorites," he said, pulling me close to him. The song ended and we were just standing there listening to the sound of the record scratching--instead of ejecting.

"I'd better get that..." I said pulling away.

He pulled me back in his arms... "Let it play again."

I did, and we danced to that record as it played over and over... As I swayed in his embrace, I looked up into his face and smiled. He looked down at me, "What are you smiling about?"

"I can tell you're an athlete."

"What makes you say that?"

"Because....you dance like one," I said and laughed.

"Kinda stiff,.....huh?"

"Yeah,...but, it's...alright."

Holding me closer, he laughed, softly. After the record played for the ump-teenth time, I said, "I'm gonna put on an album so we can sit and talk for a while."

"Ok."

I put some music on and sat on the sofa beside Deon and we talked for hours. Surprisingly, he had lived only five blocks from me growing up. I asked why he didn't attend Randall Jr. High, and he said that they had rezoned the year that he was to start, so he had to go to Hine Jr. High, instead. He said that he had played basketball with Gregory, on every court in the neighborhood, and found it strange that he had never seen me. I said that I was at most of the neighborhood games.

"You must have been ugly when you were younger....or I would have remembered you." I said laughing.

Laughing, he responded, "You must not have been too hot yourself... or I would have remembered you, too!"

I liked him....and, knowing that he was sharp enough to go tit-for-tat with me was refreshing…

Chapter 12

We must have talked about everything under the sun; where we grew up, the schools we attended.... I told him about my Ray Ja.... and Deon told me that he had a son, named Deonte', who was 2 years old. I asked where Deonte's mother was. Deon said they had dated for several years, but had parted ways when he went away to college. I asked how that could be that possible. He explained that she had visited him on campus...and one thing led to another...and a month or so later, she called and told him that she was pregnant. I asked if she was still part of his life.

"Only where my son is concerned."

"Humm........"

"Humm..., what? What's that for?" He asked.

"Let me get this straight? You and she were not going together anymore, but she traveled all the way to another state to see you, ... to have sex with you....., and the only thing that you have in common is your son?"

"As far as I'm concerned." He affirmed.

Deon continued. After she became pregnant, her parents had tried to pressure him into marrying, mainly, to protect their family's imagine. Her father is a pastor at one of the largest churches in the metropolitan area. He said he loved his son and would do anything in the world for him, but he was not going to be forced to spend the rest of his life in a marriage that he did not want to be in.... not for anybody.

"What about you?" He asked. "Are you still involved with Ray-Ja's father?"

"God no!... Not even where Ray-Ja is concerned." I stated. "That's why my parent's are so important to me. I told him that I wouldn't know what I would do without them and their support." "It's not easy being a single parent." I told him that Reggie and I had been together for about 8 years, but I felt that I had outgrown him, our goals and ambitions were not on the same path. "He is definitely not a part of my life," I said.... "And he chooses not to be a part of Ray-Ja's,.. just to hurt me."

We talked about how he got his opportunity to play basketball in Europe, all of the people that we knew in common, and were amazed...once again...that we had never met before.

It was obvious that we were both comfortable and enjoying each others company, because before we realized it, it was 3:00 o'clock in the morning! I remembered stifling a few yawns, but had no idea that it was so late. "Deon? Do you know what time it is? I asked, genuinely, surprised.

"I guess it's about 1:00 o'clock or so."

"No... It's 8 minutes after 3:00."

"You're kidding!? Man! Where did the time go? I had better leave so you can get some rest. I didn't mean to keep you up so late."

"I can't believe that we have been sitting here talking for almost 7 hours." I said.

I got up from the sofa and starting clearing the vegetable tray and chips from the table. He stood up and stretched. "By the way, I meant to apologize for running a little late, but this complex is like a maze. I must have made seven or eight turns trying to find your street."

"I know, sometimes I'm not sure how I find it."

"You might have to tell how to get back to the main road."

"Look. You look like you're as tired as I am. So why don't you just stretch out here on the sofa. I'll be getting up in a couple of hours anyway....and you can follow me out."

Deon tilted his head, looked at me, and smiled...

"I said..., on the sofa!"

"You must trust me?"

"Noooo, I just trust me more...", I said, as I invited him to kick his shoes off and try to make himself comfortable. "Besides now that I know that we know most of the same people, I could have you hunted down, if you tried anything."

He smiled and began to remove his shoes, "Naw..., it's cool, I won't try anything..., unless you want me too."

"The bathroom is at the end of the hall if you need it, and I'll see you in a few hours." I said, as I turned to go into my bedroom.

"Goodnight, Jackie," Deon said.

I turned and leaned into him for a goodnight kiss... like we had done this a million times before. Deon froze...

"I am so sorry, I didn't...", and that was all that I was able to say, because Deon pulled me to him and kissed me. My eyes were wide open from embarrassment for what I had done. Deon's eyes were closed and his hand slid down to the small of my back. I returned his kiss, and after a few seconds, pulled away.

"Goodnight Deon," I said, softly, as I backed toward to my bedroom.

"Goodnight Jackie."

When I reached my room, I closed the door and sat on the end of my bed. Across the hall from my room, I heard the bathroom door close. I sat there listening to the water running, and then the toilet flushed. A few seconds later, I heard him open the door and walk back down the hall to the living room. I didn't know what to do. I thought...I need to go wash this makeup off my face and, at least, tie my hair up or I'm gonna look terrible tomorrow. I grabbed up my nightgown and a scarf, and crossed the hall to the bathroom. As I was looking in the mirror-- washing my face, I thought, '*Jackie are you crazy? You have invited a strange man to stay in your house......a man that you really don't know anything about! He could be some kind of murderer or something.*'

I just stood there--my reflection looking back at me--wondering if I had made a mistake. How could I go back in there, now, and say, "Uh,... excuse me Deon, but, I think you need to go." I put the seat down on the toilet, sat down and tried to think. '*Jackie, girl, you* know you sleep like a log, that man could try anything with you and you wouldn't even know it until it was too late.' I stood up and shook my head clear. 'This is crazy, I'm a grown woman and if I want to let this man stay over, I have enough sense to make that decision and feel comfortable about it.' I argued with myself.

I opened the door to the bathroom and could hear a soft steady snore coming from the living room. I tipped down the hall and peaked in to see that he had fallen asleep. When I went back into my room, I decided to take the comforter from the end of my bed to cover him. I tip-toed back down the hall with the comforter and placed it over him. Just as I was turning to leave, he awoke. "Since you're tucking me in... can I get another goodnight kiss, too?" I leaned over to give him a kiss, and he pulled me down. I was hanging off the side of the sofa when we finished kissing. My head was spinning. Deon was an awesome kisser. He moved his legs so that I could sit, and I noticed that not only where his feet hanging off the sofa but most of his legs where too. The sofa stopped right at the back of his calf.

"You have got to be uncomfortable," I observed.

"I'm use to it. I'm a big guy and unless I'm in a king size bed, I usually hang off."

"I have a king size bed." I said.

I took Deon's hand as I stood up, pulled him to his feet, and lead him down the hall.

Deon was the gentlest man that I had ever been with--not that there had been that many to compare him to--but I couldn't explain the feeling that I was having for this man. We made love... It was wonderful! I turned my back to him once we were finished, and tears starting stinging my eyes, I thought, 'Oh my God, Jackie! What in the hell is wrong with you! You slept with a man on the first date! What will he....think of me...ooh,....God!?   I felt so ashamed. I tried to feel around for my nightgown that had gotten removed and tossed during our moment of passion, when Deon leaned up on his elbow, resting his head in his hand said, "Good morning."

I sat up with my back to him, pulled the sheet off the bed around me, and ran into the bathroom. I turned on the water full blast and started crying. I cupped my hand around my mouth, trying to stifle the noise, when I heard a soft knock at the door, "Jackie, are you alright?"

I couldn't even answer his question I was crying so hard. He opened the door and reached for me, I pulled away and said, "I am so sorry, I have NEVER done anything like this in my life... I don't sleep with men on first dates.. I'm not a .... I'm not like that!"

He pulled me into his arms...."Why are you crying?"

I pulled back enough to grab a handful of toilet tissue to blow my nose.... "Jackie..., he said, "ahh, baby, it's ok."

I lowered my head onto his chest and started sobbing again.

"Jackie, it's all right...., it's all right..., sssshh, stop crying...." He crooned.

I looked up into his face--with tears streaming down mine--and said, in between sobs.... "I don't even remember your last name!"

Deon held me close, kissed me on my forehead, and said, "You will."

Chapter 13

I wasn't good for anything, when I got to work that morning. I hadn't had one hour of sleep and was still feeling more than a little ashamed of myself. I had never done anything like that before and was having a hard time convincing myself that I was grown enough to make those kinds of decisions. I had been in total control of whom and how I dated, after having been in a 9-year relationship with Reggie, my son's father. In the past, if a perspective date arrived even one minute late, I've been known to open the door, inform them that they were late, close the door, and forget that they even existed until they would comply with my rules. Yet, Deon was ten minutes late and I had slept with him on our first date. I couldn't begin explain it to myself, and God knows I wasn't going to let anyone else know what had happened.

Leslie came in and walked straight over to my desk. "You look like you been rode hard and put up wet." She observed, eyeing me closely. I almost burst out crying right there in her face. Instead, I said, that Deon and I, were up late talking and I didn't get much sleep.

"Well, you look like it," she said while, putting away in her pocketbook in her desk draw.

"What happened? How late did he stay..? What did y'all talk about tell me everything!"

"Why didn't you call?" I asked.

"I forgot."

"You.....forgot?.... What if I had been stuck in there with some murderer.. or...or...a madman?" I asked her.

"Then Al would have busted down your door, because you know he was camped upside his wall with a glass at his ear, listening to everything y'all said!" She shot back.

"Ok, you're right. Besides if anything had happened..., you know, I would hold it over your head for the next 40 years."

"Yeah, I know! Well, how was your date?"

I just smiled and--looking up--saw Lula walking our way; I told Leslie that I would talk to her about it at lunch.

"Ok, I'm ready. How was it?" Lula asked.

"Lula..., he stood me up." I lied.

"You have got to be kiddin' me! I knew it!.. I knew it!.... I knew he wasn't no damn good the moment I laid eyes on him," she touched my shoulder, sympathetically, "Jackie, don't you give that man another thought, you hear me! He ain't worth the time of day."

I dropped my head and heaved my shoulders. "Alright Lula, thanks, I really appreciate you looking out for me." I turned my head slightly and winked my eye at Leslie who was about to die trying not to laugh.

"I feel so stupid...," I said, as I walked away.

Lula leaned over and whispered to Leslie, "Poor thing, she'll be alright. Keep an eye on her for me will you?"

"Sure," Leslie said, "I will."

There is no way that Lula didn't hear Leslie cracking up all the way up in the reception area. She had tears streaming down her face from laughing. I tried to tell her to stop, but I was laughing just as hard. Every time we saw Lula that day, we would fall out laughing.

"Why is she so damn nosey?" Leslie asked.

"I don't know, but she should know by now that I never tell her any of my business," I replied. "I tell her just enough stuff to get rid of her."

When Leslie and I were returning from lunch and walking through the receptionist area, I noticed a floral arrangement on the corner of the desk. I leaned over to smell the roses, just as Lula was hanging up the phone. "Those are for you." She said.

"Me?"

"Yeah, I guess he's trying to make up for standin' you up last night. If I was you, I would throw 'em right in the trash."

I picked the vase up and buzzed into the office, while reading the card that was attached. 'Hi Baby, Hope you have a wonderful day.' 'D.' My face lit up like a Christmas tree. I had never gotten flowers delivered to my job before; this was a pleasant first, just as last night had been.

Chapter 14

That evening when I got to Momma's, my sister Gloria was there. "Hey, girl, what's up," I said, giving her a peck on the cheek."

"Nothing.., I came over so that momma could hem some pants for me." Momma said, you would think she was 5 years old still coming over here to have her clothes fixed.

"Come on in here, Gloria, so that I can measure them pants."

"So, Jackie, what you been up to?"

"Nothing much, just working, and trying to keep my head above water."

"Look, I know you're going to spend some time with Ray-Ja, but do you think that you'd be able to drop me off at home later? A friend of mine has my car."

"Sure..., no problem."

"Ok, thanks.. Let me get in there, before she changes her mind and have me walking around here with high-waters on."

I stood in the doorway to the den where Ray-Ja and my Dad were watching Sanford and Son on TV. My dad was laughing at Red Foxx--walking around clutching his chest calling for 'Lizabeth..

They were so engrossed in the show, that I jumped in and hollered "Boo!" trying to scare Ray-Ja, instead my Dad almost jump out of his seat.

"Girl!!! You better stop that!!! Before somebody knock you out!" Looking like he was about to start calling for 'Lizabeth' himself.

Ray-Ja was laughing and pointing at my dad, "You was scared granddaddy! You was scared!"

I picked him up from daddy's lap and sat down to watch the rest of the show with them. Gloria came in, "You 'bout ready?"

"Ready for what?" Daddy asked.

Gloria was putting on her coat, "Jackie is going to drop me off at home."

"Where is your car?"

"I let a friend borrow it this evening." Gloria said.

"Huh! Daddy said, to her, without looking up from the TV...."Must be some friend; let'm tear it up, and then see how much of a friend dey are." Gloria looked real ready to leave...

"Let me get Ray-Ja's stuff, I'm taking him home tonight." I said.

"Jackie, you look tired, why don't you go on home and get some rest. You can come pick him up in the morning." Daddy said.

"Yeah, mommy pick me up in the morning!" Ray Ja, chimed in, eagerly.

"Thanks, Daddy, then I'll go ahead and get him ready for bed."

"I'll just be a minute, Gloria, and then I'll be ready to go."

When I pulled into Gloria's driveway, her car was there.

"There's your car...., where's your friend?" I asked.

"She must be in the house."

"In your house, without you?"

She leaned over, kissed me on the cheek, and said, "It's cool."

"Wait a minute; I need to use your bathroom, before I get back on the road."

Gloria hesitated, then said, "Oh, ok."

Gloria reached the door before me, a woman opened the door and made an attempt to kiss her. I acted as if hadn't seen what had happened and stopped at the door where they were both standing.

"Karen, this is my sister, Jackie." Gloria said, rather nervously.

"Hey Jackie, how you doing? I've heard a lot about you," she said.

"Hi, nice to meet you."

"You know where the bathroom is..." Gloria said, trying the break the tension that was gathering among us.

"Yeah, I'll be right back."

I could hear Gloria talking to Karen as I walked in the direction of the bathroom. "....Why did you do that in front of my sister?" She hissed...

"I didn't see anybody with you..., and that's how I always greet you when you get home." She defended. I stood in the bathroom a few seconds longer, then came out saying that I had to get home and get some rest, because I'd had a long day. When I got to the car, I looked back... Gloria was standing in the door looking like her world had come to an end...

As soon as I got home, I called Paige.

"Paige..., you got a minute?"

"Yeah, what's up?"

"You got to promise you won't say nothing!"

"Nothing about what...?"

"Promise me, Paige!"

"Ok, ok..., I promise. Now, what did I just promise I wouldn't say nothin' about? What's going on?"

"Paige, Gloria is dating a woman!"

"Get the hell out-a here! What!!! No! You got to be kiddin'!"

"Paige, you know how Gloria is about her stuff? Well, she let this girl, Karen, drive her Lincoln!"

"Shut...! Up...! But that don't mean that their dating," Paige denied, trying to get her head around it. "Maybe it was an emergency or something."

"I saw her try to kiss Gloria, and I overheard Gloria fussing at her for trying to kiss her in front of me!"

"Oh, my God..., what the hell is wrong with her?"

"I don't know but, something is going on."

"Do you think Brenda knows?" Paige asked.

"Girl, Brenda so caught up in her own drama that she don't know nothing."

"If Daddy finds out......he'll have a fit!" Paige said.

"Either that or it'll break his heart," I said. "Anyway, I'll holla at you tomorrow, I got to get some rest; this has been one hell of a day."

"Ok, Jackie, talk to you later. Bye."

Chapter 15

"Hey, Jackie, just calling to find out if we're still gonna to take the kids to the park tomorrow, since you got a man and all." The answering machine teased in Leslie's voice. "Just kidding. Look... Robert will drive me crazy if he can't see Ray-Ja, call me back, and let me know, bye."

"Hi, Jackie. Sorry I missed you, call me when you get in... This is Deon."

The next message said, "Hi. It's me again. I forgot to give you the number, it is 202-551-5563. Talk to you later, I hope...."

"Jackie...? This is Gloria...., just checking to make sure you got in ok.... Call me...., Love you."

'Humm,' I thought, 'I should call Gloria back, but I know that she'll be able to tell by my voice that I'm a little concerned about her situation....and, I don't feel like gettin' into that tonight?'

I picked up the phone and dialed the number that Deon had left. He answered on the third ring, "Hello?"

"Hi, Deon?"

"It's me..., Jackie."

"Oh, hey, how you doin'?" He said.

"I'm fine, I just got in and got your message. I had an errand to run and got home a little later than usual."

"How's Ray-Ja?"

I thought, 'humm, that's nice of him to ask.' "He's fine, he stayed over at momma's again tonight to hang out with my dad."

"That's nice," Deon said, "So, what are you going to do on a Friday night?"

"I'm going to catch up on some much needed sleep. I didn't get much last night."

There was an awkward few seconds of silence… "Well get some rest and I'll catch up with you tomorrow."

"Deon," I said, hesitantly, "I… um…, was wondering…, um…, about last…night…um, I hope I didn't give you the wrong impression of me. I… um…"

"Jackie, look, I really am attracted to you and I know what kind of a woman you are. I was hoping that the flowers would give you an indication of that."

"Oh, Deon, I didn't even say thank you, for the beautiful flowers that you sent! "Thank you! That was such a sweet gesture."

"You're welcome, Jackie. I really was hoping that I could see you again this evening, but I understand if you want to get some rest."

"Deon," I said. " I would really like to see you again, but it will not be a repeat performance of last night. That really shouldn't have happened, I mean not so soon, I…,"

"Jackie, I respect you, and I'll respect your wishes…I would like to see you tonight but, I understand….. Do you want to see me?"

"Yes…," I replied. "C'mon."

"Are you sure?"

"Yeah, I'll see you in a little while?"

"I'll be right over."

Deon arrived about 30 minutes later, we kissed when he came in, and as he held me in his arms, he said. "I've been thinking about you all day."

I looked into his eyes, and I knew that he really meant what he said…"I've been thinking about you, too."

I felt so comfortable with this man. I felt as if he had been apart of my life forever...not just since… yesterday. As I pulled from his embrace, I asked, "Are you hungry? There's some left- over Chinese food in the fridge."

He wasn't hungry, so we sat down on the sofa and began to talk again. Deon was so funny. He told me about his best friends, Shawn and Lennie, and how they use to do dumb stuff like, fight over who was going to ride shotgun in his old Chevy Nova. "It's not like they weren't gonna arrive at the same place, at the same time," he said. And he laughed, as told me how they would, actually, get into a fist fight over who was going to sit up front. He told me about his family, and that his father had suffered a stroke several years ago. I could see the hurt in is face when he spoke about it. He said that his father was always so big and strong, and it was hard to see him in a wheelchair, looking so small and helpless. Although his immediate family was relatively small, his dad was one of 19 children.

I was amazed…I had never heard of anyone having that many brothers and sisters. He named all of his aunts and uncles. I told him a little about my family. I told him that I was the youngest of seven and that my oldest brother had passed when I was fourteen years old. He said he couldn't believe that Gregory had five sisters. I asked him, how he thought Gregory got to be spoiled rotten? He laughed. I was so attracted to this man….. I wanted to know everything about him.

We fell asleep on the sofa. I'm not sure who fell asleep first; I woke up with my head on his chest, wrapped in his arms. He awoke, when he felt me moving. "I didn't want to wake you so, I just held you while you slept."

I skooched over so that he could lie down beside me on the sofa; we fell asleep in each others' arms. I slept like a baby--I felt like a queen.

"Would you like a cup of coffee?" I asked Deon, later, when he came out of the bathroom?

"Yes that would be nice, cream and sugar please."

"No problem." I said.

As he sat at the table, I placed his cup in front of him, "Uum that's good."

When I walked past him, he put his cup down; grabbed my hand and pulled me down on his lap. "Look Jackie, I need to ask you something." he said.

"What is it, Deon?"

"Are you involved with anyone…, I mean, I know that you told me that you weren't, but I find it hard to believe that nobody is beating down your door."

I told him that I was not involved with anyone and hadn't been for several months. "Why, I asked?"

"I was just checking." he said.

"No, it sounds like it's a little more to it than that." I surmised...

"Look, I ran into Terrence, yesterday, and I mentioned to him that I had run into you... that's all."

"Ok, and then what happened?"

"Let's just forget that I mentioned it, ok?"

"No! What did 'Terrence' have to say?"

"Well, you know how guys talk...? He just said that you were nice and all, but he stopped kickin' it with you, because you were looking for a husband."

"Really....? Did he also tell you that the one and only time I had to get my brother involved in my business was when I had to get Gregory to stop him from harassing me!?"... Did - he - tell - you - that!" I was beginning to get upset.

"Look, Deon, I ran into Terrence after Reggie and I broke up, I remembered him from school and that's how he and I started talking. Yes, over time, we became involved, but he had several habits that I didn't care for, so I ended the relationship. As a matter of fact! The night he introduced me to you, I came to pick him up, because he called and said that he was at a friend's house and was too drunk to drive! I still considered him a friend--at that time--and thought I was doing a friend a favor by not letting him drink and drive..." I stood up and walked across the kitchen, "Look Deon, I don't know what Terrence told you, but I'm telling you that I'm not looking to marry anyone, until I know that they are the right person for me.... and Ray-Ja; and that person definitely wasn't Terrence! And another thing!"--I had a real roll going, by now--"I'm doing fine by myself, so if you think what happened between us was some kind of set up or something!..."

"Wait a minute! Wait a minute! Calm down!...I didn't mean to upset you. I just wanted to know because I really am starting to have feelings for you and I was just trying to avoid any unnecessary drama."

"Well it seems the only drama that we have had is you telling me what one of your homeboys had to say about me!"

"Jackie, I know Terrence, and I know how he is. I could tell that he still has feelings for you and was trying to discourage me from talking to you." Deon crossed the room and was standing right in front of me.

"Jackie, I'm no fool. And it would take a hell of a lot more than that to discourage me from being with you."

I looked at him and smiled, put my arms around his neck, and kissed him.

"Look, I hate to run you off, but I have to go pick up Ray-Ja. I know he's probably wondering where I am." I said.

As we were walking to the door, Deon said, "And when will I get a chance to meet the little fellow?"

I paused. "Let's just see where this is going for a while," I replied. "I don't want him getting attached to someone who may not be around all the time. You understand don't you?"

"Yeah, I understand," Deon replied, as he opened the door.

"Deon," I said, "maybe I could bring him to one of your games one day."

"Yeah, that'll be fine." he said, as he descended the stairs to leave.

I thought it strange that he didn't kiss me before he left……I felt as if, somehow, I'd hurt his feelings

Chapter 16

"Deke!" Momma yelled to daddy, out the back door when I arrived. "Tell Ray-Ja his momma's here! They were playing out back waitin' on you," she said.

I had parked at the curb, in front of the house, this time, which was unusual, because there was always so much traffic on Branch Avenue.

"Why'd you come in the front?" Momma asked. "You must want somebody to tear that l'il piece of car of yours up."

"I'll only be a minute... I'm just gonna get Ray-Ja.... I'm takin' him to the park. Leslie and Robert are going to meet us there. Just then, Ray-Ja tore into the room. "I'm ready, mommy, let's go!" Ray-Ja exclaimed, excited, his face flushed.

"Can I get a kiss first?" I asked.

"Sure!" He said, as he hugged me, squeezing my neck, tightly, and kissed me.

"Ok, let's go. Robert has been waiting all week to play with you, Little Man."

"Yeeaah! C'mon, mommy!" He said, pulling me toward the front door. "Let's go!"

Leslie and I sat on the park bench watching Ray and Robert playing on the jungle gym.

"I didn't think you were coming." said Leslie. "You didn't call me back, until I was walking out the door."

"I know...., I meant to call you back last night, but Deon called, and ended up coming over."

"What? You had a date on a Friday night?" Leslie asked. "Where was Ray-Ja?"

"My parent's kept him last night." I said.

"Well, you could've called me when he left... You know I stay up late."

"Well, that still would have been this morning." I said.

"SHUT THE FRONT DOOR!!! She yelled, "YOU ARE LYING!.... HE SPENT THE NIGHT!?!"

"Lower your voice!" I said, "....before Ray-Ja hears you!"

"Jackie, he spent the night?" She asked, lowering her voice several decibels.

"Yes, Leslie, he spent the night..., but nothing happened."

"You are out of your mind, girl? You haven't had a date in... What?... six..., seven months and you have a fine black man in your house--with no kids--and you didn't do nothing!... You didn't give him...... ooooh....! What your Momma call it....? some 'Lucy!'" She said laughing.

"That's right," I confirmed, laughing, as well. "As a matter of fact, we fell asleep on the sofa."

"Jackie, as hard as your ass sleep, he probably took your 'Lucy', and brought you back in the living room...for all you know.

I laughed, "No, we just held each other right there on the sofa.... and slept."

"It's something wrong with him, then....If he didn't try, to get in your pants the whole night!"

I was cracking up laughing by now. "Leslie; there is nothing wrong with him...I assure you!"

"OH…! OH…! Assure me! Assure me! You holdin' out! You gave him some; you gave him some last night, didn't you?" She accused. "You know you can tell me, girl!?"

I looked her dead in her face…"Leslie, I swear, I did not give him any, last night! I stated solemnly. "I promise you."

"Well, I can tell that you really like him, so you'll be changin' that tune real soon." She predicted.

I just looked over at Ray-Ja, running from the jungle gym to the swings, and smiled.

It was a beautiful spring day; the first day of daylight savings time. I explained to Ray-Ja what that meant stating that it would stay lighter outside a little longer in the evenings. "More time for me to play, Mommy?" he asked.

"Yes.., more time for you to play." I replied, tickling him.

Although it was Sunday morning, I had decided not to go to church. I needed to get caught up on some washing and spend some time with Ray-Ja. I had just fixed him a bowl of Fruit Loops when the phone rang.

"Hello? Oh, hi Momma... No we're not going today...I know, I know... Ok, call me when you get back from church." I knew that call was coming! *Along with the... 'If you can go to work, every day, you can go to church on Sunday' speech.' I used to think, I should tape it, and play it everytime I ditched church--save her the time...and me the aggravation--but, that would take all the fun out of it for her...*

"Oh..., and don't forget we all meetin' over to Brenda's today for Rikki's birthday party; it's at 4:00," she reminded me.

"I had completely forgotten about that." I said.

"Well, Brenda will be upset if you don't bring Ray-Ja."

I told her that I would see her there. After breakfast, Ray-Ja and I watched some television together, and I remembered that I hadn't bought a gift for Rikki.

"Ray-Ja," I said. "Let's get dressed. We need to go shopping for a birthday present for Rikki, for her party, today."

"A party!" Ray-Ja squealed.

"Yes, all of your cousins will be there, so let's get dressed and go shopping."

"I know what she wants," Ray-Ja said, gleefully. "I want to get her the new G.I. Joe!"

"Ray-Ja, she's a girl. I don't think that she would want that," I said.

"Well, if she don't want it...., I'll keep it!" he said.

"You think you are so slick." I said laughing. "No.., I'm sure we'll find something nice for her, and it won't be a G.I. Joe."

We arrived around 4:15, and could hardly find a place to park. "Good grief," I said, "How many people are here for this kid's party?"

Ray-Ja saw his cousin, Kenya, and took out running to play with him in the back yard. I entered the house, to the blaring sound of *'Skin Tight,'* by the Ohio players. "Hey, everybody!" I said, almost screaming, to which several of my relatives turned and waved or started to walk in my direction.

"Lisa, isn't this suppose to be a party for Rikki?" I asked. It looked more like a family reunion.

"Well," Lisa said. "That's what it stared out as; but folks started coming and bring dishes, and the next thing you know, Glenn was firin' up the grill....and that's all it took! Gregory and some of his buddies went to get hot dogs and burgers; they should be back shortly."

Just then Momma and Daddy arrived bearing gifts for Rikki like it was Christmas, and hollering "Where's my grandbaby...? Where's my birthday girl? "

"Somebody turn that music down, I cain't hardly hear myself think, in here." My daddy said, as we all acknowledged their presence, and proceeded to enjoy our time together at this birthday party-turned-mini-reunion.

Momma had drawn a crowd while dancing to the chant, "Go Momma! Go Momma!" from her extended offspring, when Gregory and three of his friends returned with the food.

"Hey, baby girl," he said to me and pecked me on my cheek. "How you doin'?"

"Fine, how are you...and where in the world did you find Michael?" I asked Gregory, as Michael made a beeline in my direction.

"Hey, Jackie! How you been, girl? It's so good to see you. How long has it been; 2 years...? Damn! I see you still looking good!" He said, as he gave me a hug.

"Hey, Michael, how've you been?" I replied, "And where have you been all this time?"

"Well, you know, a brother had an opportunity to do some things..., so I moved down to 'Hot Lanta' and started my own little computer business. I was up here visiting my grandparents and ran into Garrett and Five in the Safeway. They told me that all y'all was here, so I said, man, I gots to go by and see Ms. Garrett and Jackie and dem."

"Well I am glad to see you Michael. How's Sharice?" I knew mentioning his wife would give him a reality check.

"Uhh, Reecy...? She's fine..., you know..., she's fine. She didn't come up with me this time, but, I'll tell her you asked about her."

I thought, 'Sure you will...'

"Where's Momma Garret?" Michael asked, changin' the subject real quick.

"Momma's downstairs, cutting up, dancing for the kids, go on down there..., she'll be so glad to see you."

"Ok, I'll talk to you in a few...," he said.

"...See you later, Michael."

I picked up my drink and found a seat on the front porch, where it wasn't quite as noisy. 'Damn, Michael, of all people'...I had to smile in spite of myself. I'd had a real thing for him at one time. He did everything but turn himself inside out to get with me, but I'd had held firm to my standard rule; not to deal with any of my brother's friends! But, if there was ever a time that I considered breaking that rule, it was for Michael. It was like; he could hear my thoughts because just then he came out on the porch.

"Jackie, it really is good to see you," he said, again.

"And it's nice to see you again, too, Michael. Um... How are your grandparents? Is everything ok with them?" I asked.

"Huh, yeah… You know, since my parents died, I handle a lot of their business 'n things for them. They're thinking about moving back down South, since my grandfather will be retiring soon."

"Oh, that's nice. That may be the best thing for them....have them living close to you. Look, Michael... When I heard about the accident...., about you losing your parents...., I was so sorry. You know that my thoughts and prayers where with you, don't you? I wanted to get in touch with you, but, I didn't know if Sharice would have a problem with that. So.... I'm so sorry." I said, as I got up and gave him a hug.

"Jackie, I know you...and I know that you were thinking about me. I appreciate it. Gregory called almost everyday...and that was cool. You know y'all are like family to me," He said while still holding me.

"Jackie, I wish things had been different between us."

I pulled from his embrace, and said, "Me, too."

"I'm only going to be here for a few days...I'd like to take you out to dinner or maybe for a drink or something, before I leave." Michael said.

"Michael, you know I don't drink."

"But, I bet you still like Chinese food?" He said, smiling again. "I remember, that is your favorite food." How about going over to Wah Ling's, over in the old neighborhood, for dinner?"

"That would be nice." I said, "I haven't been there in years. How about Tuesday at 8:00? I'll meet you there."

"Tuesday at 8:00..... I can hardly wait." he said, winking at me and chuckled at his silly rhyme.

It was getting dark, and the party was starting to wind down. Everyone was saying their goodbyes and leaving, so they could start preparing themselves for the upcoming work week. Gregory walked me to my car, carrying Ray-Ja on his shoulders, "You know, Jackie, Michael was real glad to see you."

"I know, it was good seeing him again, too. As a matter of fact, he and I going to have dinner before he goes back to Atlanta." I said.

"Did he tell you that he and Reecy are separating?"

"No, he didn't mention that." I said, straightening up from putting Ray in his car seat. "He told me he was here to help his grandparents take care of some business."

"Well--between you and me--he got a large settlement from his parents' death, and word is, Reecy started shopping like a white woman wit his money. Michael said she started goin' out, and he thinks she's cheatin' on him."

"I really hate that he's going through so much, but, you know, he wasn't always honest with her, either." I said.

Under no circumstances was I going to tell Gregory about the affair that Michael and I almost had.

"Anyway..., like I said. It is good to see him again, and...it will be nice to have dinner and talk about old times with an old friend."

Gregory closed my door, then motioned for me to roll down the window. "One more thing, you know Michael is sweet on you," he said.

I started my car. "Michael is married, and he is just a friend. I'm not 12 anymore, and you don't have to worry about me; besides, you know it would be a cold day in Hell before I would date any of your friends. Now let me get this boy over to momma's, so I can get him in bed by nine. Love ya... I'll talk to you later." I said and pulled off.

Chapter 17

There were no messages on the answering machine, when I got home. As it was just a little past nine, I decided to give Deon a call. He didn't answer, so I left a message and got ready for bed.

The next morning, Leslie and I got on the elevator together. "Leslie, do you remember my friend Michael, who lost his parent in that car accident about a year ago?" I asked.

"Yeah, I remember him. Didn't he move to Atlanta or something?"

"Yeah," "Well, I was over to Brenda's, yesterday, and he was there with Gregory." I told her. "Leslie..., he looks as fine as ever. I almost passed out when he walked in."

"Uh, didn't you tell me he was married? What happened to your rules? Leslie asked.

"Rule number 1: Not if they are a friend of my brothers; and, rule number 2:--especially--Not if they are married!" I chanted, in a mantra-like cadence.

"Who's married...?" Lula asked, listening to our conversation, as we passed through the receptionist area. "Jackie?! You mean after he stood you up..., you still messing with that guy?" Lula ranted. "Just 'cause he sent you a buncha tired roses...? Jackie, you better than that... an' you know it... Girl, leave him alone! Yeah...Ok...! I know he's fine and everything..., but he ain't worth it, especially, if he's married, ta boot!.... Leave that man alone!"

"Lula! What are you talking about? Why don't you get some business of your own..., so you can leave other people's alone!" Leslie snapped, in my defense.

"No, Leslie she's right…," I said.

"What?" Leslie stopped, with her mouth open.

"Lula's right." I repeated.

Leslie just burst out laughing and buzzed us in. "Why do you keep stringin' her along, Jackie?"

"Because I can… and, like you said. She's so damn nosey!……… Anyway…, as I was saying…, Michael--he's not just a friend of my brother's; he's a friend to our whole family. He's only in town for a few days, on business, and he and I are going to visit the old neighborhood and have dinner Tuesday night."

"Jackie, what is going on with you? You go from not having a date in months, to…what?.. three --that I know of--in one week….. and one was a sleepover." She recounted, incredulously.

"So who are you dating….Deon AND Michael?"

"Right now, I don't feel like I'm dating anyone. I haven't spoken to Deon, since Saturday morning, and like I told you, Michael is just a family friend."

"Yeah…, the 'family friend' that you were in love with!" She said, and rolled her eyes at me.

"No, I wasn't!"

"Uhh…, Yeah, you were, until you found out he was married." She continued.

"You know what Leslie!" I said, "I can, clearly, see right now that I tell you, entirely, too much! I'm going to have to do you, like I do Lula!" I said, closing the subject.

"Mommy, the flower man came here for you today." Ray-Ja said, as soon as walked in mamma's house.

"What? The flower man?.... Who is the flower man?" I asked, squeezing him on top of his head.

"I dunno," he replied. "But he left you some flowers."

I walked into the living room and the smell of roses hit me before I even saw them; twenty-four, beautiful, long-stemmed roses in a lead crystal vase were sitting on the table. "Oh, my goodness, these are beautiful." I said, "Who in the world is sending me flowers?"

"I started to read your card, but the envelope was sealed." Momma said. "You know that this vase is lead crystal? I had to sign for them flowers, probably, because this vase alone is worth two-three-hundred dollars."

I knew that couldn't be from Deon, because he didn't have my parent's address. I opening the small envelope, I took out the card. They were from Michael. The message read: 'Beautiful flowers, for a beautiful lady.' 'Love, Michael'.

Momma was leaning over my shoulder--not even pretending she wasn't trying to read the card, "Who they from?"

"Michael, you remember Michael, don't you momma?"

"Of course, I remember, Michael..., Jackie, I just seen him the other day," she replied. "Why's he sending you flowers, and in such an expensive vase?"

"I don't know, I was talking to him, at Brenda's, about his mom and dad, and maybe he was trying to thank me for showing him that I cared about what he was going through."

"Look more like he is thanking you for what he intends on doin' if you ask me." Momma said, walking back into the kitchen.

"What are you talking about momma? Have you forgotten that Michael is married?"

"Jackie, don't you forget that Michael is married," returned Momma. "I remember him hanging 'round here after the games, pretending to be here to see Gregory, and watching your every move."

"Momma, we were kids then... and he did have a crush on me, but that was years ago."

"I saw him lookin' at you the other day Jackie. And he wasn't looking at you like you was no kid, either." Momma said, leaving the kitchen.

"Ray, c'mon and eat," I said, "so I can get you ready for bed."

When momma went back into the kitchen, I followed her, "Momma, please don't talk like that in front of Ray, he still remembers Reggie, and I make it a point not to bring other men around him or to talk about anybody when I'm with him."

Momma put the serving spoon down and turned to me, "Jackie, Ray told me you got a boyfriend."

"What? Why would he think that?" I asked.

"He said that you and Miss Leslie were talking about your boyfriend at the playground the other day." I thought; 'The distance from where we were sitting, to the area where the Ray and Robert were playing, was too far for them to overhear what Leslie and I were talking about at the park--so why did he think that I had a boyfriend?'

When I tucked Ray-Ja in later that night, I asked him if he had told grandma that I had a boyfriend. "Yeah... 'Cause, Mr. Al was tellin' Miss Ann..., in our building..., that you had a new boyfriend." he said, "...an' I told grandma.

I kissed him. "Ray-Ja, Mommy doesn't have a boyfriend, Mr. Al is mistaken."

"Mommy, everybody needs friends...I have boy-friends and I have girl-friends." He said as he yawned, sleepily.

I just smiled at him, and laid down beside him until he fell asleep.

As I was driving home, I was hoping that 'Mr.' Al was still up, so I could give him a piece of my mind for talking about me--and for doing it in front of my child. I put the vase of flowers down in front of my apartment door, and turned and knocked on Al's door like I was the police. When he answered, I got right in his face, "Al, what did you tell Ann about me!" I asked.

"Whoa....! What, what are you talking about, Jackie?" Al backed up a step. "I just mentioned that you had a new friend."

"Al, mind your own business! Do not talk about me to anyone! Do not talk about me at all!"

"I'm sorry Jackie, I didn't mean any harm, and I was just telling Ann in case she saw a strange man coming in the building that you have a new friend."

"It's none of your business and don't talk about me again! Especially; in front of my child! Do you hear me?" I said, leaving out and slamming his door.

I unlocked my door and grabbed the vase of flowers up from the floor, threw my purse on the bar, and sat the flowers on the table. I hit the power button on the TV, kicked my shoes off, and started down the hall, when there was knock at the door. In my stockinged feet, I walked to the door and snatched it open--thinking that it was Al, coming to apologize again--it wasn't Al..., it was Deon.

"Hey! What are doing here?" I asked.

"I'm sorry to come by without calling, but I wanted to talk to you about something." he said.

"Deon. It's late, and I have a problem with you just dropping by without calling, so maybe we could talk tomorrow."

"Where have you been, Jackie? I only came by because I've been trying to reach you for two days..., I mean..., I wasn't even getting through to your answering machine."

"I haven't gotten any calls from you Deon..., I haven't heard from you since you left Saturday morning!"

"Can we not have this conversation in the doorway?" he asked.

Standing my ground and not moving from the door, I said. "Like I said, you need to call me before you come over. I would really appreciate you doing that."

"Fine, Jackie!" Deon said, turning to leave, "I'm sorry that I was concerned!"

I turned the lock off the knob, and stepped out into the hall as Deon was descending the stairs, I leaned over the railing, almost talking to the top of his head. "Deon, wait! I was upset about something that happened earlier...and took it out on you. I didn't mean to be upset with you but..., I do have a problem with people who drop by without calling."

"I did call..., I even stopped by earlier..., didn't Al tell you? I was knocking at your door when he opened his, and said you weren't home and he didn't know when you would be back."

"Can you come in for a minute?" I asked, knowing that Al was leaning on his door listening to our conversation.

Deon came back up the stairs and entered the apartment, but didn't sit down. His eyes were glued to the flowers on the table. "The florist must have gotten my order mixed up." He said, "I thought I sent a dozen roses."

"You did, those are not the flowers that you sent me." I clarified.

"Well, like I said, I just wanted to know that you were ok, since you hadn't called, and I couldn't reach you."

"You must have been dialing the wrong number, because there's nothing wrong with my phone and, neither you, nor anyone else, has left any messages," I said picking it up off of the hook to prove my point. I put it to my ear, but didn't hear a dial tone.

"What's wrong with my phone?" I said, looking down at the receiver, embarrassed, while remembering the collection call that I had gotten about the bill, last week.

"It's been disconnected." 'No wonder!' I thought. "I'll have to get it straight tomorrow," I said out loud.

Deon walked to the door, "I'll talk to you later, Jackie."

"Deon, wait a minute." I said.

He opened the door and left.

'Damn, how embarrassing was that!' I'd better remember to call the phone company when I get to work and make a payment..., Hell....I'd better call the power company, too, before that gets turned off...... Get it together, girl, you're slippin'.'

The phone was ringing, when I walked in the door that evening, I thought, 'at least it's back on,' I pulled my earring off and answered. "Hello?"

"Hello...? Jackie?"

"Yes."

"This is Michael…"

"Oh, Michael. Hey, how are you?"

"Fine…, um, Jackie, you even sound good on the phone."

"Michael, where did you get my number?"

"I stopped by your mom's today, with Gregory, and mentioned that I wanted to talk to you. Paige was there and she gave it to me. It's ok, isn't it?"

"Yeah. Yeah, it's ok." I said, "So what's up?"

"Are we still meeting for dinner?"

"Sure, I'll be there at 8:00; Wah Ling's right?"

"Right! Right.., ok, I'll see you there then."

"Ok, see ya."

I arrived at Wah Ling's about 8:10. Michael stood up when I walked in so that I could see where he was seated.

"Hi," I said, giving him a brief hug. "I'm sorry, I'm running a little late, I stopped for gas on the way over."

"It's ok, but I could have done that for you, later."

"Thanks for offering, but its ok. I just didn't want to have to stop in the morning."

We both picked up our menus and looked over the selections.

"So, are you ready to order?" He inquired.

"Sure, I'm starving." I said, in anticipation.

Just then, the waitress came over to our table and we placed our order.

"This place has not changed at all, has it?" Michael observed.

I looked around the familiar restaurant that I had patronized at least twice a week growing up. "No, it hasn't change at all." I said, "I loved this place,.... I hope the food is still as good."

Michael and I made small talk about people that he had run into since he had been home and how much the area had changed.

I mentioned that Wah Ling's use to have fast service, while looking at my watch. It had been twenty minutes since we ordered… just as Michael said, "I think this is our order now."

The food was as wonderful as I remembered! "This is really good... How is yours?"

"Just like I remember," Michael said. "I'm glad we came here; now, it really feels like old times with you."

"Michael, the flowers that you sent were beautiful. Thank you."

"I'm glad you liked them. I wanted to thank you for being so thoughtful."

"I appreciate that, but it really wasn't necessary… and that vase... Oh my God…that vase is gorgeous. You really shouldn't have sent something that expensive."

"I'm just glad that you like it." He said.

There was a moment of uncomfortable silence between us…"I'm stuffed…, this was wonderful! And it has really been nice; talking about old times… seeing you again." I began....

"Are you calling it a night already? I thought we could talk a little longer."

"I looked at my watch…, it was just coming up on 10:30…, ok.., just a while longer, but I have to get up in the morning remember. You're the one on vacation!"

"Humm…some vacation," he mumbled.

"Michael, what's wrong?" I asked.

"Jackie.., Reecy and I are separated; I'm filing for divorce when I get back to Atlanta."

"I'm sorry to hear that, Michael."

"Are you?"

"Well, I mean…, I hate to hear about anyone's marriage breaking up; especially when there is a child involved."

"To be perfectly honest, I'm not even sure if Michael Jr. is mine." he said. "I think she's been cheating on me for a while now. I'm having a paternity test done, as well. I mean..' don't get me wrong, I love Jr., but, …I need to know for sure."

"I understand, and I hate that you are going through something this painful."

He reached across the table and took my hand. "Jackie, I'm glad that I have you to talk to about this. I haven't spoken to anyone about this mess, since I found out about her cheating."

"Michael, how can you be so sure that she's been unfaithful, to you. I mean its one thing to think that someone is cheating…; but, if you don't have any real proof…?"

"I know, because I saw her with my own eyes. She doesn't know that I saw her…, but, I saw her, Jackie!" I was meeting a client one evening, about a location for a new store over in Decatur. When we left the restaurant, I saw my wife. "Can you imagine that!?!" If I hadn't been with that client…, I don't know what I would have done. I don't know, maybe it was best that I couldn't react like I wanted to at the time…… I don't know, Jackie…, I don't know."

I placed my other hand on top of Michael's.

"Have you tried talking to Reecy about it, Michael? Maybe it's not what you think, at all."

"I saw them kissing." Michael said, as he pulled his from under mine. "I was walking to the corner ...they had stopped for the light! She leaned over and kissed him! I know what I saw, Jackie!"

In his intensity, Michael had raised his voice loudly enough to attract the attention of the people sitting around us. "Michael, I know you're hurting and that you're upset, but I was just asking because maybe your marriage is salvageable. I remember once when you were not as faithful as you should have been in your marriage."

"Jackie, I'm really sorry about that.....about lying to you. I should have told you that Reecy and I had gotten married."

"Yeah, I know, but you didn't. Look, everybody makes mistakes, and, maybe, that's all Reecy has done... Talk to her, Michael." I said, as I slid out of the booth to leave.

Michael grabbed my arm, "Jackie, I really am sorry…, not about Reecy, I'm sorry that I hurt you."

"That was a long time ago.., and I got over it. Talk to her, Michael; talk to Reecy."

"Jackie, I don't want to fix this; I want to get it over with, and when I do, I want to show you how sorry I really am about what happened between us."

"Michael, I have to go now; take care, and have a safe trip home." I said, as I left.

Chapter 18

When I arrived home, I prepared myself for bed. Looked at the clock; it was just ten. *'It's too late to call, I thought,'* I'll call tomorrow. I turned on the television, but couldn't stop thinking about Deon.

"Hello?" He answered his phone on the third ring.

"Hello, Deon. This is Jackie."

"I was wondering if you would like to come to dinner tomorrow?" I invited him.

"Jackie, I have plans for tomorrow, I'm sorry."

"Oh! Ok..., well maybe some other time..."

"Yeah, maybe."

"Deon, I'm sorry about the other night. I guess that's all I really wanted say, and I thought that I could do it over dinner. Besides, I miss talking with you."

"Um..., I thought you would be talking to whoever sent you those expensive flowers." He said.

"Deon, those where from a friend of the family. I told you that I was not involved with anyone..."

"I know you did, but look..., I'm going to have to get back with you. I'll call you tomorrow."

"Deon?,.. Oh!, I'm sorry, I didn't know you were on the phone." I heard a female voice say in the background.

"I'm sorry, Deon," I said," I won't keep you any longer....I didn't know that *you* had company."

"She's a friend of the family." He said.

"Oh..., I see..., ok then, I'll let you go. Goodbye, Deon."

"G'bye.," he said, and hung up.

'....Friend of the family my ass,' I fumed, hanging up the phone. 'He IS seeing someone!

'It's after ten at night, what 'friend of the family' is there at this time of night? Yeah..., she's a friend of the family alright!' I fumed, as I fluffed and punched my pillow. 'That's it! I tried to make things right. I tried to apologize for the other night, but it's cool..... Yeah... It's cool. He makes me sick, with his smug attitude, *'She's a friend of the family...'* he says. He only said that because of what I told him about Michael. I don't have time to play games..., so whoever she is... she can have him! I don't have time for this foolishness."

I pulled the pillow from the other side of my bed, pummelled it into submission, laid my head down, inhaled deeply--exhausted-- and smelled Deon's cologne... "Damn!"

I drove to work on Wednesday, because I had a dental appointment. I hated driving in downtown D. C., especially, during the morning and evening rush hours--not to mention the cost of all-day parking.... But otherwise, I would have had to catch two subway trains and a bus to get to the dentist. The telephone call with Deon didn't help my mood any, either. As soon as I got to my desk, Leslie came over, "Jackie, I think something is going on with Carolyn. Hasn't she seemed a little distant to you, lately? She's been missing days from work, and when I call, she's always too busy to talk. I don't know..., but something just doesn't seem right with her."

"Leslie to be perfectly honest, I really hadn't thought about it, until you mentioned it. Is she here today?" I asked, looking around for Carolyn.

"Yeah, but she looks like hell. Maybe you should talk to her." She urged.

"Why do I always have to be the one to pry things out of people? Why can't you do it?" I complained.

"C'mon Jackie, you know people open up to you. You think something is going on with her son again? You know he got into that trouble with the law a few months back. Maybe it's something we can help her with..., but she won't open up to me. Are you her friend or what?" I just looked at Leslie, and she knew she had talked me into talking with Carolyn.

"Hey, Carolyn what's up?" I asked, as I sat in the chair beside her desk. "Are you alright?"

"Jackie...," she said, with tears filling her eyes. "I don't know what I'm going to do....." I saw that she was getting more upset. "Carolyn, let's go into one of the conference rooms so that we can talk."

I went over to our manager, Ms. Hoofers, and told her that Carolyn was upset and that I was going to take her off the floor to talk with her.

"Oh, by all means, Jackie, and let me know, if there is anything that I can do." Lucy said.

"Ok, thanks, Lucy. I will."

Carolyn was crying before we reached to room, I hugged her and asked her what was going on. She said that the trouble her son Troy had gotten into could cause him to have to go to jail. Carolyn is a very private person, so I didn't know all of the particulars of what had happened with Troy in the first place.

"Why? What happened?" I asked.

"Troy had gone over to his girlfriend's house and as he was leaving his car wouldn't start. He called his friend, Kenny, who works on cars, and asked him if he could come to look at it. Well, Kenny comes and looks at the car and it needed a part, so Troy and Kenny drive down to the Auto Care to get the part they need to fix Troy's car.

"I never really cared for Kenny," she continued," because he always seemed sneaky to me; but, he and Troy have been friends since they met in elementary school. Well, they get the part for the car, but on the way back, Kenny runs a light over on Alabama avenue and the police see him. Kenny keeps going, and it turns into a chase. Troy said that he is asking him, 'Man, what's wrong with you!' "And kept telling him to pull over! Kenny tells him, that before Troy called about his car, he was on his way make a drop, and that he can't stop, because he has the drugs in the car.

"Now, Troy, he's all caught up in this mess, 'cause when the police did catch 'em, they found the drugs, and since Troy was with him..., he got charged with possession with intent to distribute. Now, Jackie, I'm not saying that my Troy is no angel..., Lord knows I've had my share of problems with him..., but mostly it's the daddy-baby kind of drama, never anything, like this! His lawyer said, because he doesn't have a record or anything that it might not go so bad for him, but..., I don't know. You know all they want to do is lock our black men up in some jail somewhere."

I handed Carolyn some tissues so that she could wipe her face.

"Carolyn, where is Troy, now?" I asked.

"They still holding him down at county right now, his lawyer's trying to get him out, but they got to wait on somebody to sign off on something.... I don't know much about this stuff... Jackie, this is such a mess. I am so scared that they going to charge him and send him to jail for something that Kenny did."

Carolyn dropped her head on the desk and cried like a baby. I slid over closer to her, rubbed her back..., and let her cry. Lula knocked on the door, opened it and stepped in. She placed a box on tissues on the table and left. Apparently, she could hear Carolyn crying out in the receptionist area--and she wanted to do something to help.

Carolyn was moaning and crying, saying, over and over, that she did know what she was going to do.

"Listen....," I said, "Let me let Lucy know that you need to take the rest of the day off. You have too much on your mind to be any good at work today. I'll be right back."

When I stepped out of the room, Lula was there, "Is she alright?"

"No." I said, as I rounded her desk to call Lucy.

I didn't want to have a conversation about Carolyn in front of Lula, but I didn't want to be away from Carolyn for too long. I told Lucy that Carolyn wasn't doing well and that it might be best if she left for the day.

"Of course," she said. I asked her if she would and ask Leslie to bring Carolyn's purse up front. She said, "Of course." and hung up.

I turned to go back in with Carolyn, "Let me know if there is anything that I can do." Lula said.

I thanked her and went back in with Carolyn, who had pulled herself together, somewhat. "Look, do you need me to take you home? I scheduled for half-a-day today, anyway, and I can cancel my appointment and hang out with you for a while if you want me to."

"Could you?" She asked, looking still worried, but glad to have company.

"No problem," I said.

Leslie was waiting outside the door with Carolyn's purse. She gave her a hug and told her that she would call and check on her later.

It had been a long day.... After spending time with an emotional Carolyn, playing all evening with an energetic Ray-Ja and driving home in maddening D.C. traffic..., I was tired. I showered and climbed into bed, turned out the light, and the phone rang.

"Hello?" I said, sound as tired as I felt.

"Did I wake you?"

"No..., but I am tired, and I would like to go to sleep."

"I'm sorry to call you so late." Michael said, "But you've been on my mind since the other night."

"Michael, what are you saying? What are you trying to tell me? You're married remember? I know it this time--before, I did'nt know--and I don't deal with married men. I know you're going through a rough time... and I AM sorry, but, you are still married. So if you're talking about us being anything more than friends..., it's not going to happen." I told him.

"I understand Jackie, It's just that I have been so unhappy for so long, that spending time with you the other night was one of the best times that I have had in a long time."

"I hate that you are going through a rough time Michael, but I am not the one that you should be turning to. Go back home and talk to your wife, and try Michael...., try to save your marriage. You owe that much to your son." I said. "Michael...? Michael, are you still there?"

"I am not in love with her anymore, Jackie. I haven't been for a very long time." He said.

"Michael, if that is true, don't you think that she was aware of that? Maybe, that is why she felt the need to turn to someone else."

"Jackie, are you involved with someone?" Michael asked.

"Michael..., I have met someone, and I really like him; we're taking it a day at a time right now; but..., I'm not the issue. You are married--happy or not--and you still belong to someone else.... and I don't mess with other people's husbands." I re-emphasized.

"Do I know him?" Michael asked, clearly ignoring everything I had just said.

"Michael, It's late and I am tired, what time is your flight tomorrow?" I exhaled, exhausted and not liking the direction this conversation was taking.

"It's at 4:00, but I have to be at the airport an hour early. Are you going to work tomorrow?"

"Yes, I am, so maybe you could call me later in the week and let me know how you are doing."

"Would it be possible to take you to lunch tomorrow?" He asked.

"Michael, I don't think that that would be a good idea; I think that it would only complicate things."

"What are you afraid of Jackie?" Michael persisted. "Are you afraid that you still have feelings for me?"

"Michael you are special to me, you always have been, but we've been down that road remember?" I reminded him. "I would like to know that we can continue to be friends; I care about you...and I always will..., but that's all."

Michael held the line without saying anything...

"Hey, call me later in the week and let me know how things are going, ok?" I asked.

"Ok, Jackie. And thanks for being there for me and letting me..., you know..., vent my frustrations."

"Michael, that's what friends do for each other. Tell Reecy, hello for me. Talk to you later." I said softly, and hung up.

Chapter 19

"How's Carolyn doing?" Leslie asked, before we settled down to tackle today's load of clients.

"She was doing a lot better when I left her yesterday. Her lawyer called with good news about the case." I told her.

"What case? Leslie asked.

"Well, Troy got in a little trouble, but everything is going to work out fine, probably because he doesn't have a criminal record. Anyway, she should be coming in shortly. "What's up with you these days? We haven't had much time to talk lately." I asked, turning the questions away from Carolyn's business.

"Nothing girl, same stuff....different day; Robert is driving me crazy, but other than that everything's cool.... How about you?"

"Leslie, I haven't spoken to Deon for a few days, as a matter of fact I think that he might be involved with someone. That's probably why he took so long to call me in the first place.... Anyway, Michael was here for a few days…"

"Michael! Jackie, are you seeing him again?" Leslie asked.

"Not like you think, I told you that I ran into him over to Brenda's…, we had dinner the other night. He and Reecy are going through some rough times."

"Probably, because he is such a liar! Is he cheating on her again?" Leslie asked, keepin' it real.

"….I don't think so; it seems that it's the other way around this time... He thinks she's is cheating on him."

"Good! He deserves it! I hope she breaks his heart..., so he'll know how it feels to have someone you love cheat on you and lie to you!"

"Leslie! Let it go! I hope that they can try to work it out for their child's sake, if nothing more."

"Well, I know how much he hurt you Jackie, and I think he deserves all the pain that she gives him." Leslie said, ever a faithful friend.

"Leslie that was a long time ago and I still don't think that he meant to hurt me."

"Oh really..., he knew that you would not be bothered with him if you knew that he was married!"

"Michael and I have always been attracted to each other, since we were children, and besides… nothing happen. I'm not saying that it would not have if… I hadn't found out about him being married, but I guess everything happens for a reason. He is talking crazy, like he wants something.., or he wants us to get together; but, I know it's because of what he's going through."

"Yeah..., well I know one thing..., I know that you better not be thinking about getting back with him!"

"No, that's not going to happen; but, it was good seeing him again and he still looks good.

"He don't hold a candle to Deon, though!" Leslie said, and nudged me.

"I know, but I don't know what going on with Deon so, I might have to keep Michael on my back burner." I said jokingly.

"Don't even think about it," Leslie said, as threw she purse in her desk drawer and sat down to start working.

"Where do you want to go for lunch?" Leslie asked.

"How about getting a salad from Cerro's?" I said.

"That sounds good to me, let me find out if Carolyn wants to go."

As I was getting up from my desk, Leslie returned, "She doesn't, want to go out. She brought her lunch today."

"Ok, I'll meet you at the elevator in a few minutes then…"

"Jackie, if Cerro's is crowded, let's just get our salads to go and eat over at the park in front of the District Building."

"Ok, let's get it to go, anyway, because it's supposed to be really nice out…, and I could use some fresh air."

"Sounds like a plan to me." Leslie said.

"I could sit out here all day…," Leslie said, sitting in the sun, while stuffing salad in her mouth.

"It is nice out, isn't it? And the view of those guys playing chess is not bad either." I said.

"Hey Leslie, isn't that Jamal, playing at the board over by the fountain?"

"No, I don't think so, that guy looks to good to be Jamal."

"No, Leslie…, I think that is Jamal." said Jackie,

"I thought he moved to Baltimore…, to work for that engineering firm."

"I thought so, too. Look…! He's looking over here. That is Jamal, Leslie."

"I'm going over to speak to him, wanna come?"

"Naw, tell him I said hello." She said, not looking up, spearing a tomato with her fork.

As I was approaching, he had just finished his game and met me a few feet from where he had been playing.

"Did you win?" I asked, while opening my arms to give him a big hug.

"You better believe it! Jackie, how have you been? Is that Leslie sitting over there on the bench?"

"Fine, and, yes, that's Leslie." I said, looking back over my shoulder.

"How have you been …and what are you doing in this neck of the woods? I thought you were working up in Baltimore."

"I'm fine, and I had to come down here to present some specs for a construction site to some big wigs over at the District Building. I got finished sooner than I thought, and came over to see if I still had it goin' on with my chess game."

"How have you been, Jackie..? Man...it's good to see you! I ran into Toni, a few weeks back, down at the Harbor, did you know that she was pregnant? Almost 6 months now!"

"Get outta here, what in the world is Toni doing still having babies at her age!" I said laughing.

"I don't know, but she looked good. I met her new husband, too... Seems real cool."

"So; what's going on, over at the job since I left?" "Is Gerald Lucas, still working there?"

"No, Gerald left, shortly after you did, but Phyllis Columbus took his old job and she is really turning the department around."

"Jamal, wait until I tell Lula, I saw you, she will fall out!" I said.

"Oh my god! How is Lula; still nosey as hell?"

"You know it..., and proud of it." I said, "C'mon over and speak to Leslie for a minute."

"Hey Leslie," Jamal said, leaning over to kiss her on the cheek.

"Hey Jamal!!" "How in the world are you doing, and what in the world are you doing here?"

"Doing a little work and catching a little game in the process," Jamal said. "Leslie, you looking good girl! What you trying to do..., get high school skinny?"

"I wish!" Leslie said, "Jackie got me eating these damn salads, when you know I rather be over at KFC piggin' out on some yard bird!"

"Well, those salads are paying off because you really look good Leslie."

I leaned out of Jamal's view and raised my eyebrows at Leslie.

"So Jamal, how is...what's her name? Cheryl...., Shirley?" I asked.

"Yeah...., Cheryl... I haven't spoken to her in months; I guess she's fine though."

"Oh really, you two aren't seeing each other anymore? I just knew y'all were still kickin' it."

"Naw, I mean, you know..., we did for a minute but..., naw, ...you know we just... It didn't work out." He said.

"Aww, that's too bad." I said, guiding him to the seat beside Leslie on the bench.

"Leslie isn't that terrible.... about Jamal and Cheryl, I mean?" I asked.

"I'm not surprise." Leslie said, bluntly, while tilting her head and squinting at me, "She was always kind of strange to me anyway."

"Jamal! What are you doing next weekend?" I asked.

"Nothing, why? What's up?"

"Leslie is having a little get together, and it would be nice if you could come."

"Sure, I'd love too. Is it going to be over to your place, Les?"

Looking surprised, but managing to say through her clenched teeth, "No, Jamal, it's... uh, going to be over to Jackie's. You gotta come; she is going to cook everything; Shrimp..., steak..., barbeque ribs... you know? The works!"

Now it was my turn to look surprised, as Leslie neatly one-upped me.

"Jamal" I said, "I don't know about all that..., but, it should be nice."

"Come on over about 7:00, you know where I stay don't you?"

"Yeah, ok, then I'll see y'all about 7:00, next Saturday." Jamal said, as he hugged both of us goodbye.

"You think that you are so slick!" Leslie said, as we were walking back to the building after lunch.

"What do you mean?" I asked.

"You know what the hell I mean, Jackie. Trying to set me up with Jamal. And the way that you went about it was.....so tacky."

"Leslie, isn't that just terrible about Jamal and Cheryl?" "You are so obvious, do you think that he didn't see right through that set up?"

"Well, if he did, he must not have minded, because he took you up on your offer!" I said.

"My Offer! My Offer! You practically through me at him like a piece of meat or something!"

"Simmer down, Leslie, and don't be so dramatic. You know that Jamal has always liked you. I just gave him a little shove in your direction. And God knows you need a man, you seem so testy these days," I said teasingly.

"You're so busy trying to hook me up, but scared to call Deon and find out what's going on with him!" Leslie said, hitting below the belt.

"I'm not scared, I'm sure Deon and I will talk again, when he calls me!"

"Ok, Jackie, go on and keep being stubborn and let a good man get away. Why don't you call him to come over to the 'cook out'..., while you so busy trying to hook me up. Go ahead..., I dare you!"

Momma called me at work and asked me to stop by the Safeway, to pick up a few things that she had forgotten to get that morning. That concerned me, because my mother's mind is like an elephant's; she never forgets anything! 'Something must be troubling her, ' I thought.' I needed to know what that something was and..., was determine to do so. As I was leaving the store, I saw Gloria and Karen pulling into the parking lot. I quickened the pace to my car, looking in the other direction, but Karen spotted me.

"Hey!" "Jackie!" She shouted, while walking across the parking lot in my direction.

"Oh, Hi!" I said, trying to look surprised. "How you doing Karen? Hi! Gloria!" I said, as I kissed her on the cheek.

"What are you guys doing shopping all the way over here?" I asked.

"I was on the way home," Gloria said, "and remembered that I needed some salad dressing for dinner tonight and this was the closest store before I got home so...., I stopped here."

"The real question is, what are you doing in a grocery store! Period!! You eat at momma's every day," Gloria said laughingly.

"I do not! I denied, pointlessly. "Besides, momma asked me to stop and pick up a few things that she forgot to get this morning."

"Momma, ...forgot something. What's wrong?" Gloria asked.

"Nothing's wrong, I don't think, she said she just for got to pick a few things up that's all."

"Jackie, we are talking about our mother......, right?"

"Yes."

"Well, momma don't forget nothing, and you know it! Something must be going on. C'mon Karen, lets get this pick dressing, so I can stop by my momma's for a few minutes before we go home." Gloria said as she headed for the store. "Jackie, I'll see you there in a few minutes."

Gloria was right. Something must be on momma's mind, she never forgets anything…."HEY MOMMA, HERE'S THE STUFF THAT YOU WANTED FROM THE STORE…" I yelled, when I walked in the house and didn't see her.

"MOMMA!!" I yelled!

She was right behind me, saying, "Why the hell are you yelling like a banshee?! I'm right here. I swear Jackie; folks would think you was brought up in a barn, the way you yell all the time!"

"I thought you were downstairs…, anyway, here's the stuff that you asked me to pick up for you."

"Ok, thanks." Momma said.

"Momma, I saw Gloria at the store, and she said that she was going to stop by in a few minutes."

"Jackie, Who is this girl that Gloria been hanging with?" "Do you know her? Do yoknowwho I'm talking about?"

"Her name is Karen." I said.

"Karen who? Karen,,,,, Karen… I don't know no Karen's." Momma said.

"I met her last week when I took Gloria home." I said.

"Is that the friend that had her car that night that she came to get the pants hemmed?" Momma asked.

"Yeah, I think so; Momma why are you asking." I said.

"Cause, I talked to Lizbeth, this morning, and she said she seen Gloria last night over in the old neighborhood hanging with some lesbian girl what moved into the Williams' old house."

"Lesbian! Momma, you know Ms. Lizabeth always minding somebody else's business. What lesbian girl?"

"Lizabeth said she moved in there about 3 months ago, said she ain't never seen no man go over there, only women, and the other night she saw Gloria."

"Momma," I said, "How does she know it was Gloria?"

"Lizabeth said she spoke to her, and Gloria was acting all funny... like she was caught with her hand in the cookie jar or something." "Lizabeth said, they was hugging walking down the street, until Gloria spotted her sitting on her porch across the street. And she said Gloria like to have jumped outta her skin when she called her name. Said, Gloria walked over and chatted with her for a while, then said she had to go 'cause she was over visiting her friend."

"So, what's so strange about that I asked? I have friends that I hug when I see them." I said.

"Jackie, I know you do..., I do too! But they ain't no known lesbian!"

"Momma, like I said Ms. Lizabeth don't know what she talking about. Just because she hasn't seen a man over there does not mean that that girl is a lesbian."

"I know one thing! I know Gloria better not be messing around with no woman! Lizabeth may be old, but she ain't no fool! We had them girls like that when we was growing up, too, you know. They was called Dikes, back then, though. And I know one thing for certain and two for sure.., if it walks like duck and talks like a duck.... then....it's a damn duck!"

I heard a car door slam and saw Gloria and Karen walking up the walkway.

"Momma, here comes Gloria now, Karen is with her." I said.

"Hi, Momma, how you doing?" Gloria asked and kissed her on the forehead.

Momma never took her eyes off of Karen, "Hi baby," she said to Gloria, "I'm fine how are you, and who is this?"

"Oh, this is my friend, Karen," Gloria said. "Karen this is my momma, Mary Garrett."

"Hi Karen, how are you? You look like them Cunningham's are you related to Ned Cunningham and them?"

"No, Ma'am, I'm not. I'm not from this area." Karen answered.

"Really? Where you from?" Momma asked.

"I'm from here and there, really; my daddy was in the military so we moved around a lot."

"Oh, really, well, were your people from?" Momma asked.

"Well my grandparents live in Georgia and my father lives in Florida, now that he's retired."

"Florida? Oh, that's nice. Where does your mother live?" Momma asked, in full grill mode, now.

"She's deceased, Mrs. Garrett." Karen said.

"I'm sorry to hear that," Momma sympathized. "That's too bad."

"Well." Karen said, "It happened a long time ago; I was a little girl when she passed."

"Oh, that's so sad; your daddy had to raise you by his self?" Momma asked.

"He had help, I lived with my grandparent for a while, and after he remarried, I moved back with him."

"Momma!" Gloria said, "For goodness sake, how many question you going to asked her."

"We just making conversation, Gloria. "Why...? She got something to hide? I was just trying to make her comfortable is all. You got a problem with that...? Karen, you got a problem with me asking you all these questions." Momma persisted.

"No, ma'am, it's fine." Said Karen.

"See there. See there, Gloria…, she don't mine, so why should you?"

"Momma," I said, "look, I'm going to get Ray-Ja ready for bed."

"I'll get him ready in a few minutes," momma said. "You stay right here, and talk with me Gloria…and her new friend Karen."

"Uh, I really want to spend some time with him before he gets sleepy." I said, slinking out the room. "I'll see y'all later." I said.

"Jackie, wait a minute!" Gloria said and followed behind me.

"Jackie, what is going on with momma? I know that she never 'meets a stranger', but she is grilling Karen like the Spanish Inquisition! What is going on with her?"

"Gloria," I asked, "are you dating this woman?"

"What…? What are you talking about?"

"Gloria, I'm no fool! I saw her kiss you the other night, and apparently, Ms. Lizebeth has seen you two together."

"Damn, look, I was going to tell y'all about this, but in my own time. Look Jackie, you know what I went through with Damien, how bad he beat and abused me. I just...,"

"Gloria, if I were you, I would get back in that room..., you left her alone with momma!" And if you don't want momma takin' DNA samples..., you better get back in there!"

"Oh my god! Ok..., I gotta get back in there... Look, Jackie, I'll call you later... Can I call you later to talk about this?"

"Sure, Gloria, call me later..., but right now..., you better go save your friend!"

'Um...., Gloria was right; I do need to go to the grocery store.' I thought as I looked at the expired date on the milk carton in my refrigerator. 'Why does this always seem to happen, when you would kill for a bowl of cereal? Well yogurt'll have to do. I need to make a list.' As I went into the room to find something to write on, I noticed, the Temptations' 45, still on the record player and, immediately, started having thoughts of Deon. I can't believe that he has not called; especially, since we seemed to have made such a connection. *Jackie, I thought; stop fooling yourself, you set the rules for this game and you know what your momma always said, "Why buy the cow when you can get the milk for free."* You gave up the milk, and just like that, in the refrigerator, your relationship with Deon has expired. *'Jackie; are you going to go out like that or what?'*

'Um...,' I thought as I finished the container of yogurt, 'I'll give it one last shot and if that doesn't, work the Hell with Deon Davis.'

Chapter 20

"Hello?" He answered his phone on the third ring.

"Hello, Deon. This is Jackie."

"Hi, Jackie. How have you been?"

"Fine. I was just wondering the same about you, how have you been?"

"I'm doing ok; I started working, so I've been a little busy."

"Oh, great!" I said, "I'm glad you found a job; I know how important that is to you. Where are you working?"

"I got on with the Department of Transportation, in the shipping and receiving department," he announced.

"Deon, that's great. How do you like it so far?"

"Well, I just started a few days ago, but, it's ok, you know..., I like it so far."

"That's great Deon, I'm really happy for you."

"Thank you, Jackie, that's nice of you to say."

"I mean it, Deon; I want you to be happy."

"Jackie..., I thought about calling you a few days ago, but I wasn't sure you wanted to speak to me; you seem a little upset the last time we talked."

"Upset...? I wasn't upset. I called and you had company. I didn't mean to interrupt anything."

"You didn't..., I told you, she was just a friend of the family. She was here to see my sister."

"Oh. I forgot your sister was still at home, too." I belatedly remembered, feeling kinda stupid...

"I could tell by the way you ended the conversation that you thought she was here with me." Deon said.

"Then why did you let me continue to think that! You knew that I was upset that you had a woman over your house!" I said.

"I let you think that, because it felt good to know that you cared enough to be jealous." Deon said.

"Ok..., I was a little jealous; I do care about you Deon." I admitted.

"Well, then I guess I'll have to admit that I was a little upset, too, when I saw those flowers on the table the other night that you said were from a 'friend of the family'."

"Deon, I'm having a little get together this weekend--a few friends from work--and I was wondering if you would like to come." I invited.

"Oh...., so, you're ready for me to meet your friends; I must be making progress." Deon said jokingly.

"You will also get to meet Ray-Ja." I said.

"Jackie, what time is it?"

"Nine-thirty..., why?"

"I can be at your place by ten......." Deon said.

"What's takin' you so long...?" I said and hung up the phone.

I had just gotten out of the shower, when I heard Deon knocking at my door. I wrapped a towel around me, ran to the door, and looked out of the peephole to make sure it was Deon...and not Al.

I opened the door and let Deon in and as soon as the door closed, I lifted my arms to hug him, and as I did; the towel fell to the floor. Deon stepped back, looked at me, and said, "You are so beautiful."

I attempted to bend down to retrieve the towel when Deon pulled me into his arms and kissed me. My whole body quivered and my heart was racing. He slid his hands down to the small of my back and pulled me closer. Deon proceeded to place soft gentle kisses on my face, and then on my neck and shoulders. I closed my eyes with my face still pointing up from our first kiss, while he continued to kiss me all over. I must have swayed a little because Deon steadied me with his embrace and whispered in my ear, "Jackie, I think I love you."

I opened my eyes and looked into his, and I knew that I was falling in love with him. too.

"Deon....," I said, before kissing him with everything within me.

Deon whispered, "I want you, Jackie," and kissed me again. I moaned and placed my hands on his shoulders in an attempt to steady myself. Deon dropped to his knees and began to kiss my stomach and my thighs.

He gently brushed the valley of my sexuality. He touched me.., my whole body quivered as he began to taste the fruit of my womanhood. After several moments, I pulled him to his feet and lead him into the bedroom. I laid on the bed watching him as he undressed, admiring the broadness of his chest, the muscles of his arms, while remembering--and anticipating--the gentleness of his touch. Deon lowered himself on top of me; chest to breast, our hearts beating as one. Deon gently positioned himself. I arched my back to receive all that he had to give. We made love for hours and finally fell asleep in each other's arms. It was the most beautiful thing that I had ever felt.

Later that morning, Deon and I made love again in the shower. While we were getting dressed, I started giggling.

"What are you laughing about?" Deon asked.

"I know that Al was up all night listening to me screaming and moaning through the wall." I said.

Deon laughed, "Well, he'd better get some sleeping pills, because he will be having a lot of sleepless nights from now on."

I pulled him to me, holding his face in my hands, "I'll even pay for his prescription." I said as I kissed him. "I'll be home about eight."

Deon said, "Then..., I'll see you at eight."

I glanced, at Deon, several times in my rearview mirror, as he followed me through the maze of my apartment complex and into traffic. I couldn't help but smile and think about the wonderful night we had spent together. As he turned off the highway to go to work, he hadn't been out of my view but for a few minutes..., and I was already missing him.

Leslie was assisting a client, when I arrived at work. When she was finished, she walked over to my desk and took a seat. "Ok..?" She said. "I can count on one hand, the times you've been late for work and every time I knew why. She began counting them off with her fingers: Ray-Ja had a doctor's appointment. Your car battery was dead. Oh… The time someone ran into the back of your car; aaannd……"

I reached out and grabbed her hand, to stop her from counting, and said, "I overslept."

"Yeah…, right!" Leslie said.

"Leslie, I called Deon, last night." I said.

"And did you grovel and beg his forgiveness for being so stubborn." Leslie asked laughingly.

"No, actually we both kind of apologized to each other for all the misunderstandings……"

"Well…..? Are you going to see him again, now that all is forgiven? Things are all forgiven……….aren't they?" She asked.

"Leslie, I've already seen him…., all of him."

"Shut the front door! Oh… my… god! You slut!" Leslie squealed with laughter!

"Jackie, did you rock his world?!"

"Leslie…, I rocked him and his world…, and it was wonderful!"

Chapter 21

"What's going on?" Lula asked, walking up to my desk, also. "What's all the high- fivin' about?"

Leslie got up and walked back to her desk, and I smiled up at Lula, and whispered, "Lula we just found out that Lucy, finally, got that hearing aid that she has needed..., but she doesn't know how to adjust the volume on it, yet. So, when you see her, make sure that you speak very loud--almost yelling--so that she won't feel uncomfortable getting adjusted to it. Now..., promise me you'll remember to do that....; even if she looks at you kind of funny, just keep talking loud-- it's for her own good."

"Oh, ok... Thanks, Jackie.... I'll make her feel real comfortable, as a matter of fact..., she should be coming in a few minutes, and I want to be the first one to speak to her..., so let me go." Lula said, turning to hurry back to her place at the Reception Desk.

"Thanks, Lula. I knew I could depend on you." I said.

When I looked over at Leslie, she had slid under her desk laughing.

I was speaking to a client on the phone about his benefits a few moments later, when I heard...,

"GOOD MORNING, LUCY, ...BEAUTIFUL DAY, TODAY..., ISN'T IT!" ....that was before Lucy had even buzzed into the main office.

Apparently, Lucy responded, because Lula--true to her mission--replied, "OK...! WELL...! YOU HAVE A GOOD DAY!"

By now, I had to place my client on hold, I was laughing so hard. Leslie had to leave the area so that she could get herself together.

Lucy, stopped by my desk, and asked, "Jackie have you spoken to Lula today?"

"Yes, Lucy, I have..., why? What's the matter?" I asked.

"Well..., I'm not sure....I just came through her area, and she was practically screaming at me, when she spoke. Do you think that having her teeth pulled somehow affected her hearing... and she isn't aware of how loudly she is speaking?" Lucy asked, concern etched all over her face.

"Um..., Lucy, I don't know..., but, I do know that, generally, when people talk loud, if you lower your voice to a whisper when you respond to them, they...will, generally, start to speak in lower tone as well."

"I've never heard that before..., but..., you know what, Jackie! I'm going to try that with Lula!" Lucy said walking away, toward her desk.

Leslie was back and listening to my explanation to Lucy, with tears streaming down her face, she mouthed at me...."You are going straight to Hell!" and continued to laugh.

Chapter 22

"How is Ray-Ja?" Deon asked, after kissing me hello.

"He's fine. We must have sung the alphabet song 50 times, before he went to bed this evening. How was your day, baby?" I asked

"Good.., but better now." He said holding me.

I noticed the gym bag that Deon had hanging from his shoulder, obviously with a change of clothes inside.

He noticed me, noticing it, "I stopped by the house and picked up a few things in case you allowed me to stay over again tonight."

"That's fine, but we really need to talk about a few things, tonight." I said. "Deon, you do realize that we didn't use any protection last night, don't you?"

"Yeah, I know…, I guess I got kind of carried away, especially, after you answered the door wrapped in a towel. When it dropped and I saw you…, all I could think about was making love to you, right then and there."

"Yeah, well you do know that can't happen again. I already have a child…, and I'm not trying to have another one...; not now anyway."

"Jackie, are you on the pill?" Deon asked.

"I was, but I stopped taking them, when I stopped dating…I guess I'll have to make a doctor's appointment and get my prescription renewed."

"Ok…and I'll try practicing a little more self control." Deon said as he pulled me close and began to rub my behind.

"Yeah…, like now, huh?" I said, gently, pushing away.

"C'mon, Deon." I said laughing as he grabbed for me again. "Stop it! I'm serious!"

"Ok, Jackie. It won't happen again without taking precautions. I promise. Now..., let's seal the deal with a kiss."

Deon and I spent the rest of the evening talking and enjoying each other's company and conversation. He was so funny, and I enjoyed him. I knew that if anything ever happened, we would always remain friends.

I told him about the joke that I played on Lula and Lucy, and he fell to the floor with laughter. I, also, told Deon about the situation with Gloria and Karen, and how my mother was trying to get to the bottom of what was going on. I talked about how incredible, my parents were, and how I wish to have a relationship some day with someone, like the one they have.

Deon's parents have been married for thirty-odd years, or more, also. The very thought of it silenced me… "What are you thinking about? Deon asked.

"You know," I said, "as much as I would want what they have, I can't imagine being with someone for thirty, forty or fifty years!"

"I think it can be done. I think you just have to work at it, you know…, make it work. I think you have to be friends first; then, everything else will come naturally."

"I guess you're right, because my parents are friends and they way they jone on each other, oh.. my god…, they are insane." I laughed, remembering some of the things they've said to each other over the years.

Deon became quiet…. "My parent use to be like that…, of course a lot of things changed after my dad had a stroke."

I knew the subject of his Dad's condition was painful for him, and I wanted him to be able to talk to me about it without reservation, So, I continued to ask him questions about it--even though, initially, he appeared uncomfortable with it-- and he, slowly, opened up and shared his pain with me. I took him in my arms, and cried for the open and honest sharing that we were experiencing together.

I thought.., 'This man is so incredible…, and I knew that I was falling in love with him….and him with me…. But, first…..we were becoming friends.'

Deon stayed at his mom's, Friday night, and, even though, we talked on the phone, it was strange being in my apartment without him. But, Ray-Ja was coming home that evening and I stuck to my rules about men stay over when he was home; unfortunately, this included Deon.

"Oh!... And don't forget to bring the hotdog and hamburger buns!" I said to Garrett before we hung up.

He had heard me telling momma about the get-together, and had invited himself and a few of his buddies. He was always trying to get with Tina, who worked with me, and thought that this would be as good a time as any, to try and wear her down. This thing was turning into more that I had anticipated. Leslie, Carolyn, and a few others had already arrived; Earl and Marvin were manning the grill; and Jamal had called and gotten better directions, so he would be here shortly. Deon was coming after his game.

It hadn't been easy to get the Guesthouse at my apartment complex, but, luckily, someone cancelled at the last minute, and I was able to obtain it.

"Robert! You and Ray, stop playing so close to the grill!" Leslie yelled at the boys. "I think that this is really going to be nice." She said to me, while helping me wipe some of the patio chairs off.

"I think it's going to be nice, and you can, finally, get to give me the nod of approval for Deon. I know you're dying to feel him out." I said.

"You got that right. But, it seems to me that no matter what I say, at this point...., you have made up your mind about Deon....., and it's good to see you so happy, Jackie, it really is."

I turned and smiled at Leslie, walked over and gave her a hug. "Leslie." I said, "It's good to be happy again..., he is so good to me..., and I want to thank you for being such a good friend all these years."

"Girl, shut up, and don't go gettin' all mushy on me." Leslie said. "Besides, you just trying to soften me up, about the set up that you made with Jamal."

"Uh-uh, all I'm trying to do is have a few friends over for a good time, but, if some folks have a better time than others well...."

"Ok, I confess, I've always liked Jamal, but I don't need you pushing him at me, Jackie. Now...., if we make a natural connection.., I'll say something like, um..." Leslie began to plot out a strategy.

"Leslie don't start playing all that secret squirrel mess! Trust me..., I'll know if...., or should it say, when..., you two make a connection." I said laughing.

Jamal finally made it, just as we were getting ready to eat and he did look good.

"Leslie, would you mind getting Jamal something to eat?" I asked.

"The food is right over there..." Leslie said looking at me with her hands on her hips. I gave her a quick small-eyed stare.

"Oh! Oh! Sure! I can do that! C'mon Jamal!" Leslie said. "Let me fix you a plate." I heard her telling him how nice he was looking, as she lead him in the direction of the food.

I could see Deon parking in front of the apartment building; he waved and pointed to his wet jersey, indicating that he was going to go take a quick shower before joining us. I nodded and mouthed 'Ok'; and turned to find out what the commotion was behind me.

I should have known it would be Garrett. He made a loud entrance..., anywhere he went. Garrett handed me the bag of buns, kissed my cheek, and asked where Tina was. He looked around, expectantly.

"She's not here, yet, but..., Garrett, she's bringing a date. I thought I should warn you..., and I don't want no mess out of you, ok!?!"

"It's cool," Garret said, "I like my women even better when I take them from their men!"

"Garrett..., like I said, don't start any mess today!"

I started cleaning off some of the tables, when I was, suddenly, bear-hugged from behind and kissed on the back of my neck.

"Hi, babe!" I laughed, and turned to give Deon a kiss, but it wasn't Deon standing there. It was Michael! I disentangled myself and said "Michael, what are you doing here?"

"I hope you don't mind me crashing you little 'soiree', but, Gregory said it would be cool if I came."

I was speechless for a moment, thinking, 'Gregory should be glad I let his ass crash.'

"Jackie, hearing you call me babe sure makes me feel good." Michael stepped closer in an attempt to pull me into his arms, again. I stopped him by putting my hand on his chest.

"Michael! Stop! And I wasn't calling you 'babe'..., I thought you were someone else! What are you doing here, anyway? I asked again.

"I just told you..., He said. "Gregory invited me ....." I cut him off. "Not here!" I said angrily! "I mean here.........in Maryland?!"

Michael began telling me about....how he had left Reecy for good, but, I wasn't listening to anything that he was saying...., because Deon was standing a few feet behind him..., looking at me.

Apparently, he had seen me and Michael, and was standing there waiting for me to notice his presence. Michael, noticed my distraction, and turned to see what was taking my attention away from his conversation. Stepping around Michael, I walked over to explain the situation to a glaring Deon, who had not taken his eyes off Michael.

"Deon," I said, grabbing his hand and leading him away from the festivities. Let me talk to you for a minute. He allowed me to pull him, but I felt the resistance. I stopped. "Deon, I can explain." I said.

Deon looked down at me, took my face in his hands, and kissed me long and hard. I returned his kiss. When we finished, Deon said, "Ok, I'm listening..."

"Babe," I said, "The guy I was talking too is Michael, he is a friend of the family."

Deon raised his eyebrow, "A friend of the family..., or a friend of yours?"

".....of the family!" I explained. "Gregory invited him. He doesn't live here anymore, so he snuck up on me and grabbed me from behind to surprise me... And at first....,I thought it was you!.......Anyway..., I saw that it wasn't you and then......, that's when I saw you...and well..., I just didn't want you to get the wrong idea or anything so, you see..., there's nothing to it. He's just a friend of mine......, and Gregory's that's all."

"He wouldn't be the "same" friend of the family who sent you the two dozen roses would he?" Deon asked, suspiciously.

I shifted uncomfortably, rubbing the back of my neck as I admitted, "Uh..., yeah, but, those were because I... um..., expressed my condolences to him about his parent's death, and he sent the flowers to show his appreciation." "Deon, really, he's just a friend that's going through a difficult time and....that's all. There is nothing going on between Michael and me."

I stepped to Deon and put my arms around him. "You know that I'm not interested in anyone other than you, don't you?" I said. "Trust, in a relationship, is very important to me and I need to know that you trust me."

Deon kissed me quickly on the lips, "I believe you, Jackie, but, trust is earned... and him...." He said pointing at Michael. "I don't trust."

Leslie, having witnessed the semi-confrontation from afar, couldn't wait for Deon to start mingling so she could find out what was going on.

"Jackie. You alright?" She asked.

"Leslie, I thought Deon was going to go off! Did you see what happened? How dare Michael do that! Did you see him?! He kissed me on the back of my neck right in front of Deon! He must have lost his mind to do something like that!" I seethed, barely keeping my voice down.

"Jackie, calm down! She could see that I was clearly rattled. "Is Deon upset?"

"Not anymore, but girl..., I could see in his face, that if something wasn't explained.... and soon...... it was going to be on! I think he's ok..., now that I explained everything.... I can't believe Michael!"

"Jackie, Michael just needs to be shown that you have someone else in you life now, and I know that you will show him just how much Deon means to you. So, chill out.... and enjoy yourself...C'mon, let it go." Leslie said.

"Leslie, if you see Michael coming near me, I need you to make sure that you stop him, somehow. I don't know what will happen if Deon starts feeling that Michael is trying to hit on me."

"Ok, but I've got my own thing going on, too, you know...?" Leslie said slyly. Jamal and I are hitting it off, and who knows.... maybe you, finally, did something right." she said laughing.

"C'mon, girl.," she said pulling me back over to the crowd. "Stop worrying about Michael. He'd be a fool to try something! You see how big Deon is?!" Leslie said laughing. "C'mon!"

Deon was talking to Ray-Ja. He had introduced himself as a friend of mine, and they seemed to be hitting it off. I walked over to join in their conversation, when Deon said to me, "Uh, excuse me, but, this is men-talk."

"Excuse me." I said and left them to continue their conversation. I don't know what Deon was telling him, but he was cracking up laughing, and shortly after, they were bouncing a basketball back and forth to each other. I looked on with renewed admiration for Deon, the way he hadn't waited to be introduced, but had taken it upon himself to meet my son and start his own relationship with him. 'This guy is something else.' I thought.

Leslie and Jamal seemed be doing ok, and Deon was carrying Ray around on his shoulders. Everyone was having a good time, the evening was winding down, and I had managed to avoid Michael for the rest of the evening--even though I caught him staring at me several times.

Tina--and her date--didn't show, so Garrett turned his interest on, Shannon, another one of my co-workers, and was grinning in her face all evening. Several people had fixed plates to go and I started cleaning up.

"Need some help?"

"Deon..., you never cease to amaze me." I said. "I got this; you go ahead and entertain the rest of the guest while I clean up."

I stood on tip-toes and kissed him quickly.

"Thank you." I said, softly.

He turned as he was leaving, "For what?"

"Just 'cause...," I said.

Deon winked at me and left to see to 'our' parting guests.

Everyone who met Deon thought he was wonderful. I introduced him to everyone there, even Michael, who barely opened his mouth to speak. Deon made it known to everyone there that he was there with me. Whenever I called him over to meet someone, he would stand by me with his arm either around my waist or around my shoulder. When I introduced him to Michael, I introduced him as **'My friend.'**

Michael told Deon that he had been a friend of mine and Gregory's for years; then tilted his head to the side and paused as if to say...*I don't remember ever meeting you...*" Deon responded by holding me close by my waist, and saying, "Well Jackie and I haven't known each other for years.., but..., we're getting to know each other *very* well now." Deon looked at me, "Ain't that right, babe?" and leaned down for a quick kiss.

Michael was visibly shaken, "Well," he said, "It's nice meeting you Deon. Jackie, I'm getting ready to go so, I'll talk to you later."

Michael step to me, as if to get a friendly hug, but Deon stepped in front of me, saying that we had better finish cleaning up so that we could get Ray-Ja to bed at a decent hour. Deon put his arm around my shoulder and started walking me back toward the Guesthouse. He looked back over his shoulder, "Oh, Mike! Good meeting you, too, man."

Gregory came running across the park area with Ray-Ja on his shoulders. "Ok, little man your unk has gotta go. Got a hot date with a pretty lady! Gimme five..." He said, to Ray-Ja, with his hand stuck out.

Ray said. "On the back hand side!"

Gregory laughed at Ray-Ja saying on the 'back hand side', instead of on the 'Black Hand side!'

"See ya later, baby girl!" Gregory said to me. "I'll check on you later."

"Greg," I said, "I'm gonna punch you the next time you bring Michael around me, without warning me!"

"What you talking about Jackie? Mike has been a friend of ours...Hell....yours.. for years! Did he do something to make you mad at him or something?"

"No, just the opposite…, Michael is trying to "talk" to me, but I'm not interested in him that way…, not any more. That was in the past… That stopped when I found out that he and Reecy had gotten married."

"Oh, I see now it's starting to make sense." Gregory said, not always the sharpest knife in the drawer. "Jackie you know that he and Reecy split up don't you?"

"No, I didn't, I knew that they were having problems." I said as I walked Gregory to his car.

"Look, Greg, I like Michael–Hell! I've known him forever--but I'm not interested in dating him, as a matter of fact, I am seeing someone, and Michael could have made real trouble for me, today, if Deon wasn't cool."

"Deon… Deon Davis..,? Big D! You datin' Big D! That brother is fierce on the court! I was wondering why he was here…, I thought he worked with you or something."

"No, he doesn't work with me, but he and I have just started talking and Michael… was pushing up on me." I said.

"Damn, I missed all that! Michael better be cool, that's a big brother! Damn!" Gregory said holding his fist up to his mouth doubled up with laughter!

"Go home! Gregory...Bye!" I said walking away. "Oh! And you better be careful! Shannon's got a big ol'e husband!" I yelled over my shoulder!

"Are you mommy's boyfriend?" Ray-Ja asked.

"Well, um…Yes, I'm your mommy's special friend, and I hope you and I can be friends, too." Deon answered.

"I hope so, too." replied Ray-Ja. "Does that mean that you are going to be stayin' in my house?"

"Well…, I can stay, sometimes, if you would like me to." Deon said looking at me and suppressing a smile…

"I think you should stay, sometimes, so mommy won't be by herself." reasoned Ray-Ja.

I think that's a good idea Ray-Ja. I wouldn't want mommy to be alone, either." Deon agreed.

"Ok, Mr. Deon." Ray-Ja said.

"You can call me Deon, Ray-Ja...., just Deon."

"Oh, no I can't..., 'cause mommy said that 'children ad...dress all ad..dults' by....Mister or Misses." Ray-Ja repeated, importantly.

"That's right" I said giving him a hug. "You are so smart." I looked at Ray-Ja. "I know what; you can call Mr. Deon...., Mr. D! Don't you like that?!"

"Yeah, mommy!" "Ok, Mr. D."

"Ok, Ray-Ja." Deon said, "Gimme five!"

Ray-Ja gave Deon 'five' and ran to his room to play.

"I'm sorry, babe; I just want him to be comfortable with me, that's all." Deon said.

"I do, too, and don't apologize; but, I also want him to have manners and to be respectful to adults, as well."

Deon smiled. "How about going out to dinner, before we take Ray-Ja over to your Mom's?" He suggested.

"I would love that, but..."

Deon looked at me. "But..., what?" He said.

"Ah..., can you wait in the car, when we drop him off? It's not... that... I don't want... I mean..., I want you to meet my parents, but...."

"But, you think that it's too soon?" Deon said.

" No...that's not it. Deon, I would love for you to meet them, but... are you ready for that?"

"Why not, I'm going to have to do it sooner or later, so let's get it over with."

"Don't get me wrong, my dad is awesome and my mom is, too; but, my Mom is going to grill you like a hot dog! Are you really up for that?" I asked him.

"I think that I can handle it. Remember..., I have a black mom, too," he said laughing.

We let Ray-Ja decide where we would eat.

"How was your Big Mac?" I asked Deon.

"Delicious." He grinned, giving me a we-asked-for-it look. "How is your fish sandwich?"

"Delightful!" I said laughing and stuffing my mouth with French fries! "I think the next time, we'll have to flip a coin or we'll be eating at McDonald's every time we eat out!"

Ray-Ja was, happily, pushing a chicken nugget along the edge of the table in the new car from his Happy Meal.

Chapter 23

When we pulled up to Momma's, she was watering her plants on the back porch.

"Grandma, Grandma! Did you miss me?" Ray-Ja yelled, sprinting up the walk.

"You better know I did! Look at you! I believe you grew a whole foot, since day before yesterday." Momma said bending over and scooping Ray-Ja up in her arms!

"Oh.....!, My! She said, putting him down and rubbing the small of her back in the process. "You gettin' too heavy for Grandma to be pickin' you up! You gonna break Grandma's back".

"Go on in the house...., Granddaddy's in there waiting on you," she told Ray-Ja. He opened the door and disappeared into the house calling for my Daddy.

Momma turned her attention on me, but her eyes were on Deon. "Hi, Momma," I said, giving her a hug and whispering in her ear, "Be good!"

"Be good!?! What you mean, be good?" She said embarrassing me, while she extended her hand out to shake Deon's.

"Hi! I'm Momma! And you are?" She zeroed in on him.

"Hi! I'm Deon." He said grinning. Then Deon, respectful, but amused, submitted to being questioned, by this delightful, but fiercely protective mother of the woman he was growing to care for.

"MY goodness, how tall are you?" She said, stepping closer to Deon, as if she were measuring herself against him. "I thought Gregory was tall, but I believe you got him beat! You must be 7 feet tall!"

"Six- foot- eight." Deon replied, laughing.

"Momma..., you can let go of his hand, now." I said.

"Oh, Lord, Chile, I forgot that I was holding it!" She patted Deon hand a few times and, finally, released it.

"Deon, you say?"

"Yes Ma'am."

"Deon, c'mon in and make yourself comfortable." Momma said, opening the back door. Deon extended his hand to indicate that momma and me should enter before him. "Ooh..., and he's a gentleman, too." She added, jokingly, in her 'company' voice.

"Mr. D..., this is my granddaddy." Ray-Ja said, pulling my daddy into the dinning room.

Deon stood up and shook my father's hand, "Nice to me you, Sir." he said.

"Nice too meet you too, Son." My daddy said, "Call me Deke."

"Ok, Sir." Deon said "I mean Deke."

"Mr. D. is mommy's special friend." Ray-Ja said and beamed with pride because he remembered what he was told.

"Oh..., your "special" friend." Momma said tilting her head. "And what exactly is a special friend?"

"Deke, am I your special friend?" Momma teased, laughing at my embarrassment.

"Leave the girl alone, Mary... Stop embarrassing her." Daddy said.

Momma went in for the kill, "Deon, what... exactly... is a special friend?"

"Well, I guess it means that Jackie and I are dating..., Mrs..."

"Mary." Momma replied, smiling.

"Ms. Mary," Deon said.

"Oh, I see." said momma. "You and Jackie... dating?"

"Momma, would you leave him alone? Yes..., Deon and I are dating."

"And how long has this been going on?" Momma asked.

"About two weeks now...?" I said looking at Deon for confirmation.

"Uh..., yeah....about two weeks." Deon replied.

"And you are bringing him to meet me and your daddy?" She asked.

"That was my idea, Ms. Mary; I wanted to meet you and Mr... Deke. He answered her.

"Jackie is very special to me..." Deon said. "And because she is very important to me...,"I wanted to meet everyone who is important to her."

"Well, that's all right!" Momma said "I like him, Jackie! I like this young man!"

Deon and I spent another hour or so being interrogated, mostly by momma, and as we were leaving momma pulled me aside, and said. "I like this young man, Jackie, he seems really nice."

As I kissed her goodnight, I told my momma...., "I like him too."

"You must," she said, "Because you don't bring nobody around Ray-Ja. That's good, Jackie. It's real good to see you trusting someone again…I think you made a good choice."

"I hope so momma, it feels right, but I don't want to be hurt, again…, and I certainly don't want Ray-Ja to get attached to anyone who isn't going to be around."

"You can't stop livin', 'cause you been hurt. Hell...! Everybody been hurt one time or another; you have to keep on living. I'm glad to see you with someone as nice as Deon." Momma said.

"He is nice, Momma. We'll see," I said, kissing her on her forehead.

Momma gave Deon a hug as we were leaving.

"Your parents are cool." Deon said when we got in the car.

"I know...., I thought Momma was going to sit you in a chair with a bare light bulb over your head…with all the questions that she was asking." I said laughing.

"I thought so, too!" Deon said laughing, "But it was cool. Your Pops is cool, too. I like them."

Deon and I were entering the apartment building, arm-in-arm, when Al came up the stairs from the laundry room. "Hey folks, what's up?" Al asked.

"Nothing much. How you doing, Al?" Deon spoke.

"Fine. Oh! Jackie, I signed for a delivery for you, wait a minute and I'll get it for you."

"A delivery," I said, grinning at Deon.

"I haven't sent you anything." Deon said.

My smile vanished. Al brought out a bouquet, of no less than one hundred red roses in a lead crystal vase. Al could hardly carry the thing!

"I was taking my laundry down, when the delivery came. I didn't want the kids in the building to mess with it, so I told the guy I would sign for 'em. Hope you don't mind." Al said.

"No, not at all, Al. Thank you!" I said.

There were so many flowers that once Al handed me the bouquet, I couldn't see him or the lock to open the door.

Deon took my keys and opened the door; he didn't attempt to help me with the flowers. I sat them on the bar and looked at Deon.

"Aren't you going to read your card?" Deon said, sarcastically.

"Oh, um… yeah." I reached for the card and slid it out of the envelope. I read it to myself and stuffed it back into the envelope.

I knew before I read it that they were from Michael; the vase was just like the one that he sent before.

"Nothing on the card?" Deon asked.

"Yeah...they are…, um...they're from Michael" I said.

"Really?" Deon said.

"Deon, I'll talk to him and make him understand that you and I are in a relationship and not to send me anymore flowers." I said.

"Jackie, Michael knows that we are in a relationship! Those flowers weren't meant for you! They were meant to send a message to me!" Deon said, angrily. "Michael is flexing his muscles, to let me know that I have competition!"

"That's ridiculous! Deon, Michael knows that I'm not interested in him!"

"Jackie, it's not about you being interested in him! He's letting me know that he's interested in you and that my presence don't mean a thang!"

"Deon, he's really not like that, you don't know him."

"Jackie, I don't have to know him! He's a man and he's trying to have a pissing contest with me!"

"That's not true, Deon." I said, trying to embrace him.

Deon stiffened in my arms, "What did the card say, Jackie?"

I pulled the card out of the flowers and handed it to Deon. "Read it…, read it yourself."

Deon opened the card, threw it on the table, and walked out of the room.

It read. "I lost you once, I won't again." Love, Michael.'

Deon was lying across the bed looking at TV when I entered the bedroom. I laid down beside him and leaned up on my elbow. "Deon? Can we talk?" I asked.

"Sure, what you want to talk about?"

"You know what I want to talk about, Deon, the fact that you are upset about Michael!"

"Jackie, gimme a kiss." Deon said.

"What?"

"Gimme a kiss." Deon said.

I kissed him, passionately, and slid down to be closer to him.

He turned me so that he was lying on top of me and kissed me… again. "Jackie, I'm not worried about Michael."

"You don't have to be."

"I'm not. He can send you all the flowers in the world…, just as long as he doesn't try to pick this one…Deon said, sliding down, kissing my body, until he reached my *Lucy!*"

Chapter 24

The next day Leslie couldn't wait for me to get to work, so she could tell me all about her date with Jamal.

"Jackie, I swear he is the sweetest thing! He is so nice. We went to the movies and to dinner last night..., and he's coming over for dinner tomorrow!" She gushed...

"Calm down, Leslie." I said, and tell me all about it.

"Well... After we left your house, the other night, Jamal walked me to my car and told me that he really enjoyed spending time with me...., and asked if I would like to grab a cup of coffee or something. Well, I said I didn't want to drink coffee this late, that it would keep me up. And he said well, all right, I guess I'll talk to you later then."

"Leslie, he was trying to spend more time with you, fool!" I said.

"Will you let me finish!" Leslie said, impatiently. "That's when I realized what he was really asking sooo..., I said, "How about a drink instead?!... Huh! Huh! Jackie! You would have been proud of me for being so si-dit-ty!"

I just looked at her.

"Anyway, he said, jokingly, 'My place or yours!' I said, mine and he said, 'Ok then..., lead the way and I will follow!' Girrrl!" She said, pushing me on the shoulder. "I almost wrecked my car, lookin' in that rearview mirror to make sure that fine thang was still following me!"

"And then? What happened?" I asked, trying to give her time to catch her breath.

"....Well, like I said, he came over, and I fixed him one of my 'Sweet Lucy' specials! You know, when I mix punch wit bitters and Bacardi rum!"

"I know, Leslie..., how did he like it?"

"He loved it! I made a whole pitcher full, and we sat and talked and drank the whole thing!"

"Uhh huh..., and was that the only 'Sweet Lucy' Jamal got last night?" I asked.

"Girl, I'm grown! *Whhhyy, you all up in my business?*" She said, laughing, as she sashayed away.

"Uh..Huh, I knew it!" I called after her!

At lunch, Leslie and I finished our conversation; it was good to see her speaking about a guy--any guy--in a positive way. I told her about the rest of my weekend and about the flowers that Michael had sent.

"He gonna be trouble, Jackie. I can smell it." Leslie predicted.

"I'm not worried about him..., and neither is Deon." I said.

"Really.... How do you know that Deon isn't worried about him?" Leslie asked.

"Trust me, I know." I said, remembering last night...and smiling.

"I know one thing," I told Leslie. "I'm going to get in touch with Michael and make sure that he knows that Deon and I are a couple and that he needs to accept that and leave me alone."

"Well it looks like you're gonna get your chance." Leslie said. "He's walking over to our table right now..."

"I'm going to the lady's room and I'll be right back, ok, Jackie?" Leslie said, looking at Michael with disgust.

"She still can't stand me, can she?" Michael asked.

"Michael, what are you doing here?" I asked.

"You know what, Jackie, that seems to be all you are asking me these days... 'What are you doing here? What are you doing here?'" He said, mockingly.

"Ok, Michael. Let me ask you another way. 'What the *HELL* are you doing here?'" I asked.

Michael laughed. "Now that's the old Jackie that I know! I was just in the area and stopped to get something to eat and saw you and the Grench sitting over here eating, so I came over to speak."

"Ok, well you've spoken, now you can leave!"

"Whoa! Jackie what's with all the attitude?" Michael asked.

"Michael, let me make something perfectly clear. I am seeing Deon. You remember Deon…? The guy I introduced you to the other day? Well, he and I are seeing each other and…. Guess what? He's not married! He hasn't lied to me…., and you know what else? I'm really into him sooooo…, I would really appreciate it if you would respect that!"

Michael appeared to give what I said some thought. "I can respect that," Michael said. I can respect that! I'm not trying to start no trouble Jackie!" Michael said holding his hands palms up as if surrendering. "I mean no harm," he said smiling. "And if I caused you two any problems… please, forgive me, because that was not my intention."

Michael's sudden change in attitude caught me off guard. I calmed down a little. "It's ok, but, like I said before, Michael, there's nothing between us anymore but friendship and I hope that we can continue to be friends.

Michael leaned over, innocently, as if to kiss me. I offered my cheek, but he turned my face and kissed me on the lips.

Leslie cleared her throat to let it be known that she had returned, just as Michael excused himself. "Jackie, I heard what you said, but I meant what I wrote on that card! I'll talk to you later." He said and left.

I was so angry I couldn't finish my lunch.

"Leslie, he is crazy?!" I said.

"I just sat here and told him that Deon and I are seeing each other and he acted like it went in one ear and out the other! I think he has lost his mind!"

"Don't tell him nothing… Let Deon beat that ass one good time, and he'll get the message."

"I don't want it to come to that ...maybe Gregory can talk to him..., I don't know... But, what I do know is that Deon is not going to take Michael disrespecting him. I know that!" I said.

"Like I said..... Let him keep on....and somebody gonna get dey ass kicked!" Leslie said laughing.

I started giggling.

"What you laughing at?" Leslie asked.

"Michael called you, 'the Grinch'!"

"He called me what! 'A Grinch!' Like the one that stole Christmas!" Leslie said angrily, looking around. "Where he at? I'll beat that ass myself!"

I was cracking up laughing at how angry Leslie was. "I just want to be there when it happens!" She said, placing her tip on the table. "Call me, pleeease! Call me!"

"Shut up and c'mon..., let's get back to work." I said laughing.

"I never did like that bastard, anyhow." Leslie said.

"It's about time that boy's luck changed," Gregory was saying when I walked into Momma's.

"What boy and what luck are you talking about?" I asked.

"Michael's..., I'm talking about Michael."

"What about Michael?" I asked.

"He landed a big contract with is computer business.... and that brother is getting paaaiiiid!" Gregory said.

"That's good. I'm happy for him. He deserves something good to happen in his life for a change. I know he's worked hard for it." I said.

"Yep, and he said that he's moving his business back here. That's alright." Gregory said, getting ready to leave, "I'm real proud of that brother. That's alright!"

"His momma and dem would be so proud of him." Momma said. "Bless his heart."

"Hey, Gregory," I said. "You got a minute?"

"Yeah, Jackie, what's up?"

"It's about Michael." I said.

"Oh, so now you wanna get with a brother, huh?" Gregory said laughing.

"No, I don't wanna to 'get with a brother'." I said. "As a matter of fact, I would like for you to talk to him and tell him to chill."

"What's' going on?" Gregory asked seriously.

"Well, like I told you, I'm seeing Deon, and Michael keeps sending flowers and showing up where I work and he's…, um, kinda being a nuisance, you know."

"Damn! I thought he was kidding when he said now that he's landed this contract he can make things right with the woman he loves, but I thought he was talking about fixing things between him and Reecy. I didn't know that he was talking about you! Ok, Jackie, I'll talk to him, but I don't know how much good it will do. You know how Mike is when his mind is set on something? You'll see what I mean, when you go back in the house." Gregory said, leaving that last statement hanging.

"Well, I'd appreciate anything you could do. I like Michael, and I'd like for us to remain friends, but I will not let him mess up what I have going with Deon. Make sure to tell him that, ok?"

"Alright, baby girl, I'll talk to him…, you just keep cool. I'll see you later. Oh…, tell Big D, I said, 'What's up'."

"Alright, I will." I said.

"Ray-Ja, where are you baby?" I yelled when I went back in Momma's

"I'm in here playing." He replied.

"Oh, my.., isn't that nice." I said, looking at the tricycle that Ray-Ja was sitting on. "Where did you get this from?" I asked.

"Mr. Mike brought it over for me today." Ray-Ja said.

"Um hum." Momma said standing in the doorway. "Isn't that a nice tricycle." Momma asked.

"Yes, it is." I said, through clenched teeth.

"Jackie, what's the matter?" Momma said, as I stormed past her.

"Nothing Momma…, Look…. can you tuck Ray-Ja in for me, tonight, I gotta go take care of some business."

"Sure, but are you alright. Where's Deon? Is everything ok?"

"Everything is fine." Momma I said, as I walked out the door.

I was hoping that Michael was staying over to his grandparent's house. I drove down the street where they lived and there was a new car with Georgia tags; parked out in front of their house.

I parked and walked through the gate and up to the door. Before I could ring the bell, Michael opened the door. "Hi, Jackie. Now it's my turn to ask; 'What are you doing here?'"

"You know, damn well, what I'm doing here, Michael. Why are you buying Ray-Ja toys? Who asked you to buy him that bike?! You know what, Michael, I have been trying to understand that you have been going through a rough time..., but I will not let you intrude on my life! You had no right, buying Ray-Ja anything..., without my permission! He is not your son... and I am not your woman! Don't do it again....Do you understand me!...Don't do it again!" I was furious.

"Michael? Who's that at the door?" His grandmother asked from behind him.

"It's Jackie Garrett, Grams," Michael answered. "You remember Jackie, don't you?" He said, stepping a little to the side, so his grandmother could see me.

"Hello, Mrs. Simpson," I said, "How are you doing?"

"Oh, my goodness, Jackie Garrett..." "Don't you look beautiful? Look, Michael, don't she look beautiful... all grown up and everything?" She said.

"Yes, she does, Grams..., she does look beautiful," he said, smiling at me.

"C'mon in here, Jackie, and sit a spell." She invited. "C'mon in here an tell me what you been up to. How your Momma and dem doing?"

"They're doing fine, Ms Simpson. How have you been, you lookin' good?!" I said.

"Well, I'm doing the best I can, with the few tools I got." she said laughing.

"Michael, where your manners, get Jackie something cold to drink. Jackie, you want something to drink?"

"No, ma'am, as a matter of fact, I really need to get going. I just wanted to stop by to tell Michael something." I said.

"Well, ok, it sure is good seeing you." Ms. Simpson said, "Now, don't you be no stranger.... You come by and see me sometime. Ok?"

"Ok, Ms. Simpson, I will. You take care."

"Michael I'll talk to you later." I glared at Michael, as I turned to leave..., my irritation with him, seeping through my perfect façade.

He stood in the door watching me, until I pulled off. I was so angry with him for overstepping his boundaries! Hopefully, what I said got through to him this time I thought...

I was still a little upset when I got home, and even more so, because Deon had been sitting outside of the building waiting for me. When I pulled up, he jumped out of his car and rushed over to wait for me to exit my car.

"Are you ok? Is everything all right?" Deon asked.

"Yes, everything is fine. I'm sorry that I'm running late. I guess we'll have to talk about getting you a key, so you won't have to be kept waiting outside, until I get home, huh?" I said.

"I'm not concerned about that," Deon said. "I was just concerned about you."

"Aah, Babe, that's so sweet, but I had an errand to run before I came home. Let's go in..., and I'll tell you what happened."

I fixed sandwiches for us, as I and brought him up to date with what was going on.

"What did he have to say when you confronted him, Jackie?" Deon asked.

"He said that he didn't mean any harm, but he thought that Ray-Ja would like it, so he got it for him. I know one thing. I made it perfectly clear where he stands with me and that he knows that I am in a committed relationship with you." I said, getting up to go sit on Deon's lap.

"Jackie, I know that Michael is your friend..., and I wouldn't want to do anything to jeopardize that, but if he doesn't stop; I'm gonna have to say something to him myself." Deon said.

I kissed Deon. "I don't think he'll try anything else, babe…, but if he does, I understand where you're coming from."

"By the way, Jackie, it's my weekend to get Deonte'. Yvonne is going to bring him over to my mother's Friday evening."

"Are you going to bring him here?" I asked.

"I'll probably bring him over Saturday to meet you and Ray-Ja, but Yvonne would have fit if she found out that I took him somewhere other than my Moms to spend the night."

"You mean if she found out that he spent the night over your woman's house, right?"

"Well, yes, I guess that's what I'm saying; think about it Jackie, how would you feel if Ray-Ja spent the night over to his father's girlfriend place? Would you be ok with that?" Deon asked.

"Hell, no! I mean, I understand what you're saying--so it'll have to be Saturday, I guess."

"I have a game Saturday afternoon. Why don't you bring Ray-Ja; that'll be a good time for Deonte' and Ray-Ja to get to know each other."

"Ok, I can do that. What time is your game?"

"It's at two, over at Sherwood Recreation Center. Do you know where that is?" Deon asked.

"Sure, I know where Sherwood is…Would you like me to meet you there?"

"Yeah, it that would be great if you could get there about 1:30, so that you can meet Deonte' before the game."

"Sooo…, you want me to baby sit him, while you play; is that it?" I asked, half-jokingly.

"If you don't mind keeping an eye on him for me, during the game--I understand if you don't want to--I can bring my sister to the game, if it's a problem?" He said, quickly.

"It's not a problem. ….Well, we'll see how he takes to me first… I don't want to force a relationship with your son." I said.

"That's cool, I understand, but I assure you that once he meets you, he'll fall in love with you…., just like his dad…and besides he'll have Ray-Ja to keep him busy too."

"Deon, are you falling in love with me?" I asked.

"Nope…, I am in love with you." Deon said, awkwardly.

"I love you, too." I said.

We were both a little quiet after that conversation; drinking in the realization of what we had confessed to each other…, and so soon. I knew that what I had just said to Deon was what I felt for him, and I prayed that he was feeling the same.

Friday night, Deon and I talked on the phone. I was missing him being there with me, but we both knew what we had decided was the best thing to do…, for now.

"What time is Yvonne bringing Deonte' over?" I asked.

"She called a little while ago and said she was on her way." Deon said.

"Does Deonte' look like you?" I asked.

"Just like I spit him out! I couldn't deny him, if I wanted to." Deon said, laughing, proudly.

"I'm looking forward to meeting him tomorrow."

"Maybe we can hang out or take them to McDonald's after the game to get a bite to eat or something." Deon said.

"Sounds like a plan…I agreed. I'll talk to you tomorrow, babe."

"Ok, Babe, goodnight."

The next morning, Deon called. "Hi, Babe, how are you this morning?" I said to him.

"I'm good…, but I wanted to call and tell you that Yvonne is coming to the game today." Deon said.

"Oh…, does she normally come to see you play?" I asked.

"No…, never," Deon said. "When she dropped him off last night, she asked what our plans were for the weekend and I told her that I was taking him to see me play. She asked who would be watching him, while I was playing, so I told her a friend of mine would be keeping an eye on him for me during the game." He explained. "She asked me who this friend was, and I asked her why she wanted to know. Well…., she went off about… how she is his mother…. and she needs to know who is going to be watching him while I'm playing ball. I told her that a lady friend of mine would be watching him, and I guess you know that did not sit well with her. She was so upset, until she started not to let me keep him last night. She can be such a trip sometimes....Anyway, like I said, she said that the only way that Deonte' was going to the game was if she was there to watch him herself so....Look...., if you just want me to stop by later; I can do that?"

"So, are you asking me *not* to come to the game?" *I asked.*

"No! I'm just saying that Yvonne will be there, and I didn't know how you would feel about her being there..., even though she'll only be there for Deonte'." He tried to clarify.

"Deon, I can handle it..... The question is..., can you? I mean..... is there something that I should be concerned about.... other than the fact that Yvonne is Deonte's mother?"

"Not at all!" Deon said, definitely.

"Ok then...., I'll see you later at the game, ok?"

"Ok, babe, see you at the game." Deon said.

'Deon was right, with the exception of being a much shorter version, Deonte' looks just like him,' Jackie thought. Yvonne was also short, or at least, shorter than I had envisioned, but she was kind of attractive--when she wasn't looking at me with daggers in her eyes. Apparently, she hadn't gotten over Deon, and she was trying to make her presence known. Seated on the opposite side of the court, from me; I could feel her staring at me....and hating my very being. Ray-Ja and I were watching the game, Deon was a great basketball player, and I was really enjoying the game.

Deon would glance in my direction every chance he got, while he was playing and wink at me. I could hear Deonte', 'yell out, "Daddy!" Every time Deon ran up or down the court. As half-time was approaching; I decided to walk over to the other side so that Deon wouldn't be made to feel guilty about which direction he would be coming off of the court. As Ray-Ja made our way through the crowd, I saw Deon pick Deonte' up and I could also see Yvonne smiling and telling Deon to put him down, before he got him covered in sweat; she was still smiling at him..., until she saw me walking up.

As I approached them, I smiled and said, "Hello."

"Hi, Babe." Deon said.

"Jackie, this is Yvonne...and this little man is Deonte'." Deon introduced us.

"Hello, Yvonne," I said. "Nice to meet you... Hello, Deonte', how are you?" I said bending down to shake his little hand.

Yvonne never opened her mouth, she just looked at Ray-Ja and me like we were dirty or something. I, immediately, turned my attention to Deonte', who was asking Ray-Ja if he would like to go get on the swings.

Ray-Ja looked up at me for permission. "Yes, you can.., until the game starts again." And off he and Deonte' ran, in the direction of the playground.

Deon, in an attempt to make conversation, said, "Uh, Yvonne, Jackie grew up in Southeast, too. You two have probably seen each other before."

Yvonne tilted her head slightly to the side, looked me up and down, and said, "I don't think so."

I smiled, "I don't think so, either," I said, and stepped closer to Deon.

Yvonne's eyes became slits. She was obviously upset that I was there and that I was being so familiar with Deon.

"I'd better go check on the boys." I said, and gave Deon a kiss.

"No stay here...I can see them. They're fine." Deon said.

He appeared to be ok with the situation, so I knew that she was the one who still had feeling for him but it wasn't reciprocated. Yvonne rolled her eyes at Deon. "Where are you planning on taking Deonte' after the game"?" She asked.

"Jackie and I were going to take the boys out to get something to eat." Deon replied.

"Well, I don't think that Deonte' will be able to go." Yvonne said, peevishly. "In fact, I'm going to take him with me and maybe you can get him next weekend, when you don't have so much company and you can spend some one-on-one time with him."

"No, this is my weekend to have him. Michael said, "I'm going to take him to get something to eat, and then he is going to spend the night with me tonight, just as we planned."

There was nothing being said....., no breathing......Not even mine. I began to feel like I was eavesdropping, so I excused myself to go check on the boys...., while they continued to argue about Deonte'.

I was giving each of the boys one last push before making them get off of the swings, when Yvonne came over and stopped Deonte' in mid-swing.

"It's time to go!" Yvonne said.

"Why?" Deonte' asked.

Yvonne yelled! "Because, I said so!"

She turned and looked at me and rolled her eyes.

"Say, 'bye." She said, pulling Deonte' away from the playground.

I turned to see Deon staring from across the playground, he turned and went back to finish his game. I got Ray off the swing and walked back up to the basketball court and finished watching Deon play. I could tell that the was upset. 'Maybe, I shouldn't have come,' I thought; Deon and I are really going to have our work cut out for us in this relationship; that Yvonne is really going to be difficult--a real pain in the ass.

"I'm sorry about today." Deon said, when we got home. "I knew that Yvonne would do something stupid! I'm going to have to go to court and get visitation rights, so that she cannot tell me when and where I can take Deonte!"

"Deon, calm down! I know that you're upset, but I think that the realization that you have moved on was a little bit more than she could handle and her first instinct was to hurt you. She'll get over it and things will get better."

"You don't know how spiteful she can be." Deon said.

"Babe," I said, putting my arms around him, "I'm just sorry that you didn't get to spend more time with Deonte'. Maybe, you can call her and still go get him for the night, if she's convinced that you will take him over to your mom's. I know you want to spend time with him... So why don't you call her...?"

"Because, he is my son, too!" Deon said, "And I shouldn't have to clear it with her as to where I want to take him! I'll talk to her about it, but not tonight.... I'm to upset to talk with her tonight."

"Deonte' is so cute." I said, trying to change Deon's mood. He smiled at me..., "Yeah, looks just like me, don't he?!"

I slapped him on the arm, playfully, "No! He's cuter than you!"

Deon smiled, "Babe, I'm sorry about today."

"It's ok." I said, as I kissed him. "We'll get through all the bull that Yvonne tries to throw at us."

"Do you think Ray enjoyed the game?" Deon asked looking down at me while still holding me in his arms.

"I'm sure he did, and he said that he had fun with Deonte', too.

"Give it time, Deon." I said. "It'll all work out..., you'll see."

"I hope so, Babe, because I want you and Deonte' to get to know each other."

I put my head on his chest, held him close and said, "We will, Babe, we will."

Chapter 25

The next few weeks were uneventful, with the exception of Momma trying to find out anything she could about Karen. Gloria and I, finally, had a heart-to-heart talk about her new-found lifestyle. And in the end--although, I don't understand it and I wasn't a fan of it--it was her life to live. She'll have to deal with all of the repercussions from her choice; my only concern is the effect that it will have on my parents--not to mention that Brenda and Sherry are still in the dark about it, but I'm sure they'll find out at the party that Gloria is having tonight.

"Jackie! What are you wearing to this shin-dig?" asked Paige, as soon as I picked up the telephone.

"I don't know....Why? Is it supposed to be formal or something?" I asked.

"No, I don't think so. All Gloria said was that she was having a little get together..., and we could come if we wanted too." Paige said.

"That doesn't sound like she really wants us to come, but more like if she don't invite us and we find out that she had a party that they'll be hell to pay... don't it?" I said, with sisterly intuition.

"All I know is she said a few of her friends will be stopping by on there way from New York to Florida and she decided to have a little get together." Paige said.

"I didn't know that Gloria had any friends that lived in New York, huh..., she's never mentioned anybody to me that lives there...,; has she to you?"

"Noooo. Hey, Jackie!" Paige said, as a horrifying thought occured to her. "You don't think that this is one of those lesbian parties do you, 'cause I'm telling you right now, I'm not going to have no women looking a me like I'm a piece of meat...or...or something....!"

"Girl, you are crazy! Gloria wouldn't dare invite her sisters to something like that." I said, laughing at Paige.

"Well, you said yourself, that her invite didn't sound like she really wants us to come..... maybe that's why!" Paige said.

"Look, we don't have to stay long--I know, I'm not. I'm gonna 'show my face in the place', for a few minutes and leave...., and that's all you have you do, too," I told her.

"Ok, but I haven't really been spending a lot a time with Gloria, since you told me about her and that Karen girl." Paige said.

"I know, that is why I think she needs to see that we're not turning our backs on her. Just because she is going through this, woman thing..., that she's going through right now."

"Look, have you said anything to Sherry or Brenda about all of this? Asked Paige, probably looking for reinforcements.

"No, but I'm sure Momma probably mentioned it to them, and you know they'll be there-- like detectives--looking for solid evidence of lesbianism." I said laughing.

"Jackie..., Brenda is going to pass out, if she finds out on her own! Don't you think we should give them a heads up?"

"A heads up about what, Paige? We don't know what kind of party Gloria is having, so I don't think we need to say anything."

"Ok, well..., is Deon coming with you?" Paige asked.

"No, he offered to keep Ray-Ja tonight, so that I can hang out with my sisters for a change." I said.

"Ok, I'll see you about...what..., eight-eight thirty?" Paige asked.

"Yeah, I should be there about eight, see you later ... Oh! And, Paige, don't be coming in there acting like Perry Mason." I said, jokingly.

"Shut up and get off my phone." She said laughing, as she disconnected the call.

Paige was sitting in her car when I arrived. She got out after I parked and exited my car.

"Hi! Did you just get here?" I asked.

"No. I got here about ten minutes ago."

"Why didn't you go in, then?" I asked.

"Jackie..., I've been sitting out here...., and about ten people have arrived since I've been here...."

"Okay... and that's what people do when they are going to a party." I said chuckling.

"Jackie, I ain't seen not one man go in there, yet!"

"Paige you are so paranoid! Have you been in there, yet? No! So you don't know if men are already in there or not, do you? Look, you can stand out here all night but, like I said, I'm gonna show my face for a few minutes..., and then I'm going home to be with Deon and Ray-Ja. You coming...., or what?" I said, as I started walking towards the front door.

"Wait! I'm coming!" Paige said, "But if there ain't no men in there you better stick close to me, Jackie, and I'm not playing!"

"Ok, but don't get upset if someone mistakes *us* for a couple." I said laughing and ringing the door bell.

Karen opened the door with a look of surprise on her face that Paige and I were there.

"Hey, Jackie!" She said.

"Hi Karen... Karen. I asked. Have you met our sister Paige?"

"No... No, I haven't had the pleasure," Karen said and extended her hand to Paige, who was standing there like a deer caught in the headlights.

I nudged her with my shoulder and Paige snapped out of her stupor..."Hello, I'm Paige." Where is Gloria?"

Karen said. "She's out back taking stuff off the grill. Go on out there, she'll be surprised to see you two.

As we were walking through the living room there were several women standing around chatting and laughing in conversation. Paige was almost walking in my shoes; she was so close to me. I stopped and turned around to face her. "What is wrong with you?"

I asked. Why are you about to pull my shoes off my feet..., walking so close to me?!

"Jackie, did you see that woman in the black shirt? She was smiling at me!" Paige said, completely ignoring my objection to having her walking on my heels.

"Paige, they were all smiling, you know..., like... saying 'hello'. That's all! Why are you so homophobic? Get yourself together, and stop acting so crazy...., before I grab you and kiss you!" I said laughing!

"Jackie, you think you so funny... Let one of them say something to you..., and see how you feel then." Paige said.

"Nobody is going to bother anybody...," I said. "These people ain't thinking about you! Stop, being so paranoid!"

I crossed the kitchen and went out onto the patio where Gloria was cooking and entertaining several other ladies. She turned and saw me and Paige and almost dropped the pan of grilled chicken she was holding.

"Hey, y'all," Gloria said, trying to compose herself. "I didn't think that you guys were coming, I didn't hear back from anybody about coming." she said.

"You know we wouldn't miss a party of yours." I said.

Paige was looking around as if she had lost something. "I told Paige that we would stop through for a few minutes and see if there was anything that we could do to help you; but it seems like you have everything under control. Is there anything that you need me to help you with?' I asked Gloria.

"No, I think everything is ok." Gloria said.

"Well, I don't." Paige mumbled, under her breath.

"Paige, are you ok?" asked Gloria.

"Me...? Yeah.... I'm fine..., but, uh..., Gloria, how come I don't see any men here."

Gloria looked at Paige..., and then sneered at me, "Because..., none where invited, Paige. This get-together is for a few friends of mine and Karen's, who called and said that they were on way to Florida and they where thinking about coming through D.C. They asked if we would mind if they stopped by...., and we told them that it would be good to see them. Karen and I decided to have this little get-together for them... Gloria explained, her voice a mixture of defensive guilt and anger. Is... that... ok... with... you..., Paige??" Gloria asked, enunciating each word clearly.

Gloria looked at me, and asked, "Didn't you tell her about me and Karen?"

"Of course, I mentioned something to her about Karen..., she asked me who she was; I told her she was a friend of yours....But, don't you think you should tell Paige, if you want her to know what's going on with you." I said. Not allowing her to palm her responsibility off on me.

Gloria scanned the patio area with her eyes, "Paige. Have you met Karen?" Gloria asked, while looking around for her."Have you met her..., because, if you haven't..... I want you to meet her.... She and I are in a relationship....and I want you to meet her."

"Yes. She has," I said. "She opened the door for us when we arrived."

Paige and Gloria were standing there....staring at one another.... Each looking at the other...not like they were sisters, at all......but, as if they were just seeing each other for the first time.

"Look, Gloria, stop getting so self-conscience, about this." I said, trying to break the awful tension that was growing between them. "Nobody's trying to judge you..., or Karen. Paige is just a little shocked about this new life style of yours..., but that doesn't mean she's judging you..., or anything. C'mon and enjoy your party and your friends. If you two want to talk about this later, then do that; but..., now, is not the time... or the place."

Karen, who had come to the doorway, in response to Gloria's summons, was watching the three of us. She walked over to Gloria, "Is everything ok?" She asked.

Paige turned and walked back into the house, without saying a word.

I looked at, both, Karen and Gloria, "It's going to take time for all of us to adjust."

I turned to follow Paige into the house, when I heard Brenda's voice.

"Gloria! What the Hell is Paige talking about? She said you are dating a woman! What in the Hell is she talking about...., and who are all of these bitches, up in here! Gloria?!"

"What, is going on around here?!" Sherry chimed in, loudly.

"I don't believe it!" Brenda said. "Gloria... is... gay!?!"

"Would you lower your voice!" I said, to Sherry. "You're embarrassing her!"

"I'm....embarrassing her!!...... "Embarrassing...her............!?! She 'round here datin' a woman and you worryin' about me...embarrassing her!?! Shut up, Jackie! Who the hell is she suppose to be dating around here, anyway?! You...!!!" She pointed to a woman, who was staring at the spectacle we were making.

"I'm Karen...." She said, walking into the kitchen.

Sherry looked her up and down.

"Where is Gloria?!" Sherry demanded.

Gloria came in and stood beside Karen. "Can I see all of you in the other room?" She asked Sherry, Paige, Brenda, and I.

Do you want me to come with you, "Karen asked, concerned.

"Did she say your name!?! No!! I don't think so!!! Sherry barked. "So keep your ass outta here, while we talk to our sister!"

"Sherry, don't talk to her like that." Gloria snapped.

She pulled Karen aside and talked to her for a moment, in private, then led all of us into her room to talk.

"Before, any of you, say anything..., let me say this!" Gloria said. "This is my life and I will live it as I want to...., and I will love who I choose! I'm old enough to make my own decisions and--contrary to popular opinion--this is not some phase that I am going through....I really love Karen, and..... she loves me, too!"

"Gloria," Brenda said. "We're just concerned about you. We love you and this..., this..., woman thing is not good! It's just not right. Women are not suppose to be with women. Why are you doing this?!"

"It's not something that I'm DOING, Brenda! It's the way I feel... No one was more surprise than I was to find that I had feelings for this woman..... I can't explain it..., but..., I need you all to try to understand what I'm telling you. I love Karen..., and I want to be with her!"

"Your ass must be on drugs!" Sherry said! "Did she give you some drugs or something?! You can tell me, Glo! We'll get you help...if that's the case."

Jackie started laughing and everybody looked at her like she'd lost her mind or something.

"What the Hell you laughing about?" Paige asked.

"Y'all...., I said. That's what, I'm laughing at..., y'all. Look.., like Gloria said, this is what she wants. She seems to be happier now than I can ever remember her being soooo.... Why don't we just get off of her back and let her do her thang. I mean look at you Brenda; you act like you have always made the right choices. And, Sherry...! You need to be better to your man...! This is none of our business!"

"Who you talking to like that, Jackie...! You gonna make me come over there and knock the...!!!

"Hey!" Gloria said forcefully, "Can we not fight about this anymore; I have made up my mind and I hope that this doesn't affect our relationship. I love all of you..., but, I'm happy. Happier than I have been in a very long time...., and I feel that this is what I need in my life at this time. Who knows...? Maybe it is just a phase...., but, if it is then it's a phase that I have to go through…, not you."

Everyone was quiet.., digesting all that Gloria had just said, when Paige asked, "Does Momma know?"

"I think so," Gloria said, "or at least she suspects...., but once she gets to know Karen, I think that she'll be ok with it... I hope so anyway."

"What about Daddy?" Sherry asked.

"I don't think so..., but Daddy is a little more understanding about things than Momma, I think I'll tell him myself." Gloria said.

"Look, I know that this a shock to all of you...., and, you know that last thing I want to do is to see any of you hurt about anything--especially something that I've done--but I'm hoping you will try to understand..., and give Karen a chance to show you how wonderful she is."

"Just long as she don't try to hook me up with none of her friends!" Paige said.

"Paige, don't nobody want you, but that tired old man that already got you!" I said laughing.

"Girl, you crazy." Paige said, "I still got it! Men... and women... would die to get a piece of me!"

We all looked at each other started laughing.

"Paige, you right girl!" Sherry said, winking and handing her a mirror from Gloria's dresser. "You still the high school prom queen!"

"Y'all go to Hell," Paige said laughing, "do not pass go, do not collect two hundred dollars....! Just go straight to Hell!"

"GROUP HUG!!! I yelled, gathering them to me, and, then, spoke for all of us.

"Gloria, I don't understand what you are doing, but I respect your right to do it. You are my sister and I love you." I hugged her again, and said, "You have guests! Go on back and enjoy your party."

Gloria looked at each of us...., assessing us; this had to be a difficult time for her--even though we were struggling through different degrees of tolerance and understanding, we loved her--and, we all knew it.

"Thanks, for understanding. I have been dreading this...., you don't know how much!"

"I can't imagine..," I said. "But, hey! We'll get through this, just like we get through everything else that happens in our lives... Right...?" I said looking around for affirmation.

"Right," everyone said in low voices..."

As we were leaving to go back out to the party with Gloria, Sherry mumbled...., "Wait 'til Gregory finds out. He's gonna shit a brick!"

"Shut up, Sherry!" We all said at the same time!

Chapter 26

We spent the rest of the evening talking with Gloria's guests and attempting to make Karen feel like we were trying to accept our oldest sister's new-found lifestyle. Their friends were nice; intelligent, informed women....ranging from doctors to school teachers. Paige was engrossed in a conversation with Dr. Keesha Smith, about a recurring pain in her left shoulder, when I said my goodbyes.

Ray-Ja was asleep in his bed, when I arrived home, and Deon had fallen asleep on the sofa. I kissed him awake and asked how his evening had gone. He said, he had just put Ray to bed a few minutes ago.

"What...? It's almost twelve o'clock!" I said, surprised.

"Hey, we were having a boys night out. He tried to hang, but could barely keep his eyes open." Deon said laughing.

"How was the party?" Deon asked.

"Don't ask." I said.

"Why, what happen?" Deon asked.

"Well....Gloria is out of the closet." I enlightened him.

"Whaaaat!?" Deon said, "I didn't know that she was IN the closet.."

"Neither did we...., until tonight." I said.

"Well, Gloria is grown and it's her life." Deon said.

"Yeah, well we'll see, Daddy and Gregory still don't know yet." I said.

"Like I said, It's her choice and they'll just have to accept it or not." I responded.

"Can we change the subject, please?" I said, with tired resignation. "Believe me, I have heard enough about this subject for one night!"

"Ok, Babe," Deon said, holding me in his arms. "Let's go to bed."

As I was turning out the lights, Deon, suddenly, asked, "Who's the man?"

"You are, babe...." I said, smiling.

"No, Jackie..., I mean..., between Gloria and Karen."

"Shut up, Deon..., and go to bed."

Deon laughed.

I got up very early the next morning. I don't know; I guess.., even though, Deon and I were practically living together; it was still out of my comfort level for Ray to see us in bed together. I was still extremely guarded about that. I left the room to start making breakfast. Ray-Ja was still fast asleep, when I peaked in on him, and it felt good having my two men at home. I was just about finished cooking when I heard Deon talking, so I went back into the bedroom to ask him how he wanted his eggs.

"Ok, I'll be there to pick him up at nine. What? Look, Yvonne, don't tell me where I can take Deonte'! This is my weekend with him and whatever I choose to do with him is my business!" "What.....? I would appreciate it, if you wouldn't call her that...! Her name is Jackie! Look...! I'll be there to get him at nine..., just have him ready. Thanks! Bye!"

"Man! She can be such a B-i-t-c-h sometimes!" Deon said after hanging up the phone.

"What's a B-i-c...? Ray-Ja started spelling...

"Uh, nothing," I said, noticing--only now--that Ray-Ja was standing in the doorway behind me. I rolled my eyes at Deon and lead Ray-Ja into the bathroom to wash up and brush his teeth.

I walked back into the bedroom, and before I could speak, Deon said, "I'm sorry babe, I shouldn't have said that, but Yvonne makes me so damn mad sometimes!"

"I know she does," I said, "but you have to remember that she is still Deonte's mother, so please; respect her. She'll come around, but it's gonna take time. She's angry right now because you have chosen to go on with your life; but..., she has to consider what or who, her son should be exposed, too. I know how she feels."

"Jackie, I wouldn't take him around just anybody. I love him, too! And she is going to have to except that fact whether she wants to or not." Deon grabbed a towel from the linen closet and slammed the closet door.

"C'mon, Babe," I said. "Breakfast is ready... C'mon and eat, so you can get dressed and be on time to pick up Deonte'."

Deon got up from the bed and gave me a kiss. "I love you." He said.

"I love you too, but you got morning breathe." I said fanning my hand in front of my face.

Deon tried to grab me for another kiss, but I managed to slip from his grasp. Laughing I said, "You need to handle that! 'Dragon'... I mean.., Deon!"

"Ok. Babe, I'll be in there in a minute." He said, breathing into his hand and smelling it, on his way to the bathroom. "It ain't that bad," he yelled after me, "that's a manly smell!"

"Fix it!" I yelled back, laughing at him, just before he closed the bathroom door.

Deonte' was adorable! He and Ray-Ja got along great and played all day together. Deon made more noise than the boys did. He was so happy and I knew that he had not been able to spend this kind of time with Deonte' in a while.

"Who wants McDonalds?" Deon yelled down the hall.

"I do! I do!" They yelled back, and came running down the hall to go. "Jackie, I'm gonna take them to McDonalds, you want something?"

"No, I'll just sit here and enjoy the peace and quiet.....Oh! a fish sandwich, please."

"Ok," Deon said.

"And... some fries...and a chocolate milkshake." I added.

"Is that all....?" Deon asked.

"Yeah..... And a kiss."

"That..., I can give you right now." Deon said, leaning toward me.

"No... No food... No kiss...." I teased, pushing him away.

"Oh, it's like that!?!" Deon said.

"Yep! See you later, and.... don't forget the ketchup...," I said pushing them out the door.

"C'mon guys, before she ask for something else," he said laughing and ushering them out the door.

Deon had rented some movies for the kids to watch after they ate and they were engrossed in that, when I asked Deon how it went, when he went to pick Deonte' up.

"You know, she was angry, but we were cool in front of Deonte'. I could tell she wanted to kill me, though. Especially, when Deonte' asked where we were going today, and I told him that we were just going to hang out and have fun."

"You know he'll talk about Ray-Ja when he gets home." I said. "She'll know that he was with me."

"Jackie, she will just have to get use to it, because I won't have her telling me who my son can be around."

"Did she want you to bring him back tonight?" I asked.

"She tried to get me to go for that, but I reminded her that I have him until tomorrow afternoon..... and that's when I'll be bringing him home." Deon said.

Deon and I sat there in silence for a while; I had placed my head on his chest.

"Listen to them laughing in there." I said, "There's nothing better than the sound of children laughing."

I looked up and Deon was asleep. The kids had worn him out.

I nestled my head on his chest listening to his rhythmic heartbeat and the children's laughter and smiled.

Deon was home watching, TV when I got home from work.

" Hi, Babe." I said leaning over to give him a kiss hello.

"Hi, Babe. How was your day?" He asked.

"It was fine. How was yours?"

"Actually...., it was good. I got a promotion today." Deon said.

"That's great! Babe! Maybe we can go out to dinner, tomorrow, to celebrate."

"Sounds like a plan! Let's do that. Oh! Before I forget…, you had a phone call, Deon said. It was ringing when I came in. I thought it might be you, so I answered it, instead of letting it go to the answering machine. It was Gail. She said she wanted you to call her no matter how late you get in. She asked who I was. So, I introduced myself…, and she said to tell you to please call when you get in."

I started laughing and said, "Babe, Gail, is one of my oldest friends…, and I'm sure that she was shocked that a man answered my phone."

"She sounded like she was a little shocked, now that you mention it…. I could tell that she wanted to ask me some questions, so I told her that I would have you call her no matter how late you got in."

"Um, something must be going on," I said, reaching for the phone to call Gail.

"Hey, Gail it's me, Jackie. What's up?"

I started laughing and looking at Deon.

"She's talking about me isn't she?" Deon asked.

I nodded my head, yes.

Deon turned his attention back to the TV, and I continued my phone conversation.

"Gail, I was going to tell you about him… So much has been going on….What…? I know! I know…! No…! I'm not holding out…, I said laughing! "Ok, will you shut up long enough for me to tell you!"

"His name is Deon, and we've been dating for a few months now. Who? NO!" I said, looking at Deon to see if he was listening. I almost felt him 'hear' Gail ask me about Michael. But he appeared to continue to be engrossed in his program.

"No, Gail….Yes, you will meet him very soon, I promise…. Yes, Momma and dem have met him…. They get along fine; and Deon has a son and he and Ray get along, too." I said.

"Look! What's going on with you?" I asked, turning the conversation back to the reason for the call in the first place.

"WHAT! You are lying! WHEN! OH! Gail, that is great! When..? Gail that is so wonderful!"

Deon was looking at me, I covered the phone and whispered, "Gail is getting married. I knew it was going to happen! Larry is so good for you.... I am so happy for you two. Tell Larry I said congratulations..., and that I can't wait for him to meet Deon."

I could hear Gail telling Larry what I'd just said. Larry asked..., "Who is Deon? Yeah..., I got to meet him if he going to be dating my sister," I overheard Larry saying in the background.

I told Gail that I'd heard Larry. And then I told her that they will, both, like him very much.

"Have you set a date?" I asked.

Gail said that she was thinking that it would be in June of next year, and she wanted me to be in the wedding. I told her that I would be honored and that I would call her later in the week so that we could continue our conversation.

"Kiss Larry for me, and I love you, talk to you later." I said, and hung up.

"I can't believe it. Gail is getting married!" I said, to Deon.

"Didn't you think that it would ever happen to her..., or what?" Deon asked.

"Of course, I knew that she would one day that's all we used to talk about when we were little. ...How wonderful our weddings would be! ....How wonderful our lives would be...! I am so happy for her and Larry. They've been dating about a year and a half. I knew he was right for her." I said, kicking my shoes off and curling up on the sofa beside Deon.

"So, she thought that you were still dating Michael?" Deon asked.

"Deon. Gail and I have been friends for over twenty years, we don't talk everyday, we might talk about once or twice every three of four months, and it's just like we spoke to each other the day before. The last time we spoke I, purposely, didn't tell her about Michael, because she would have worried about me. She knows Michael, and she has, never liked him. I guess, I was trying to avoid her..., 'I told you so', so when it ended..., I didn't tell her. ...Anyway...., she is really looking forward to meeting you. She said she could tell by my voice that I am happy..., and she wants to meet the man that put that song back into my voice."

"I would like to meet them, too." Deon said. "I can tell that she is special to you, too; you haven't stopped smiling since you hung up the phone."

"You don't know, Gail and I have been through thick and thin together! When Reggie and I split, she was there for me... I could tell her things that I couldn't even tell my sisters. She is a good friend and I love her. Boy... that girl and I have had some crazy times together, "I said laughing, "from boyfriends to séances! I am so happy for her!"

"She must think a lot of you, too," Deon said, "to ask you to be in her wedding."

"When we were little girls., we always said that we would be in each other's weddings. I thought that I would have gotten married before her though..., Reggie wanted to, but I am sooo glad I didn't make that mistake. Anyway, at least one of our dreams will come true." I said smiling at Deon.

Deon didn't say anything; he looked at me and, then , looked away kind of nervously.

"I'm going to bed." I said, getting up. "Are you coming?"

"I'll be in, in a few minutes." He said.

I leaned over, kissed him, and went to bed.

Chapter 27

Deon was very quiet, the next morning, and I was wondering if he thought that I was trying to feel him out about marriage or at least his feelings about marriage. So, when he came in to fix his coffee I asked him if everything was ok.

"Yeah, everything is fine, Babe. I was just thinking about my new position on the job, why? Are you ok?"

"Yeah, I just noticed that you got real quiet after our conversation last night, and I didn't want you to feel like I was feeling you out about your views on marriage or anything that's all."

Deon looked uncomfortable for a second, and proceeded to add sugar and cream to his cup of coffee. "Jackie, I do plan on getting married one day..., if that's what you wanted to know?"

"Deon, I'm sure I will one day, too. Who knows," I said, "miracles happen..., huh?" I said, as I took a sip from my cup.

"Yeah, they do... Look, Babe, I got to run. I don't want to be late for my first day as a supervisor..., wouldn't look good." Deon gave me a quick kiss and practically ran out of the house.

"Ok, I been watching you all morning... and something is wrong. What's the matter?" Leslie asked.

"Nugh.., nothing is wrong." I said. "As a matter of fact, everything is going pretty good. Deon got a promotion to supervisor on his job."

"That's great. Are you two going to celebrate? Are you going out to dinner or something?" She asked.

"Yes, we are. As soon as I get home tonight. Probably, nothing fancy just celebrating the occasion." I said.

"Would you like for Jamal and me to join you?" Leslie asked.

"I think that would be a good idea, and it will probably take some pressure off of Deon." I said.

"Pressure...? What kind of pressure?" Leslie asked.

"Oh...., I'm probably making more out of it that it really is..., but, my oldest friend, Gail, called--she's getting married. Deon and I were talking about it and..."

"And... you feel that he feels, that that's what you want from him. Huh?" She said, sagely.

"Yeah, how did you know?" I asked.

"Jackie, I know you! I know when something is on your mind, girl, before you do!" Leslie said laughing and rubbing my shoulder.

"Leslie, I'm not trying to pressure him; but, to tell you the truth, if he wanted to get married right now..., I would do it. I love him."

"Would you really, Jackie?" Leslie asked.

"Yeah, I would...., but, that doesn't mean that I want him to ask me...., not right now anyway. But maybe one day..., you know, maybe one day." I said.

"Ok, I'll call Jamal and let him know, and, believe me..., I'll talk about everything except marriage at dinner... God knows that talking about marriage would probably make Jamal get right up from the table and run out of the restaurant!" Leslie and I both laughed and she went to call Jamal about dinner.

"Deon, I hope that you don't mind, but I invited Leslie and Jamal to meet us at the restaurant to celebrate your promotion, tonight."

"Naw, that's cool; where are we going anyway?" Deon asked.

"Well,' I said hugging him, 'I know you like steak, so I thought the Steakhouse would be a good idea. Is that cool with you?"

"You know what I like more than steak?" Deon said kissing my neck.

"No, what?" I asked, smiling and lifting my head to give him better access.

"What time are the reservations for...?" He asked between kisses.

"We have time..." I said, and pulled him down to the floor.

Jamal and Leslie made a nice couple. They complemented each other, I noticed as they entered the restaurant. Leslie was glowing. I looked at her and smiled and she raised her eyebrows to confirm that she and Jamal had just spent quality time together, too!

We all greeted each other, ordered our food, and had a wonderful evening talking about everything under the sun except…marriage.

As we were leaving the restaurant, Jamal leaned over and thanked me for hooking him and Leslie up. He said that he thought she was incredible and he was glad that I made them get together.

I mouthed, "you're welcome," and gave him a hug.

Deon gave Leslie a hug and we said our goodbyes in the parking lot.

"Thank you, Babe." Deon said.

"What for?" I asked.

"For being you." He said.

I reached over, touched his thigh."You're welcome, Babe."

"All right, now," he said. "You'd better stop that or you know what will happen."

I slapped him on the leg. "Stop being so fresh." I said.

He reached over and squeezed my thigh, "Then stop looking so good." He said.

"I love you, Deon." I said placing my hand on top of his.

We were coming to a stop light; when we stopped Deon leaned over and kissed me passionately. "I love you, too." He said.

We drove the rest of the way home in silence.

Chapter 28

"Jackie, you have a delivery up front." Lula said over the intercom.

"Ok," I said, "I'll be right up. Thanks."

When I arrived at the receptionist's area, there were a dozen long-stemmed red roses sitting in the desk. I signed for them.

Lula said, "I thought you were still at lunch. Who are they from?" She asked.

I smiled at her and removed the card from the little evelope.

'I really miss you, please, forgive me.' Is what it read. 'Love M.'

"Lula, who delivered these flowers?" I asked.

"I don't know..., but now that you mention it...., he didn't have on a uniform; just jeans and a shirt. Why...? Who they from?" She asked, again?

"An old friend." I said, buzzing myself back into the office with the flowers.

"Girl, that Deon got class!" Leslie said cupping one of the roses in her hand to smell it, "These are beautiful!"

"They're not from Deon." I said, looking at her.

"Oh, Shit! Not Michael." she said. "That brother just won't give up! Jackie what did you do to that boy!" She said trying to make light of the situation.

"You like 'em....? Here! You can have them and any other flowers that he sends to me!" I said.

"Jackie, maybe if you talk to him again, you can make him understand that he is wasting his time and his money trying to woo you." Leslie said.

"Leslie, I've...tried that, I have even had Gregory talk to him, and if Deon finds out that Michael is still after me....He's going to have a talk with him! But he'll be talking to him with his fist!" I said.

"Maybe you should let Michael know that! Maybe that is what it will take, for him to get the message." Leslie said.

"I'll call him; he has got to stop this! I want him to leave me alone, Leslie. He is going to cause problems between Deon and me, if he doesn't stop." I said.

All the way over to Momma's, all that I could think about was how childish Michael was acting. I'll call him as soon a I get there and get this mess straightened out...., once and for all.

"Hello, Michael?"

"Hi Jackie, did you like the flowers?"

"Michael. Please do not send me anymore flowers. I am in love with someone and you sending me flowers all the time could really cause a problem." I said.

"Really? Jackie, you know that I wouldn't do anything to hurt you. I'm not trying to cause you any problems. I'm sorry if I have." Michael said.

"You said that the last time. Michael, like I said, we have been friends for a long time..., and I want us to remain friends. But that is all that we are..., and that is all that we will ever be! I asked him, "How would you like it if someone was sending your woman flowers? Huh? Wouldn't you feel disrespected? Well..., that's how my man would feel if he found out! So, please, don't do it again or he may want to take matters into his own hands."

"Am I suppose to be frightened, Jackie...? Am I supposed to be afraid of Deon or something?" Michael asked.

"No, and he is not threatening you, Michael, I am!! Please, just leave me alone."

"Welllll....Then you had better get home before he does and hide the flowers that I sent... Oh..., and let me know if that ring is right size!" He said and hung up.

"What!?!" I said into a dead phone. "What, ring!?!"

"Momma, I got to go!" I said, grabbing my purse and heading for the door, in a hurry.

"Ok.. Is everything all right? I heard you say Michael's name. Is everything all right? His grandmother's ok isn't she?" Momma asked, concern etching her face.

"Yeah, momma, Michael's grandmother is fine. So is Michael; although, he's trying to ruin my life, I said, exasperated.

"Ray-Ja dozed right off while you were on the phone. I'll tuck him in..., go on home and I'll see you tomorrow." Momma said.

"Ok. Goodnight, momma," I kissed her. "Goodnight, daddy!" I yelled on my way out the door.

When I got home, Deon was heating up some leftovers.

"Hi, Babe." I said, giving him a kiss.

"Hi. Want some spaghetti?" He asked.

"No, I'm not hungry."

"Did you eat over to your Mom's?"

"Uh, No..., I, uh... don't have an appetite, for some reason." I said.

I walked out of the kitchen, back into the living room, and sighed, 'That damn Michael was yanking my chain! He knew that I would fly home to prevent Deon from seeing a floral delivery from him! He is such a jackass!' I thought! 'How could I have ever had feelings for him...,with his immature self!'

"Babe, would you mind fixing me a cup of coffee?" I asked "since you're still In the kitchen. Oh, and some toast, please!" I yelled, walking down the hall to change out of my work clothes.

"I thought you weren't hungry!" He said. "Do you want some of this spaghetti, too?"

"No, just coffee and toast, please. Thanks!" I said.

When I turned the light on in my room there was a UPS package on my dresser. My heart sank. "Babe, where did this delivery come from?" I asked.

"Oh, it was at the door when I came home, I forgot to tell you." Deon said. "Did you order something?" He asked from the other room. I could smell the fresh coffee brewing.

"Uh... Yeah, some earring I saw in a magazine." I said.

I sat on the side of the bed looking at the small package, I had lied to Deon and I hated myself for that. I will take it out of the house in the morning and get in touch with Michael one last time!

I threw the box and my purse on my desk, and flopped down in my seat. Leslie walked over to my desk, picked the package up and asked, "Aren't you even going to open it?"

"It's from Michael, he sent it to my home!." I said, "....And no! I'm not! I'm not going to open it! I'm going to return it, unopened. Maybe then, he'll get the message that I'm not interested in anything that he sends me."

"Jackie, don't you at least want to look at it?" Leslie asked.

"No, Leslie, I don't!"

"Jackie, look, I know Michael is trying to break you and Deon up; the flowers and expensive gifts are more to hurt Deon than tempt you...." She said, "OK, do you want me to send it back for you? .... UPS?"

"No, I can do it. I'll take it down to the mailroom on my way out to lunch, but thanks for offering." I said.

"Just remember to insure it and send it registered mail; you don't want a gift this expensive to get lost in the shuffle." Leslie said.

"How do you know that it's expensive?" I asked.

"Why wouldn't it be?" Leslie said, "Jackie, look, this man is trying to win you back..., now, do you think he got that ring out of the Cracker Jack box...or something? I bet it's at least three carats!"

"I wouldn't care if it was fifty carats! I don't want it! And, somehow, I think you are still trying to get me to open it, Leslie! C'mon don't make this harder for me than it has to be!"

"Ah-ha! I knew you, at least, wanted to look at the thing!" Leslie cajoled. "C'mon, Jackie, just one little peek..., and I'll wrap it back up so that you can mail it back! I might never get a chance again too see a fifty carat ring in person! You wouldn't deprive me of this one little wish would you?" Leslie said, pleading.

"I don't care what you do with that ring! But, I don't want it..., and I don't want to see it!"

"Ok, I'll just take a little peek, and I will wrap it back up, and you and I can take down to the mailroom together, how's that?" Leslie said.

"Fine, Leslie, open the damn box." I said. Walking away.

I had barely gotten back to my desk, when I heard Leslie yell.

"OH MY GOD! Jackie you have got to see this thing! It's humongous! Look at that diamond! Oh! My GOD!" She ran over to me with the ring box open and inside it was the biggest diamond I had ever seen!

"Jackie! Oh! My God! What have you done to this man for him to give you a ring like this! I need to know so I can get Jamal to lose his mind and get me one like this! Hell...! I'd settle for one half this size!" Leslie said in amazement! "Are you really going to send this back?" Are you crazy? There is more that one way to teach Michael a lesson! Girl, I would keep this ring..., and still not give him the time of day!"

"See...., that's why I didn't want you to open it! I knew that you would lose your mind and try to get me to keep it! I knew it!" I said.

"But, Jackie! Look at this thing!" Leslie said.

"Leslie, I can't keep it. Michael needs to know that I cannot be bought! Michael needs to know that I don't want him or anything that he tries to bribe me with! And more importantly, He needs to know that I am in love with someone else and that I am not interested in him anymore! He had his chance! He blew it! Not me!"

I looked at the ring once more, before closing the box in preparation to be wrapped.

"Leslie like I told you, he must be crazy! Why would you send someone that's not interested in you a ring like this?"

"TO MAKE THEM INTERESTED!" Leslie said, louder than necessary. "I don't know Jackie, you're better than me, 'cause I would never send it back!"

"Yes you would..., if it meant destroying what you and Jamal have." I said.

"Umm, I don't know..," Leslie said and laughed. "Yeah you right..., but, damn, that's a gorgeous ring! Can I see it one more time?"

"No! C'mon let's get this thing in the mail, before I have to knock you out!" I said.

When Leslie and I got on the elevator to go to the mailroom, I said, "Leslie, I'm going to have to call Michael, before I get home, and cuss him out! He knows exactly what he's doing. He wants me to see that Deon can't afford to give me a gift like that..., and I don't appreciate him trying to belittle him. God, if Deon ever found out about this, he would be furious!"

"Do you really think that that's why, he's doing this?" Leslie asked.

"I know it is, because Michael and I took a trip to Atlanta, once, and we stopped in a jewelry store. I was looking at the diamond rings, and the ring that he sent is one of the rings that I saw and fell in love with; but this one's bigger than the one that I saw in the store that day. He thought it would be hard for me to refuse it, because I loved it so much. But..., guess what? I love Deon more, and won't he be surprise to find that I don't want it, or him!" I said.

"How can he afford it, I mean, I know that you said he had his own business and all, but that thing must have cost twelve or fifteen grand! Does he have that kind of money...?" Leslie asked, as we stepped off of the elevator heading for the mailroom.

"Michael just came in a small fortune. One of his engineering ideas was recently patented and he is not hurting for money." I said, while filling out a UPS shipping label.

"Well, Reecy, must not know about it, because his fortune would be cut in half!" Leslie said laughing. "If she had any sense, it would, anyway!"

I stopped dead in my tracks!

" Leslie! That's it! I bet Reecy doesn't know, but I have a feeling she will if Mr. Michael doesn't get the message this time." I said.

"What? Are you going to tell her?" Leslie said.

"I'm sure she would be interested in knowing about his little windfall; besides. They have a child together so we talking alimony and child support!"

"Jackie, I hope that you know what you're doing, remember she cheated on him." Leslie said.

"Leslie, I don't want to hurt him... But..., I will not let him hurt me again, ever!" I said.

"Michael, this is Jackie."

"Oh, Hi Jackie! How are you? Did you like your present? I remembered how much you loved that ring, when we saw it in the store. I couldn't afford it then, so I felt that since you had to wait so long for it; then I needed it to be bigger and better than the one we saw." Michael said.

"I sent it back." I said.

"What!?! Why!?! You picked that ring out yourself. It's the same ring that you said you wanted!" Michael said.

"Michael! That was a long time ago! When we were together! We are not together, anymore! You are married! You were married! You know what I'm saying, and if you don't stop trying to buy Ray-Ja and me..., I'm going to tell Reecy everything! Do you hear me...., everything!" I threatened.

"Jackie, no one knows better than me, the mistake that I made letting you go. I should have been honest with you...., and even more so..., I should have been honest with myself. Tell Reecy! He challenged. "I don't care! I think she knew all the long that I was in love with someone else, and now she'll know who. Tell her! Do you want her number?" Michael continued.... "Oh, and by the way, the florist called today to apologize for the mix-up. Apparently, he had a new driver and your flowers weren't delivered, yesterday; however, he assured me that they will get there today. Talk to you later, Jackie! I love you." And he hung up.

I cannot believe the stuff that has managed to find its way onto my pocketbook, 'Where is my phone book?' "Oh, here it is... Al...., Al..., here it is! Alvin Johnson, 301-555-1215.'

"Hello, Al!"

"Yeah? Who is this?"

"Al.., it's me, Jackie!"

"Oh, Jackie..., wait... let me turn this music down, I can hardly hear you. Ok, I'm back. What's up?" He asked, finally getting himself together.

"Al, I need you to get the flowers from in front of my door, and keep them in your place until I come to get them. Can you do that for me?" I asked.

"What flowers? I just got in a few minutes ago, and I didn't see any flowers at your door."

"I did hear Deon over there playing some music though. Do you want me to go over and see if he got them?"

"No! No! Don't do that; I'll..... um... see them when I get home if he got them." I said.

"Jackie, what were you trying to do surprise him or something?" Al asked.

"Yeah! That's what I was trying to do..., but, if they got there already, I guess I blew the surprise." I said, sadly.

"Jackie, wait a minute, I hear someone coming up the stairs now.... Hold on!

"...No, but I will take them for her. The kids around here might mess with them if you leave them out here, ...Sure, ...Sure, I'll sign, ...ok, have a good day! Thanks!" I heard Al's door shut.

"They just came. He was about to knock on your door when I caught him! What's the occasion? These flowers are beautiful!" Al said.

"Oh! Our three-month anniversary is tomorrow!" I lied, maybe not about the anniversary--but, definitely, about the flowers......God, forgive me.....

"Jackie, I'm not trying to get in your business, but he's suppose to be sending you flowers; not the other way around! But.....anyway...., I got 'em and you can pick them up when you want too."

"Al, thank you! I really appreciate that."

"Ok, Jackie, no problem. Talk to you later."

"When I got to momma's my head was aching. "Momma, do you have any aspirin, I have a splitting headache." I said.

"Sure, baby, in the cabinet. Get yourself some water and I'll get them for you. What are you doing with a headache?" She asked.

"Tough day. Where's Ray-Ja?" I asked.

"Oh, Gregory and Michael came by and scooped him up. They're taking him down to see the basketball game tonight."

"Why didn't Gregory call me! He knows that I don't like Ray being out late. Where are they playing?"

"Well, Gregory is playing, Michael said he would watch Ray for him, since he carried on so about going to the game with his Uncle Garrett.

"That Michael sure is nice. It's good to see him so happy again, after all that he has been through." Momma said.

"Did you know that he and Reecy are getting a divorce?" Momma asked.

"I heard. Look, I'm going home. My head is hurting, and I just want to lie down." I said.

"Ok, baby, you go on home. They should be back, shortly, and I'll tuck Ray in. And don't worry about him; he'll be fine with Garrett. I'll call and check on you, later. You just get some rest." Momma fussed.

"Momma, call me when he gets in. I want to say goodnight to him, ok?" I said.

"Ok, baby, I promise. Love you." She said, planting a kiss on my aching head.

When I got home, Deon's car wasn't in the parking lot. I went in to the apartment and there was a note on the table. "Jackie," he'd written. "Gone to play ball. Be back by nine, love D."

I walked down the hall to the bedroom and crawled across my bed to lie down. I had just closed my eyes when a thought suddenly made me sit straight up on the bed. What if Deon and Garrett are playing at the same game.... and Deon sees Michael with Ray-Ja! I fell back on the bed. Trying to talk myself out of the odds of that happening..., but I couldn't. I'll just wait until Deon comes home, if they were are at the same game, I'm sure he will mention seeing Ray-Ja. "......Please let them be playing at different games." I prayed.

My head felt like it was about to split, I got up to check the cabinet for Tylenol extra strength and I didn't have any. 'Let me see if Al has anything for a headache,' I thought. 'Shit! Al! Al has the flowers!' I slipped on my house shoes, took the lock off the door, and knocked on Al's door.

"Hey, you got anything for a splitting headache?" I asked as soon as he opened the door.

"Sure," Al said, "Jackie, you look like Hell. What's wrong with you?"

"Al, you wouldn't believe the day that I've had." I said. "I just need some medicine and rest, and I'll be fine."

Al got the Tylenol, and asked, "Do you still want me to keep the flowers, until tomorrow?"

I hadn't even noticed them, until he mentioned them.

"Oh..., uh...yeah...., I mean, no... No, I'll just take them now. Al. I can't thank you enough for being such a good friend. I mean it. Thanks." I said, really meaning it.

"Jackie, it's no problem, really....not a problem at all. I hope Deon appreciates what a good person he has." He said.

"Thanks, again." I said, as I was leaving with the bouquet of flowers. I went back into my apartment, and as soon as Al shut his door, I ran down stairs to the dumpster to get rid of the flowers... expensive vase and all.

Chapter 29

Deon got home around nine-fifteen; I had showered and was almost asleep when he entered the bedroom. I turned over, to face him.

"Hi Babe, how was the game?"

"We won." He said, nonchalantly.

"What was the score?" I asked, trying to make conversation.

"I don't remember." He said, pulling his shirt over his head. He balled it up and made two points throwing it into the laundry basket.

"Babe, is everything ok, you seem a little upset. Are you ok?"

"Yeah, I'm fine. Why are you in bed so early?" He asked."

"Headache. It's just starting to ease up." I said.

Deon went into the bathroom and started the water for his shower.

"Oh, Jackie, I saw Garrett at the game. He played a good game, tonight." Deon said.

"Yeah, I knew he had a game tonight, but I didn't know it was the same one that you were playing." I said.

"Yeah, he said that I had just missed Ray-Ja. He said a friend of his took him on home, because he fell asleep....I sure hated that I missed him." Deon said.

"I know, Babe, I hate that you missed him, too." I lied.

"I'd better call momma and make sure he's home and tucked in." I went into the living room and called my mother.

"Momma, did Michael bring Ray-Ja home, yet? I asked her. "Deon said he saw Garrett at the game and he told him that his friend took Ray home, because he was sleepy.

"Yes, he's home and in bed. I thought you were going to try to get some rest young lady." Momma said.

"I am, I just wanted to make sure that my baby was home safe, before I fell asleep. Goodnight, momma."

"Jackie, you worry too much." she said before she hung up.

I could hear the water running in the shower, but when I turned around Deon was closing the door to the linen closet. The look on his face let me know that he had overheard my conversation with my mother.

"Was Michael the friend that had Ray-Ja?" Deon asked.

"Yes. He went to the game with Gregory and offered to watch Ray-Ja, while he played. Deon, I didn't know about any of this, until I got to momma's, tonight. It's not unusual for Garret to take Ray to his games, but he usually tells me in advance. Since, I never objected in the past, I guess he just cleared it with momma, this time, and took him. I didn't know that Michael would be watching him."

Deon turned and walked into the bathroom and closed the door.

When Deon finished his shower, I told him there was something that I wanted to talk to him about.

"What is it?" He asked.

"Deon, I need to be truthful with you about a few things; it's not that I haven't been, but, they're some things that I think that you should know," I began.

Deon sat on the side of the bed and looked at me..."What is it, Jackie, what's wrong?"

"There is nothing wrong. It's just that it seems; that Michael has become more of a problem than I thought he would be." I said.

"What do you mean?" Deon asked, "Has he been bothering you?"

"Not in the sense that you mean; he hasn't been threatening me or anything! He has been trying to shower me with expensive gifts and flowers. I asked him to stop on several occasions, I even went to his house to ask him to respect our relationship and to leave me alone but it's like it's some sort of game for him. He says that he made a mistake letting me go and that he wants to make it up to me. I just want you to know what is going on. And now he's trying to get to me through Ray-Ja. I told him that I would like us to remain friends, but that I will not let him destroy what you and I have. I mean it Deon. I told him that I love you and that he and I will never be anything more that friends; and not even that if he continues."

"You…, went over to his house?" Deon asked.

"Yes, he is, or was, staying with his grandmother; that was the only way that I knew to get in touch with him."

"Why didn't you tell me about this before?" Deon asked.

"I thought that I could stop him; I even told him that I would call his soon to be ex wife; and he offered me the number to call her. It's like I'm not even talking to him, when I tell him to leave me alone. I didn't want you to become involved in this Deon. I thought, based on Michael and my friendship alone, that he would honor my wish to be left alone, but, apparently, I was wrong."

"Jackie, I know that you and Michael have been friends for a long time, and I know that you and he were involved for a while but that was in the past. What you are telling me seems like some kind of obsession or something. I knew that something was going on! I could tell when I met him at the cookout that he was still attracted to you. You said he sent you expensive gifts. What did he send you?" Deon asked.

"The UPS package that you put on the dresser, the other evening, was from Michael. I told you that it was something that I ordered, but, I lied. I'm sorry. I didn't know what to tell you. I knew then it was really becoming a problem when I had to lie to you about it. That's when I tried to talk to him, again. I will not lie to you. I felt so bad having done so."

"What was in the box?" Deon asked.

"It was a diamond ring," I said.

"Where is it?"

"I sent it back," I said.

"Deon, I know this is a strange request, but I don't want you to do anything. I just want you to be aware of what is going on. I will make Michael understand, but I don't want you to do anything to him." I said.

Deon looked at me as if I was crazy, then said, "Jackie, let me get this straight! You want this guy that is bothering you to stop, you want me to know about it, but you don't want me to get involved? Does that sound crazy to you or is it just me that it sounds crazy to!"

"I know it sounds crazy; but I don't want an altercation between you and Michael! He is only interested in me, because he is rebounding from a failed marriage, and, in the past, I have always been there for him when something's gone wrong in his life. He'll come around, but it will take time. I know he will!"

"...And what am I suppose to do in the meantime?" Deon asked. "Just let him keep trying to steal you away from me! Is that it Jackie!"

"NO! That is not it! Because, he can't steal me or buy me... Period! Like I said, I felt that you should be aware of what was going on because I didn't want you to find out that he was sending flowers and things..., and think that something was going on behind your back! I don't want Michael Deon! I want you. I just wanted you to know; maybe I shouldn't have told you after all." I said.

"Jackie, I know guys like Michael, " Deon said. "He's not going to stop, until he gets what he wants; unless something is done."

"Something like what Deon? What! What you gonna do? Punch him in the face like we're in junior high school or something? Beat him up on the playground? What?"

"Jackie, I'm trying to respect the relationship that you have with this guy, but on the real; he is trying to see how far he can push me! Not you!" Deon said angrily.

"Babe," I said. Look, I can handle Michael. I only wanted to make you aware. I promise you he will stop when he realizes that no matter what he tries it will not affect what you and I have. I need you to trust me to handle this. Will you do that? Please, for me. I swear the minute that I feel that you need to intervene, I will let you know, ok?"

"Jackie, you are asking a lot. You are asking me to keep letting this guy disrespect me! You are asking me to give this guy permission to try and steal my woman! I think that you are asking too much! I tell you what I'm gonna let you handle it! But if I see that bastard I'm gonna kick his ass, and that's a promise! Do you understand me!!!" Deon said snatching the covers back and getting into bed.

I slid into bed beside him and turned the light out. We laid there in silence for a few minutes. I knew that Deon was angry. I wondered if I had done the right thing in telling him. I just didn't want Michael to do something that would make Deon not trust me. As I was lying there regretting my decision Deon turned over to face me.

"Jackie, I appreciate you telling me everything…, I really do. I even understand why you lied about the package, but I think that you are wrong about this guy. He's not going to stop until I make him stop. But I'm willing to try it your way for now, only because you asked me to."

"Thank you, Babe, I said I'm sorry that this is happening."

"I can almost understand why he's so determined," Deon said taking me in his arms, "I wouldn't want to lose you either."

"You never will." I said, as I returned his embrace, kissed him passionately and proceeded to express my love to him.

Chapter 30

The next evening Deon and I arrived home at the same time. I had gone over to mommas to be with Ray-Ja after work and Deon had gone over to his mom's when he got off work. As we entered the building, Al was coming out of his apartment.

"Well if it isn't the Love Birds of Atwood Street," he said.

I blushed; thinking that he had heard us through the walls last night.

"What's up, Al?" Deon asked. "How you doing?"

"Hi, Al." I said.

"I'm fine," Al said. "Oh, Deon! Hope you liked the flowers that Jackie got you for you anniversary. I told her that she had it all twisted, you should have been sending her flowers but you know Jackie!"

Deon looked at me and then back at Al. "Yeah, she's something else, always trying to do the right thing. But you know, I guess it's the thought that counts…," Deon said.

"Yeah, you right man!" Al agreed. "But boy did we have a time trying to keep you from knowing about 'em. Anyway, y'all go on and I'll talk to y'all later."

When Al walked away, Deon looked at me.

"Michael." Deon said.

I just looked at him and didn't answer. Deon walked up the stairs and entered the apartment without saying another word.

It was going to be a long evening.

After dinner, Deon said that we needed to talk. I was dreading having a conversation after what Al had just told him but I knew that it was inevitable.

"Jackie. When I went over my mom's this evening, I got my mail and there was a letter from an attorney. Apparently, Yvonne is taking me to court for child support. I knew that she would try something. I wasn't even surprised. The thing that pisses me off is that I pay her more now than the courts would order me to pay. This is being done out of anger. I swear I don't know what I ever saw in her." Deon said.

"When do you have to go to court?" I asked.

"In two weeks."

"Would you like me to go with you?" I asked.

Deon got up from the sofa and threw the letter on the table. He started pacing back and forth across the room.

"I don't know, Jackie, why would she do something like this? I have always given her more than enough for Deonte'," he said.

"It's because of me that she is doing this, Deon," I said, trying to console him. He looked at me sitting on the sofa.

"Damn, aren't we a pair...," he said. "You got a nut job after you..., and I got a woman scorned on my ass. A match made in heaven," he said sarcastically

"Deon, just as you are handling my issue with Michael; I'm handling your issue with Yvonne. Nobody is going to come between us! Not Michael or Yvonne. If Yvonne wants to take us to court then let her! And if it gets to the point where I need to get a restraining order put on Michael...or something, then we'll do that, too! We're in this thing together and that's what we need to show them," I said.

"You know what, Babe? You're right. I just get sick and tired of Yvonne always trying to do things to stop me from seeing my son."

"Well, she may have bitten off more than she can chew this time. Because when we go to court we're going to ask for visitation rights. If she wants to have her child support court-ordered..., then we'll have our visitation rights court-ordered, too!" I said.

Deon smiled, "I can't wait to see her in court," he speculated, ... To know that it won't be her decision anymore if or when I can see Deonte'...."

"Yeah, Babe, to answer your question, yes, I want you to come with me to court."

I could hardly contain myself when the judge reprimanded Yvonne. The child support was not increased but Deon did get visitation rights. Yvonne was furious! She whizzed out of court with her entourage, consisting of her sister, her mother and her dad, who was the pastor of one of the local churches. Her dad stopped in front of Deon and me and said something about how busy the devil was in court today…I remarked that "he" wouldn't be if he had a better handle on HER! I also reminded Yvonne that I would be there to pick Deonte' up, in, two weeks. Court ordered!

"It seems like I'm always saying 'thank you' to you." Deon said as we were leaving the courtroom--arm in arm.

And I'm always wondering for what…? Thank you for what?" I asked.

"For, always being here for me, especially today," he said, "Jackie, I couldn't have done this without you."

"Aw, sure you could have. But I'm glad I was here for you. Let's go home."

As we were leaving the courthouse, I heard someone yelling my name. I turned to see Leslie and Jamal running across the lawn in our direction. Deon and I waited until they reached us-- both of them panting and out of breath.

"What are you doing here?" I asked Leslie.

"Girl, we were trying to get here for moral support but, we got stuck in traffic! What happened?"

Deon was so surprised that he could hardly speak.

"You guys didn't have to do this," he said.

Jamal, who was still leaning over hands-on-knees, while trying to catch his breath, said laughingly "Well, obviously we didn't!… But it looks like things turned out all right by the look of you two."

"It did!" I commented.

"Great!" They both said; as we all hugged one another.

"Let's go get some breakfast! I'm starving!" I suggested.

In between ordering and eating, I told Leslie and Jamal what happened in court. Especially, the part about Deon having court-ordered visitation and being able to pick his son up every other weekend, without basing it on how Yvonne felt.

Deon mentioned again how much he appreciated their thoughtfulness in trying to be there to support him.

"Man, look, we fam , and I'm sorry that we weren't there in time," Jamal said.

Leslie looked at him over the rim of her coffee cup and said, "If, you had taken the South Capitol Street exit, like I told you, we would have been there on time, but noooo…, you had to go down Pennsylvania Avenue."

"Look, Leslie…! Jamal said.

And I cut them both off…."It's ok, I said believe me when I tell you; your trying to be there has just as much effect as if you were there, so stop arguing about it. We love you guys. Let's just enjoy our breakfast and each other's company."

"Yeah, you right," Leslie said, rolling her eyes at Jamal. "Let's just enjoy each other's company."

"I saw that!" Jamal said!

"I meant for you to!" Leslie said laughing!

We arrived home, and the mental stress of the morning in court, in conjunction with a hearty breakfast, had taken its toll on both of us: we were exhausted. That had never stopped anything in the past, so, I laid across the bed anticipating the cat and mouse game that always proceeded our lovemaking, only to hear a soft snoring coming from Deon. I nestled behind him spooning him and fell fast asleep as well.

I awoke and looked at the clock; it was 7:45 pm. Deon was not beside me and I could hear the television in the other room. Deon had ordered Chinese to be delivered and was talking to the television, "Who is Ann Boleyn?" He answered the question being asked on Jeopardy.

'That's correct,' Alex said to his contestant. "What was the question I asked as I sat beside him on the sofa?"

"What was the name of the queen who was reputed to have six fingers?" He repeated.

"How did you know that?" I asked?"

" 'Steel Magnolias'," he replied.

"You've seen 'Steel Magnolia's'?" I asked.

"One of my favorite "chick flicks," he said.

"I swear, Deon, you never cease to amaze me." I said laughing and began to quote several lines from the movie, making a poor attempt to mimic the accents of the actresses...when the phone rang.

I answered. It was Paige.

"Jackie, Sherry just called Russell is in the hospital.," she said.

"What! What happened? What's he in there for?" I asked.

"He's in a comma, apparently, his insulin level dropped and now he's in a diabetic coma." Paige said.

"Oh my God! How is Sherry?" I asked.

"She's freaking out, Jackie. I'm on my way over there now, you coming?"

"Yeah, have you told Momma and Daddy?"

"Yeah, Garrett told them, and Miss Ellen is watching Ray-Ja. You coming?"

"I'm on my way. I'll see you in a few minutes," I said hanging up.

"Sherry's husband, Russell, is in the hospital." I said getting up to get my purse and shoes.

"I'm coming with you," said Deon. "Besides, you look to upset to drive."

We arrived at the hospital's entrance the same time as Gloria and Karen.

"Have you heard anything else?" Gloria asked as we waited for the elevator.

"No, I haven't. I hope everything is going to be ok, though." I said.

Gloria turned to Karen, "What do you think his chances are of coming out of this?"

"I don't know, Gloria, I'm not familiar with his case," Karen replied. "But I'll be more than happy to speak to the physician in charge if you want me to."

I looked at Karen, "Please would you do that for us? I would really appreciate it."

Unconsciously, I extended my hand towards her.

"Sure," Karen said taking my hand in hers. "I'll do all I can to find out his status."

When we exited the elevator Garrett, Momma, Daddy, Paige, Brenda and Russell's parents were standing in the hall outside his room. Everyone greeted each other solemnly.

"How is Sherry?" I asked to no one in particular?

Momma answered. "Not good, Jackie; Sherry had gone to the store and when she got home she called out to Russell's and he didn't answer. She said when she went to see where he was she found him on the floor beside the bed. She has no idea how long he had been down there. She's blaming herself for not being there."

I comforted my mother as she began to cry; Paige just held her hand prayer like over her nose and mouth to muffle the sound of her crying. Karen asked my Daddy if the doctor was in with Russell.

"I believe, he just ordered some test to be done." Daddy replied.

"Are you a doctor?" My father asked.

"Yes," Karen replied. As we all realized that this was the first time that Daddy was meeting his daughter's girlfriend. Paige stopped crying, briefly, and realized that this was not the time to incite a riot.

"Daddy, this is Karen." Gloria said. "She is a doctor."

"Oh, nice to meet you Karen, I'm sorry it's under these circumstances..., but maybe this is the right circumstance, do you know anything about comas? Diabetic..., comas?"

"Yes, I do," Karen replied and began to explain what could have taken place. She informed everyone that she would be more than happy to speak with Russell's physicians on our behalf. Daddy thanked her while explaining how important Russell was to all of us..., and that anything she could do would be appreciated.

When the nurse came out of Russell's room, she instructed us to wait in the visitors' waiting room and told us that she would keep us informed of any changes. Karen informed the nurse that she was a physician and asked to confer with the attending. The nurse told her that she would let him know and left us all there to wait. Nurse Johnson came back a few minutes later to inform Karen that she could speak with the doctor and Karen assured us that she would update us as soon as possible. It seemed like hours had passed already, but it had only been a few minutes since we arrived. While we were sitting in the waiting room Daddy attempted to lighten the mood, saying, "I tell you, leave it to you to come to the hospital with a doctor," he said to Gloria.

Paige, Brenda, and I just smiled at Gloria who was very much aware of our thoughts.

"Yeah Gloria, nobody but you travels around with their own personal girlfriend, who just happens to be a doctor."

"Paige you mean her own personal doctor, who happens to be a girlfriend." Daddy corrected her...

"Yeah! Daddy, that's what I mean to say..." Paige said, "Her own personal doctor who happens to be a girlfriend."

"I could see where this was going, so I interjected, "Everyone should be so lucky as to have a friend like Karen..." narrowing my eyes at Paige. "I just hope she can help to shed some light on this situation."

Karen came back with hopeful news. She said that the test results indicated that although he was in a comma, Sherry had gotten him to the hospital before any irreversible damage had been done. Unfortunately, all we could do at this point was... wait. She said that she saw Sherry and told her that we were all out here for her. Karen said that all Sherry asked was for us to pray; so we all joined hands and prayed.

Russell's doctor came out to speak with us and pretty much said the same thing that Karen had informed us of. He suggested that we all go home and get some rest and he promised to keep us informed of any changes. Momma said that she wasn't going until she saw Sherry and proceeded down the hall to do just that. They did give her, Daddy, and Russell's parent's permission to see him briefly. Deon and I followed Garret who was taking Momma and Daddy home. I needed to see Ray-Ja.

I could not imagine something happening to my only son. I couldn't imagine what Russell's parents, the Templeton's, were going through. I needed to see Ray-Ja.

Ellen had just put him to bed, but I still went in and kissed him goodnight, and whispered how much I loved him in his ear.

Chapter 31

On the way home, I was telling Deon about Sherry and Russell. They were so much in love and had been since high school. After graduating, Sherry went to a local community college for a few years, but Russell went away to school. They stayed together through all of that and when Russell graduated they got married.

"I can't imagine what Sherry is going through…" "Not knowing, if Russell is going to come out of this comma. I pray that he gets better." I told Deon.

Sherry and Russell had been married for four years and their daughter, Taylor, was only two years old.

Deon asked where Taylor was and I told him that her Aunt Cynthia, Russell's sister, was watching her; she usually did while Sherry and Russell worked.

Riding in silence, I began to cry.

Deon reached over, rubbed my neck, briefly, and then took my hand.

"I'm sure he'll be alright," he said, attempting to console me.

I appreciated the gesture; but my heart was feeling that something was very wrong.

I called Momma the next morning, "Have you spoken to Sherry?"

"Yes, and, unfortunately, nothing has changed," momma said. Russell was still in a coma. I asked her if she wanted to go to the hospital with me when I got off work.

Momma said she would probably be going earlier in the day; she said that she and Daddy would take turns going so that someone would be there to watch Ray-Ja.

After arriving at work, during break I was telling Leslie and Carolyn about everything that had happened, when Lula came into the break room looking for me.

"Jackie, Deon is here to see you...," she said.

"Les, Carolyn, and I looked at each other and then at her. I couldn't believe how calm she was, especially, since she didn' know that Deon and I were still seeing each other."

Lula turned and walked out of the break room, when it hit me that something must be wrong. I knew it to be true, when I saw Deon's face. Deon did not smile when I came into the receptionist area, "Babe, your mother called me and asked me to come pick you up."

I knew without him saying another word that Russell had passed.

Everyone had gathered at Momma's when we arrived. Garrett was the first to get there so that Momma and Daddy could go to be with Sherry, to help her to make the funeral arrangements.

"Where is Taylor?" Paige asked.

Brenda, who was being consoled by Bruce, blew her nose and answered tearfully that Cynthia was on her way over and that Taylor was with her. Gloria was being consoled by Karen and Garrett was just sitting with his head in his hands. Deon was watching over me; reassuring me with his eyes; that he was there for me.

Bruce and Paige's husband, Gerald, introduced themselves to Deon.

"Man, I'm sorry that we are meeting under these circumstances." Deon said. "Jackie has told me so much about you," he said to both of them.

Gerald and Bruce both agreed.

"I wish you'd had a change to meet Russell; he was good people," Bruce said.

"Yeah, I heard," Deon said. "Jackie thought the world of him." I heard him tell them, how upset I was when I heard about Russell's passing. "Man, I thought that she was going to faint." I heard him say, attempting to whisper.

"I know," Bruce said. "Brenda took it hard, too."

"Ya'll ain't seen nothing yet, wait until they see Sherry... that's when our work is going to be cut out for us." Gerald said. "The Garrett girls are tight! And when one of them hurts... Man, all of them hurt... You know what I mean...?"

"Man, this is the first death we've had in the family since Joe Hot-Dog died,"said Bruce. Russell was only thirty three years old.... It's a shame. Russell been dealing with the sugar all his life man..., I feel so bad for Sherry and Taylor."

Word was spreading fast about Russell's passing and the phone was jumping off the hook; people calling to offer their condolences and bringing food over to Momma's.

When Momma, Daddy, and Sherry arrived, we all cried.

Deon, Bruce, Gerald, and Karen really did have their hands full attempting to console all the Garrett sisters. Ray-Ja and Taylor didn't know or understand why everyone was crying. Ray-Ja hugged me and asked me what was hurting, so that he could rub it and make it better; which sent Paige; who was sitting beside me, into another fit of crying. I walked outside with him and tried explained about Uncle Russ going to heaven.

"Will he come see me sometime?" Asked Ray-Ja.

"Precious" I said, holding him close and fighting back tears, "Whenever you want to see him; just close you eyes and touch your heart."

"Like this!" Mommy he said, doing as I had just explained. A small smile brightened his face as he exclaimed..., "I can see Uncle Russ Mommy! I can see him just like you said when I close my eyes."

I kissed his forehead and told him that I wanted him to be extra nice to Taylor and to teach her how to see him, too.

"I will, Mommy. I'll be extra nice to Taylor." Ray-Ja said.

Everyone was sitting around sharing memories, condolences, and stories, when I came back in the house. Neighbors and friends had come with food and offers to help in anyway that they could. I looked around for Sherry; I needed to be with her; she was not in any of the rooms that I looked in. In the living room, Deon was talking to my Daddy; I smiled to let them know that I was ok.

Sherry was lying on her side on Momma's bed--staring into space. I refreshed the tissues that were soaked and balled up in her hand, climbed over her, and laid down beside her. Paige came in; followed by Gloria and Brenda who positioned themselves somewhere on the bed, close to Sherry, as well.

No one said a word.......

The service was beautiful; the funeral home had done an excellent job on Russell. He, honestly, looked like he was asleep. I could not believe the people; there had to be four hundred or more attending the service. Nobody knew more than we did; Russell was loved.

The repast was in the banquet room of the church. Momma had wanted to have it at her house, but then thought better of it, once she realized how many people would be attending Russell's funeral. She couldn't have accommodated this crowd.

Sherry was holding it together as best she could, and by instinct; Brenda, Gloria, Paige and I were always in close proximity in case she couldn't. Deon was talking to Garrett and Bruce across the room, but positioned so that he could keep a watchful eye on me. It was comforting to know that he was there for me and so supportive. I stood there torn between the pains of Sherry's loss and feeling so loved; Deon smiled from across the room and a tear ran down my face.

"I have a shoulder..., if you need one to cry on," A voice said from behind me. I turned to see Michael. He was smiling and pointing to his right shoulder.

"No thank you, I'll be fine," I said.

"Jackie, I am so sorry for your loss. How is Sherry holding up?"

"As good as can be expected," I replied. "I know she appreciates you being here, thanks for coming," I said, as I started to walk away.

"Wait a minute," Michael said, as he grabbed my arm, "Can we talk for a minute?"

"Michael..., I don't think that this is a good time; besides, I need to check on Sherry."

"Jackie, it will only take a minute, I know how close you were to Russell and I know that this is not an easy time for you."

"I appreciate your concern Michael, but I'd really rather not talk about it right now," I said, as my eyes welled up with tears.

Michael stepped to me and embraced me.

I pulled away…"Don't do that! Really, Michael, I'm fine."

"Is everything, ok, Jackie?" Deon asked from right behind me.

I turned to him and embraced him, laying my head on his shoulder.

"Yes, everything's ok," I said. "Michael was just offering his condolences and I got a little upset. It's been an emotional day," I said, talking into his shoulder.

Deon leaned back so that he could look in my face, "Babe, are you sure that you're ok?" He asked again.

"Yes, Deon, I'm sorry for causing such a scene. I need to get myself together before Sherry sees me; I don't need to upset her."

Deon handed me his handkerchief to wipe my face.

"I was just trying to be a shoulder for Jackie; she looked as though she needed one." Michael said.

"Well, as you can see…, she has one. As a matter of fact you don't ever have to worry about Jackie, ever! I got her."

"I can see that, yeah; well Deon, Jackie; take care." Michael said as he started to walk away.

"Uh.., Michael you got a minute, I'd like to talk to you?" Deon said.

"Sure, man, what's up?" Michael said.

"Jackie. Babe, why don't you go check on Sherry. I'll be over in a minute," Deon said as he stared at Michael.

"Babe, this is not the place." I whispered.

"Jackie, everything is fine. I just want to have a few words with Mike, that's all. I promise you. I'll only be a minute and I'll join you, ok."

Deon leaned over, gave me a quick kiss, and dismissed me at the same time. I took a few steps away and turned, they were both watching me. Michael had a look of confusion on his face as Deon turned to face him, turning his back to me. I cannot tell you how reluctant I was to walk away, but I trusted Deon's judgment not to use this forum to start a scene with Michael. I stared from across the room at the two of them in conversation. Deon was talking..., and I was trying to read Michael's face.

Michael smiled and tilted his head slightly, while listening, intently; to whatever it was that Deon was saying to him. He gave a short reply, folded his arms across his chest, and tilted his head; as if he didn't hear what was just told to him.

I looked at Michael and Deon staring at each other and my heart was racing. I thought, 'Oh God! Should I go back? Should I find Garrett and send him over?'

Just as I started to scan the room for Garrett, Deon put his hands in his pockets, turned and headed across the room in my direction.

Looking past him, I could see Michael still standing there, watching Deon walk away.

"What happened?" I asked.

"Nothing," Deon said.

"It didn't look like nothing," I replied. "Michael is still looking over here."

"He'll be ok," Deon said with such finality that I thought that I had better leave it alone..., for now anyway.

Chapter 32

The next few weeks were solemn. We all made it a point to try and be as natural as possible, but to watch over Sherry and Taylor, too. Deon and Garrett went over on a regular basis to cut the grass or repair things. I told Leslie that Michael had come to the repast and that he and Deon talked.

"What happened?" Leslie asked, "Did Deon punch him in the face?"

"No! He just talked to him for a few minutes. I told her, "I still don't know what he said. I tried to be subtle and ask him, but he just said it was man talk."

"What the hell is man talk?" Leslie asked.

"He probably told him that if they weren't at that repast that he would beat his ass!" Leslie said laughing.

"Whatever it was; it left Michael standing in his tracks." I said.

"Good! I hope Deon got him strait! I bet he won't be bothering you no more."

"Well, it's been three weeks and I haven't heard from him, so maybe it worked. I hope so for his sake."

"Hey! Are we still on for the game this Saturday?" Leslie asked.

"Yeah, do you need me to pick you up, or what?" I asked.

"Naw, I'll meet you there. Jamal said he was coming, so we'll see you guys there, about 3:00?"

"Yeah, ok. Oh! Yvonne will be there dropping Deonte' off. You'll get to see her and meet Deonte'." I said.

"Girl, she is gonna be hot as fish grease, about having to leave her child with you! But, I got your back if she starts anything!" Leslie said putting her fist up and taking a defensive stance!

"Shut up! You are so crazy!" I said laughing.

"I mean it, Jackie!" Leslie said as she bobbed and weaved, from side-to-side, while thumbing her nose and sparing around in a circle, "I got your back!"

The bleachers were packed; it was almost half-time and Yvonne had not arrived with Deonte'. Deon was playing a great game and I was hoping that Yvonne wouldn't do anything dumb and not honor the court-ordered visitation. At the half, just as Deon was leaving the court, I heard Deonte' call out to him. Apparently, Yvonne had come and was sitting a few rows down from us on the bleachers.

Deon scooped Deonte', up and swung him around just as Ray-Ja, Leslie, Jamal, and I joined him.

"Have him home at 7:00 Sunday." Yvonne said, as she dropped his overnight back on the ground and walked away.

Deonte' yelled goodbye to her but she didn't respond; she just continued to walk.

"Oh, she's a real Bitch," Leslie whispered.

"As real as they come…," I said picking up the bag and shouldering it. "….As real as they come!"

The remainder of the weekend was wonderful! Ray-Ja and Deonte' became the best of friends. I had never seen Deon so happy and relaxed. They almost drove me crazy. Deonte' told Deon that he was having so much fun that he didn't ever want go home. I reassured him that he would be coming over on a regular basis and that his mother would miss him if he didn't go home.

"I have a great idea! Deonte' said. "Mommy can come live with us too!"

Kids…, I thought, 'Ya gotta love 'em!'

After dropping the kids off, I observed that Deon was noticeably quiet.

"A penny, for your thoughts…" I said.

"I was just thinking about what a great weekend this was..,"

"It was great wasn't it?"

"Babe, I know it's hard for you not having Ray-Ja with you. Why don't we start bringing him home every night?"

"Deon, I wasn't leaving him with my parents because I wanted to. I did it because, when his father left he took it hard. He really missed him..., and.., I had some adjusting to do myself so; my parents suggested keeping him. I really miss not having him at home, though."

"Oh..., I didn't know that," Deon said.

"Oh, don't get me wrong! I was ready for Reggie to be out of my life; however, I did think he would be more responsible, though, and remain a father to Ray-Ja...I don't know why I thought that, because, he was never a responsible person. His revenge on me for breaking up with him was to ignore his son. I just out-grew him emotionally, mentally, and financially. I have not regretted that decision for one second, and, in the long run, I think it was better to have him out of Ray-Ja's life."

"I understand why you did it," Deon said, "But, I'm sure Ray misses him."

"I tried hard to be civil with him, after the breakup, but he thought that it meant that we would get back together. He would call and say he was coming to get Ray, and would never show up. I can't tell you how much it hurt, to see my son standing in the door, watching cars going up and down the street waiting..., only to be disappointed-- again and again. I wanted to kill Reggie for doing that to Ray; it broke his little heart. So, I decided I would not let him hurt him, anymore. When he would call, I would let him speak to him, but if he promised him that he was coming to see him, I would plan a day out with Ray so that he wouldn't be disappointed."

"I was so worried about whether I had made the right decision. I don't know what it's like not having a father. I didn't want that for my son but, not everybody... that is a father is a daddy. Reggie made me very aware of that fact."

"I spoke to my parents about it, and they understood. I'm in the process of saving, to buy a home for Ray-Ja and me....a home our own. I plan on bringing Ray-Ja home--to a real home--within the next year. That, is a goal that I have set for not only myself…, but for Ray-Ja, as well."

"Jackie, I don't understand why brothers neglect their kids…," Deon said. "I could never neglect Deonte'. I know that Yvonne was hurt because I did not get back with her, especially, after she became pregnant. We had been apart for several months when she made that trip down to my school."

"I'm not going to tell you that I wasn't glad to see her, you know, to be with someone that you were familiar with. But, I asked her if she was still on the pill and she said that she was. Six weeks later she calls talking about missing her period. Here I am in school, struggling, and she calls to tell me she is pregnant. I felt like she was trying to trap me."

"Yvonne is not a bad person, but we were both young and foolish. I feel bad that I let her go through that by herself, but, I wasn't even sure if she was really…, pregnant by me, like I said…, we had been apart for several months. Anyway, after she had the baby, my mom and sister went to see her. My sister said Deon," 'That baby is yours! He looks just like you.' "I called Yvonne and told her that I wanted to see him, she said ok, and as soon as I laid eyes on him, I knew that he was my son.

"It hasn't been easy for either of us. I guess she was embarrassed, because here she was a preacher's daughter having a baby out of wedlock. Plus, we had been together for seven years and I guess everybody thought that we would get married one day. I guess it's kinda like…what you felt about Reggie…it just wasn't connecting anymore. Our goals and ambitions were not the same anymore. Yvonne wanted to get married; I wanted go to school and to play pro ball. She felt that that was just a dream of mine, and I guess I felt that she had lost faith in me. Like I said, it was like we were on the same street but going in different directions. I knew that I would break up with her when I went away to school; what I didn't know was that she had a slight breakdown after I left. I mean…, we talked a few times and she sounded fine, and then one day she just popped up on campus and…, well…, you know the rest."

"Life is a trip ain't it! I never thought that my life would turn out like this…," I said.

"Hey, I don't think it's so bad. I try to learn from my mistakes. I believe that you have to go through some things to learn to appreciate other things." Deon said, philosophically.

"I guess you're right, Babe, I know that Reggie sure has made me appreciate you." I said.

"Well, as your mother always says…, 'I appreciate anything 'preciateable', Deon said laughing.

"Jackie, you said that you have plans to get a house?"

'Yeah, I…, um… have been pricing a few, and I finally have enough for a down payment on some I've seen in my price range."

"Oh, I see." Deon said, sarcastically?

I knew from his response that I needed to choose my words carefully, so we road in silence for a few minutes.

"Deon, this is a goal that I set for myself…, I had no idea that I would meet anyone; especially, someone like you," I said.

"So, what are you saying, Jackie?" Deon asked.

"What I'm saying, Deon, is this is a goal that I have set for myself; and part of the agreement that I made with my parents. I wanted to save enough to get a home. They don't charge me anything for keeping Ray-Ja….to help me save for a home." I explained.

"Sooo. That's why….," Deon said, under his breath.

"That's why, what…?" I asked.

We had just pulled into the apartment parking lot. Deon turned to me and said, "That's why you won't let me pay half the expenses. I was trying to figure out why you never mentioned anything to me about sharing the expenses."

"Deon, it's no different from the goals that you set for yourself." I said starting to feel defensive–and not understanding why.

"Jackie, all of my goals and plans include you, Deonte' and Ray-Ja!" Deon said getting out of the car and slamming the door.

"Would you please try to understand?!" I said following him into the building. When he reached the door to the apartment, he used his key to open the door, then turned and handed the key to me.

"What's this? Deon, what are you doing? Why are you giving me your key?

"Somehow, now…, I don't feel like I should keep it." Deon said.

"Don't be silly!" I said trying to hand the key back to him.

"Naw, Jackie, you keep it." Deon said, walking away heading for the bathroom.

"Deon! Deon! Can we talk about this?" I asked, through the closed door.

Deon opened the door and walked into the bedroom. He started pulling his things out of the dresser drawers and stuffing them into his gym bag.

"Wait! Deon, what are you doing?" I asked.

"Jackie, you know what…? This is not working out!" He said.

"What! What are you talking about! You're upset because I have a dream! A goal! Is that what you are upset about Deon?" I asked, completely confused and upset at what he was doing.

"HELL NO!" Deon shouted, "Jackie, I feel like a complete idiot. Here, I'm talking to you about bringing Ray-Ja home to be with us, and you're telling me that you are going to buy a house. Tell me, Jackie, when were you going to mention this to me?"

"You don't let me pay for anything, because when you make this move YOU won't have to feel guilty about me, because I don't have a leg to stand on, or anything to say about it! Jackie, did you equate me into your plan? When you move; were you planning on me moving with you…, or are all of these decisions yours to make--alone?"

"Deon, when I made my plans you were not in my life; but, now that you are, I think that this is something that we can talk about. Please, let's talk about this…" I pleaded.

"It seems to me that you have already made your plans and I'm not a part of them so, I think it best if I go ahead and leave now, so that I won't make things difficult for you."

"Deon, please, sit down and talk to me." Jackie pleaded.

"I'll call you tomorrow," Deon said, and walked out the door.

I had taken just about all I could take… I just sat down and cried.

Chapter 33

"Ok! Are you going to tell me what's wrong with you or are you just going to continue to snipe at me and the rest of your co-workers, for the rest of the day?" Leslie asked.

"Umm..., Rough night." I replied.

"Well, you need to get it together. What's wrong with you anyway?" Leslie asked, again.

"Leslie, I really don't want to talk about it." I sniped.

"Ok, we'll talk at lunch...," Leslie said walking away.

I smiled, a little smile to myself, knowing that Leslie was concerned about what went on in my life. It wasn't like Lula, who just wanted to be noisy. I knew that Leslie really cared.

"Ok," I told her, capitulating, "But if I'm talking..., you're paying!"

"You got it!" Leslie replied and relieved to see her friend smile again, at least, a little.

When they were seated at the restaurant, Leslie took a sip of water. Cleared her throat and said, "Ok, what?"

"Leslie." I began, "Remember, when I told you that I was looking to buy a house?"

"Yeeaah..., and..." Leslie said.

"Well..., Deon and I were talking last night, and I mentioned that I had been saving to buy a house and that I had recently been looking into some property within my price range."

"Ok, soooo..., what's the problem?" Leslie said.

"Well, I have been planning this for a long time; even before I met Deon, you know that." I said.

Leslie's right eyebrow lifted, as she began to understand where I was going with my case.

"Jackie, did you tell Deon that you were moving into this house without him?"

"No, well.., kind of..., I guess, he took it that way." I said.

"Jackie. What happen to... 'I love him.... He is sooo... amazing. If he asked me to marry him tomorrow I would?' "Leslie quoted in a syrupy, sweet voice that was supposed to be me.

"I still feel that way, and I do love Deon, but, Leslie, I want to but my own home, I need to know that I have accomplished this one thing by myself! That's what all of the sacrifices that I have made have been for..! I want to but a home for me and Ray-Ja...., and I don't think I should be made to feel guilty for making my dream come true!"

Leslie leaned back in her seat, "Did you explain it to Deon, like you explained it to me?"

"I tried..., but he refused to listen to me."

"Jackie, how did this all come up, I mean did you just blurt out, 'Hey, Deon! Did I tell you that I am buying a house for me and Ray-Ja?!'" Leslie asked.

"No! I wouldn't just blurt it out like that!" I said.

The food arrived and we didn't talk for a few minutes, as we started eating our lunch.

"Deon asked me if I was ready to bring Ray-Ja home every night."

"Whoa..., you mean like..., let's be a real family?" Leslie asked.

"Yeah, that's what he was saying." I said.

"Damn, Jackie! Deon is telling you, 'Hey, Babe, I want us to be a family. You have been there for me through my custody battle, and since we are living together, why don't we live as a family.' and you said..., what, 'I am going to bring him home..., when I buy this house that I have been looking into.' And YOU don't include him in that equation?"

'You make it sound so selfish!" I said.

"I.... make it sound selfish, Jackie...?" Leslie said.

"I didn't plan on Deon being in my life! I didn't plan on anyone being there except me, and Ray-Ja." I defended myself.

"Well, so now what? Deon is in your life and you two have been living together for the past four months; why didn't you mention your plans to him before now?

"It just never came up! And when it did and I tried to explain everything to him, he just got upset and left." I said, remembering and hurting.

"Jackie, let me ask you something. How would you feel if he had done the same thing to you?" Leslie asked.

"I know what you are saying! I know that it hurt his feelings..., but that is not what I intended to do! You make it seem like I'm trying to hurt him on purpose! All I'm trying to do is something that I promised myself that I would do for me, and my son! Why, is everybody trying, to make me out to be the bad guy here?!" I argued.

"Jackie, Deon knows what you've gone through, and he knows why you are so determined to do this. I think that it was just bad timing and that you need to make him understand that you are not saying that you want him out of your life..., but that this is something that you need to do..., for you." Leslie said.

"I tried to tell him that last night. He was really upset when he left, Leslie; I don't know what he is thinking." I said.

"Call him, Jackie."

"He won't talk to me, Leslie."

"Call him, Jackie."

"I'm telling you that I practically begged him to talk to me about it last night, and he just walked out." Jackie said

"Call him, Jackie."

"Ok, ok, I'll call him." I said, getting up from the table, "But I'm telling you, Leslie, he won't talk to me."

Chapter 34

By the time I had gotten over to mommas, I was mentally drained. I could not help thinking about what I was going to do if I couldn't make things right between Deon and me. I love him so much.

Why was I being so hardheaded about this house thing? Did it really matter if he moved in with Ray-Ja and me? 'I should have told him about my plans before now. I should not have let him move in with me. I should have told him that his staying with me wasn't really in my plans. Everything has happened so fast. I cannot change my focus! If Deon can't understand how I feel, then maybe this is for the best. I made this sacrifice, so that I could make a secure home for my son and that is what I am going to do! I don't have to bend over backwards to make anybody understand my reason for doing anything!'

I'll call him when I get home, and if he doesn't want to talk to me..., then he can't say that I didn't try.

"Everything ok," Momma asked as I was preparing to leave for the night.

"Yeah, Ma, I just have a lot on my mind. I'll call you when I get home." I said as I was unlocking the door to leave.

It felt so strange coming home and Deon was not there. Al was coming out of his apartment with a bag full of trash as I was walking up the stairs.

"Hey! Jackie, how you doing?" Al asked.

"Hey, Al, I'm fine, how are you?"

"I'm ok, where's Deon? Working late?"

"Uh… Yeah, as a matter of fact, he is." I lied.

"Well, tell him don't work too hard." Al said descending the stairs.

"Ok, I'll tell him…," I said more to myself, than to Al.

The answering machine was blinking; I threw my purse down and push the button….'Ms Garrett, this is Mava Hayes from Family First Reality, I have a new listing that I think that you will be interested in. I'm sure this one won't be on the market long, so please return my call at your earliest convenience so that we can discuss this listing further. My number is 301-555-1212.'

'Jackie; call me.' Leslie.

'Hey, Jackie, this is Gail, haven't heard from you in a while, call me girl. Love ya'

You have no more messages.

I don't know why I was surprised that Deon hadn't called. I knew I would have to make the first move. So. I called him. His sister sounded little put out when I left a message for him to call me. I wondered what he'd told them…, or what they thought about him moving back home. I went to bed with Deon on my mind.

I woke up to the sound of the telephone ringing and realized that I had fallen asleep with the television on. I felt around for the remote and turned the TV off, and tried to go back to sleep.

'How can something so right, feel so wrong. All I want is to make a home for my son and be happy, but how are both things going to be possible without Deon in my life? I gotta fix this!'

I looked at the clock, but it was too late to call again tonight. I hope he calls.

I was running late the next morning, which was a good thing, because it didn't give me time to think about all of my problems. I got work and knew that I had to face Leslie. I told her that I did try calling and that I had left a message, but that I hadn't spoken to Deon.

"If I don't hear from him, today, I'll go by his mother's house to talk to him." I assured Leslie, trying to feel as hopeful as I sounded.

Chapter 35

When I got home, there was another message from the realtor, but none from Deon. I returned her call and set up an appointment to meet with her the next evening to look at the property she had called me about.

I called Deon… he answered.

"Hi, Deon, this is Jackie."

"Oh, hey. How you doing?"

"Are you asking just to be cordial.., or do you really care how I'm doing…," I replied,

Deon was silent.

"Deon, can…can we talk? I really need to talk to you."

"We are talking," he replied. What's up?"

"I'm sorry." I said.

"Sorry…Sorry about what?" Deon asked.

"Oh, I don't even know anymore…, about everything…. About our misunderstanding."

"WE didn't have a misunderstanding. I misunderstood." Deon said.

"You're not going to make this easy for me, are you?" I replied.

"Look, Jackie.., I gotta get up early in the morning so, let me give you a call tomorrow."

"Deon, don't do this. Can't we talk about this?" I asked him, again.

"Maybe, tomorrow, I gotta go." Deon said.

"How long are we going to do this?" I asked, getting tired of the one-liners.

"You tell me." He retorted.

"Well I'll tell you this..., I'm trying to repair our relationship, but it seems as if you are not interested in doing that." I snapped, thoroughly frustrated and getting angry.

"You know what, Jackie, you really are crazy? All I wanted was for us to be together! You did this! And now you are trying to make it seem as if this my fault. You really are crazy!" Deon snapped back.

"But you love me." Jackie said teasingly, abruptly changing the tenor of the discussion.

Deon laughed. "Yes..., yes, I do."

"I love you, too, Deon... So can we talk?" I asked in that baby-like voice I use when I want my way...

"Ok, Jackie, but not tonight. I'll meet you at the apartment after work tomorrow. Oh, and don't forget, I don't have a key anymore, so don't have me waiting in the parking lot like some vagrant."

"Ok, I'll see you at 7:00. ok?"

"Ok, goodnight."

"Goodnight."

As soon as I hung up, I grabbed my pillow and gave it a big hug! I was so happy that at least we were on speaking terms again. I laid back on the bed smiling and, suddenly, remembered that I had an appointment with the realtor at 7:00 tomorrow night! I'd have to call her and reschedule.

Deon and I arrived at the apartment at the same time. He looked so good.

"Hi, Babe," I said, leaning in to give him a kiss. He barely grazed my lips with his cool response.

"I'm sorry, I'm just glad to see you," I said.

"Jackie, I can't stay long. I have an appointment later that I have to keep."

"...And you didn't know this last night when we spoke? Deon, why didn't you tell me this, yesterday?" I asked.

"...Because, you said that you wanted to talk. And, honestly, I had forgotten about it until I was on the way over here," he responded.

"Well, what time is your appointment?" I asked. "Maybe we need to reschedule our talk."

"Jackie. What do you want to talk about?" Deon asked.

"I wanted to tell you that I'm sorry that I didn't tell you of my plans about a house. It just never came up in our conversations, and I didn't think I was anywhere near having enough for a down payment, but I'd invested a little in some stock, and between my savings and my investment, I think I have enough. Anyway, I can tell that you feel that my plans don't include you..., but Deon; I can't imagine my life without you..., and I'm sorry if I made you feel differently." On the one hand, I was genuinely sorry to have hurt him...to have hurt us; however, I couldn't help but resent that I was being made to feel guilty about....what...trying to accomplish my goals...or was it simply dealing with a damaged ego? "Jackie. Listen. I think what you've done is great. I thought about our conversation, and I think you're right. This is something that you want to accomplish on your own, and I'm proud of you. I've been thinking, since all of this stuff about the house came up. You have a right to do your thing..., about purchasing a home..., I mean. It made me think about the fact that I get visitation rights every other weekend with my son, and that it would be nice to have a nice place to bring him. I'm not in a position, right now, to buy a house, but I did look at some apartments, today, and that's what my appointment is about. I promised the lady at the complex that I would think about whether I wanted the apartment and get back to her by 8:00 tonight. I'm going to get the apartment."

"Just like that!" I said. "Just like that, you're going to get an apartment? Just like that?! What about us, Deon? Where you even planning on telling me about this?"

"I was going to tell you." Deon said. "I guess you made me realize that I should have my own place. It really didn't feel good the other night having to return to my Mom's to live. I thought that we were going to live together, but like you said; everything happened between us so fast...I just assumed...but, hey, it's all working out for the best. You'll have your place and I'll have mine."

I stood there wondering what the difference was between what he was doing and what I was being accused of--the exception being that my goals had been set and my plans in motion long before we'd even met--Why couldn't he see that! "So, are we moving apart or breaking up?" I asked,

"Moving apart," Deon replied, succinctly.

"You don't sound very sure." I said, not sounding very sure myself.

"Jackie, it will be different, you and I both know that. I'll be living in Northeast; the apartment is closer to my job. I'm not saying that we're breaking up, I'm just saying that we probably won't see each other as much... But, look..., we'll take it a day at a time and see how it works. Look," Deon said as he reached to take my hand, "I gotta run, can we finish this conversation later?" Deon lean in, kissed me quickly, and got in his car, "I'll call later," he said and pulled off.

I just stood there for a few minutes in shock. I could not believe what had just happened. Here, I had cancelled her appointment with *my* realtor to meet with Deon only for him to tell me that he was getting his *own* place. *'I can't believe this!'* Deon should have told me that he was thinking about getting an apartment. Jackie thought as she unlocked the door to hers.

'This is just pay back. That's all this is! And why does he have to move all the way to Northeast! It's his way of telling me that it's over, that's what this is! Well, you know what! Fine Deon Davis, if that's how you want this to play out; then it's fine with me! I never told him that I didn't want him to live with Ray-Ja and me..., but I sure didn't hear any invitation for me to live with him!' I fumed, getting a glass and slamming the kitchen cabinet door. 'You know what, the hell with it. I thought. *"We'll take it a day at a time...,"* my ass! He knows damn well that between my schedule and his; his weekends with Deonte'; and his playing ball-- we'll never see each other.'

"You know what? FINE!!! THE HELL WITH HIM!!!" I yelled, swiping at the tears that had started falling from my eyes.

The next day at work was Hell. I could hardly concentrate. Deon hadn't call as he promised he would, adding to my frustration.

"Jackie, are you ok?" Leslie asked.

"Leslie, I really don't feel like talking right now. I know that you're concerned and I appreciate it, but, I need to think some things through," I told her.

Leslie could tell that something was really bothering me, so for once she respected my wishes.

"You know, if you need to talk...." Leslie said.

"I know..., thanks, Leslie."

Chapter 36

"Hey, baby girl." Gregory greeted me.

"Hey, Greg, what are you doing over here? I thought you were a permanent fixture over to that new girlfriend's house these days." I said as he gave me a brother hug.

"What's up with 'the... Greg'?" Gregory said, "You only call me that when you're mad at me for something?"

"No..., I'm not mad at you and that's not true. I call you Greg all the time." I said.

"Whatever... Hey? Where's Deon? Tell him he missed a good game over at Sherwood last night. I thought for sure he would have been there." Garrett said.

"Oh, he, uh, he... had some business he had to take care of last night, but I'll tell him that you asked about him."

"Ok, well, look, I gotta run. Take care, baby-girl, and tell Deon that the play-offs start this weekend. Don't forget!" Garrett said giving me a kiss on the cheek; leaving.

"Ok, I'll tell him. Now let me get in here before Ray-Ja falls asleep."

"I'll talk to you later, bye. I said turning to go into the house."

Deon must have completely forgotten about the game last night. He's so busy trying to get an apartment, all of a sudden. Maybe I'll stop by his Mom's house before I go home...

After spending the evening with Ray-Ja, and tucking him in. I said goodnight to my parents and left. As I starting driving home, I remembered of my earlier thought of dropping past Deon's mother's house and talked myself out of it.

I'm not gonna stalk you Deon! I'm not going to force myself on nobody! If you don't want to be with me then fine..., I'll just go on...just like I did before.

'Damn, I miss you.' I thought...

"Hello? Ms.. Garrett this is Mava Hayes. I guess we got our signals crossed yesterday, but if you are still interested in that property give me a call. Thanks and have a nice day."

"Hello? Jackie, this is Leslie; just checkin' on you. Call me if you need to. Ok? Love you."

"Hello? Jackie, this is D…. talk to you later." Deon said, electronically.

'Dammit! I just missed his call by ten minutes,' I thought, frantically dialing his number, 'I can't believe I sound so desperate…. what is wrong with me…?

"Hello, Deon…, Jackie."

"Oh, hey, Jackie, how you doing?"

"I see that you called. Sorry, I missed it. I just got in and got your message." I said.

"Yeah…, look…, sorry 'bout not calling you back last night. I got in late and I thought that you were asleep, so I figured I would catch you tonight." Deon said.

"Yeah, well, I probably was…, but tell me; how'd it go with the apartment?"

I asked reluctantly...

"Oh, I put a deposit on it, and I'll know in a few days if I got it." Deon said.

"Oh, that's good." I said, trying to sound happy for him, but feeling her heart break.

"Yeah, I should know something in a few days. How are things with you? How's Ray-Ja?"

"Deon," I explored"…Do you hear us? Do you hear how we sound; talking to each other like we're strangers. Deon, what is happening to us?"

"I know…, we do sound like strangers don't we?" Deon replied.

"Baby, I don't want you to have to ask me how I'm doing…" I was crying. "I want you to know how I'm doing and I want to know how you are doing! I want to see you everyday..., and wake up beside you..., and hold you before I go to sleep at night..., and listen to your snoring when I'm trying to read at night and ...."

"I miss you, too, Babe," Deon said.

"Deon..., can..., you come home? I need you," I said.

"Jackie... What about your plans? I can't afford to buy a house, right now, and I know that's what you want." Deon responded.

"Babe, we can work that out, I..., I thought that getting a house was so important because I felt as if I had failed in so many other things where Ray-Ja was concerned..., but, he loves you and I love you..., and that's what's important." I said.

"Jackie, I don't want you to think that what you want is wrong. You have made a lot of sacrifices and you deserve to get what you have worked for. I'm sorry, if I made you feel that what you were doing was wrong. That's one of the things that I love most about you..., your focus..., your desire to always better yourself and to make things better for those you love." Deon said.

"Sooo..., You still love me?" I asked sheepishly.

"Give me an hour... and I'll be there to show you how much." Deon replied.

"Babe, I love you!"

"I'll be home in a little while..." Deon said and hung up.

Chapter 37

"Babe, are you going to work today?" Deon said.

"Uummm, what time is it?' I replied without opening my eyes and snuggling closer to Deon.

"7:30." Deon replied.

"I'll call in, if you do..." Jackie whispered seductively.

Deon reached for the phone.

"You know, Babe, we need to do this more often. It's nice spending the day in bed with you." Deon said.

"I know, it's been wonderful, but I have to get up in a little while, and go spend some time with Ray-Ja."

"I'll come with you, if that's alright?" Deon said.

"Ok, I know he'll be happy to see you, and, you know, Momma would like to see you, too. She asks about you all the time."

"What's in there to eat.., I do believe I've worked up an appetite." Deon asked.

"Ummm, let's see...Left over Chinese, ...left over spaghetti; what would you like?"

"Either..., neither..., unless you would like to go out and grab something to eat? Why don't we order in. How about pizza, that way we can stay right here and relax?" He offered, "I'll call it in."

"Just as Deon reached for the phone it rang; he looked at Jackie as if asking permission to answer it.

"Go on," I invited.

"Hello." Deon said.

"Hello?" The gentleman asked. "May I speak to Ms Garrett."

"May I ask who's calling?" Deon asked.

"Tell her it's Michael." Said Michael.

"Uh-huh..." Deon said, handing Jackie the phone and getting out of the bed.

"Who is it?" I whispered, reaching for the phone.

"Michael." Deon said, pausing at the bedroom door.

"Michael? Why is he calling me...??? Hello..., Michael. What do you want? Why are you calling me!?!"

"Damn, Jackie, is that any way to answer the phone?" Michael scolded.

"Look, I'm not trying to cause a problem... I just thought about you and wanted to see how you were doing..., that's all," Michael said.

"Michael, I would really like for you to stop calling me." I said loud enough for Deon to hear from the bathroom.

"Jackie, I told you that it's not over between us--and that little talk your so-called boyfriend had with me at the repast--let me know just how insecure he really is. Oh..., yeah, was that him that answered the phone, tell him I said 'what's up'," Michael said.

"You know what Michael, I have been trying to stop him from whippin' your ass..., but you are blatantly trying to disrespect him, now! You want to tell Deon, 'what's up?' Why don't you tell him yourself..., here he is... DEON!!!" I yelled! "Michael wants to speak to you!"

Michael disconnected the line before Deon came to answer it.

"Jackie!?! What's going on?" Deon asked, coming, quickly, out of the bathroom.

"Deon, I am finally convinced that Michael is delusional! He really thinks that he and I are getting back together! I don't know what's wrong with him!" I said.

Deon sat on the bed and held me in his arms, "Don't worry about it, Baby. I got this...," Deon assured me. "You still want me to call in for a pizza?"

"No, I just lost my appetite."

"Babe, don't let this thing with Michael upset you. I know he's an old friend and I promise you, I won't kill him," Deon said jokingly.

I just looked at Deon.

"I'm joking," Deon said hugging me, "I'm joking! Look, he's only doing this to upset you. He's trying to abuse the friendship that you to have. I know you've made it perfectly clear to him that you don't want him; but he knows how caring you are and that it would upset you to know that he's still hurting. Don't let him upset you, Baby... Believe me, I made things perfectly clear to him the night that we spoke. He isn't going to try anything... That's why he hung up. Michael ain't no fool... He'll play these stupid games for a while and then he'll stop... Trust me on this..."

"I hope you're right, Babe, because I don't want you two to get into it." I said.

"He don't either..." Deon said laughing. "Gimme me a kiss.... Now..., pepperoni or cheese..." he said picking up the phone.

"Babe..., whatever you want..., is fine with me," I said smiling.

"One slice left you want it Jackie?" Deon asked.

"No, you eat it." Jackie said.

"You sure? "...'Cause for somebody that lost their appetite, I thought four slices was a bit much!" Deon said teasing me.

Punching him, I laughed, "Shut up!" And it wasn't four! It was five!"

"You 'bout ready to head over to your mom's?" Deon asked.

"Oh, yeah..., Deon, Garrett wanted me to remind you, about the playoffs this weekend. Are you playing in this year's tournament?" I asked.

"Yeah..., I need to call Guy to find out what's happening. I'll call him tonight." Deon said as we were leaving.

As we were pulling into the alley behind momma's house, Garrett and Michael where getting into Michael's car.

Deon stopped the car and jumped out."Hey! Garrett, wait up man!" Deon shouted!

"Hey Deon! What's up?" Garrett said, giving Deon some dap!

"Nothing man. What's up with you?" Deon asked.

"Nothing, look..., did Jackie tell you about the games?" Garrett asked, obviously, not sure I'd remembered to tell him.

"Yeah, man, I'm in... I'm in; I'm gonna call Guy this evening and find out what's up." Deon said.

"Yeah, ok, then," Garrett said dapping Deon again. "I'll see you on the court then…"

I walked up to the two of them talking and looked at Michael leaning against his car door.

"Hey, Jackie. How you doing?" Michael asked.

I didn't respond; I just looked at him. Deon followed my glare and put his arm around me.

"What's up, Michael?" Deon said hugging me and smiling.

Garrett noticed the tension, "What's going on?"

"You might want to ask your boy. He seems to be fixated on your sister. For some reason, he can't seem to make him understand that he's not wanted. I know I can make him understand, if it's clarity he's looking for…" Deon replied.

Garrett looked at Michael and then at Deon.

"Garrett man let's go; I got things to do." Michael said.

Deon removed his arm from around me, and started walking towards Michael.

I grabbed his arm to pull him back, as Michael took a step towards us.

They stood there looking at each other.

"Hey, y'all, come on y'all… Be cool," Garrett said.

Momma had walked down to the gate…to the alley, where we were standing. She looked at our faces… "Is everything, ok?" She asked, obviously feeling the tension.

We all answered… Yes…, Yes, Ma'am, everything is fine.

Deon and I walked her back to the house and spent time with her and Ray-Ja. We didn't talk about Michael on the way home.

"What are you going to do about the apartment? Did you call the lady back and tell her that you are not interested anymore?" I inquired.

"No, I haven't had a chance, but I'll call her tomorrow and let her know," Deon replied. "What are going to do about the house?

"Well, actually the night that you stopped by to talk, I was suppose to meet with the realtor. I cancelled but I still have her number if you would like to go see the house with me." I suggested.

"Jackie, do you think we're ready for that kind of move? I mean…, do you really want us to get a house together?" Deon asked.

"Yes. I think we are, why…? Are you having second thoughts?" I asked.

"Babe, that's…, that's a big step, buying a house. I mean…, what's the rush? Can't we talk about this a little more before we jump into something that serious?" Deon asked.

I just took a deep breath and tried to calm myself down by looking at the passing cars in traffic. "Ok, we'll talk about it later." Jackie said reluctantly.

When we got home, Mava Hayes had left another message. I listened to the message twice, hit the delete message button, and went to bed.

Deon came into the bedroom, "She sounds pretty anxious for you to see that house." Deon said undressing.

"I know, she said it's really nice." I said fluffing my pillow and getting comfortable in bed.

Deon sat on the side of the bed with his back to me. He sighed and turned to look at me.

"What?" I asked.

"Nothing," Deon said, and went in to take his shower.

'Another dream differed…,' Jackie thought as she laid there listening to the running water from the shower. By the time Deon emerged from the bathroom, she was fast asleep.

"Jackie…! Jackie! Wake up!" Deon shook me.

"What? What is it, Deon? It's 3:00 in the morning. What's wrong?" I asked half awake

"Jackie, do you want to get married?" Deon asked.

"Yeah, Deon….I don't care," I said, yawning and dozing back off to sleep.

Chapter 38

"Deon were you talking in your sleep last night?" I asked as we were getting dressed for work.

"Uuh... No, why do you ask?" Deon asked, with a puzzled look on his face.

"Oh, I..um..., was just asking..." I was looking at him, "I thought I heard you say something last night..., but I must have been dreaming."

"Naw..., I wasn't talking; what were you dreaming about?" He asked.

"Uh..., oh, nothing," I said jokingly, "I just thought that I heard you talking, that's all. It seemed so real. Um..., strange."

"Look. Babe, I'll talk to you tonight... I gotta go or I'll be late for work." Deon said.

"Ok, have a good day, Baby? I'll see you tonight. Bye." I said, as he went out the door.

"Leslie," I said, when they were seated at lunch. "I need to tell you something."

"What's the matter?" Leslie asked uninterested.

"Leslie, you know, Deon and I made up."

"I knew you would." Leslie pronounced, sarcastically.

"Ok, what's wrong with you?" I asked, "Is that all you have to say? No five minute speech..., no fifty questions...? What's wrong with you, today?"

"Nothing!" Leslie said angrily, "Does every conversation have to be about *you*, Jackie? Did you ever think that maybe the sun would still come up, and the moon would still shine if, we didn't talk about you and your problems for just one day?" She said with an attitude.

"Ok, Leslie...? What the hell is wrong with you, today? Aunt Flo visiting you or something...? You've been in a funky mood all day! I heard you yelling at poor Carolyn about one of her clients this morning. What the hell is wrong with you!" I asked her, not intimidated, in the least, by her unearned diatribe.

"I'll tell you what's wrong Jackie!" Aunt Flo, is not visiting! "As a matter of fact, she hasn't visited for two months, now. Get the picture!" Can you figure it out, or do I need to spell it out for you?" Leslie said.

"Les," I said reaching across the table to take her hand, "Are you pregnant? ...Are you sure?"

Leslie leaned back and exhaled, "I think so, Jackie. Hey..., I'm sorry for snapping at you, Hell..., it ain't yo baby!" Leslie said, trying to make a joke of the situation. "God, I feel so stupid, Jackie. A baby is the last thing I need in my life right now. Hell..., I'm barely making ends meet as it is, just raising Robert." Leslie said.

"Have you told Jamal?" I asked.

"What makes you think it's Jamal's baby?" Leslie asked, with a straight, serious face.

"I...I...just assumed..." I stammered.

Leslie fell out laughing, "No..., I haven't told him.....yet." Leslie, finally, responded.

"Leslie! Stop playing! What are you going to do?"

"Girl, I don't know..., I think I am... but, I'm scared to take a test to even confirm it. Jamal is gonna hit the ceiling! Jackie, I am not going to have another baby without being married. That's just trifling and my momma brought me up better than that. I mean one mistake is bad enough...I mean..., it's not that I don't love Robert... you know... what I mean? I just can't." Leslie said fighting back tears.

"Look, before you get yourself all worked up; let's find out for sure." I said, trying to sooth her at least a little, but understanding exactly what she was saying.

"Leslie, I will support you in whatever you want to do, but if you are pregnant, I think, you should let Jamal know…, before you decide to do anything."

"It was good, while it lasted," Leslie said under her breath….

"What was good?"

"My relationship with Jamal." Leslie said sadly.

"This doesn't mean that it's over… What kind of person do you think Jamal is…? He loves you, and you know he does." I said.

"Yeah…, you ever seen love run…?" Watch Jamal, when I tell him that he gonna be a daddy!" Leslie placed her tip on the table and got ready to leave.

"I think you're underestimating him. He's not like Bobby. Jamal loves you and I know you love him, too. You just need to confirm this thing…, and take it from there." I stood up and gave her a hug, "It's gonna be alright, Les."

"Jackie, I haven't slept in over a week, worrying about this. Jamal thinks I'm PMSing."

"Well…, let's just hope he's right." I joked.

"Love you, Jackie…;" Leslie said, looking ashamed at her outburst, earlier.

"Even if the sun doesn't rise and the moon don't shine……" I quoted.

"Shut-up and don't you tell nobody…, you hear me!?? Not even Deon!" Leslie said.

"I promise, Leslie…, not even Deon." I swore, as I raised my right hand.

"Now. What was it you wanted to tell me, before I bared my soul to you?" Leslie asked.

"Huh…, Oh! I thought I heard Deon propose to me last night." I said, narrowing my eyes and slowly shaking my head, from side-to-side.

Leslie stopped dead in her tracks… "What..? What do you mean you *'thought'* he proposed? I mean…, was it during the throes of passion--which probaby doesn't count--, or while water was running, or was he yelling over the roar of a passing airplane…??

What was goin' on at the time? What do you mean, you thought?" Leslie interrogated me.

"You know, Les, now that I think about it...; I'm sure I was dreaming."

Leslie just stood there looking at me as if I had lost my mind.

"You know how *I know* I was dreaming?" I said, thinking it through.

"How?" Leslie asked, slowly walking back towards the building.

Now, I stopped in my tracks, "Because..., no one, in their right mind, would wake up in the middle of the night and propose to someone. That's how! It was just a silly dream. Pizza always, either, gives me heartburn..., or makes me have strange dreams."

Chapter 39

"Jackie…, this is Gail. I would like to invite you and Deon over for dinner next Saturday. If you can make it; give me a call and let me know. Love you. Talk to you later."

"Deon.., Gail, has invited us over for dinner next weekend, wanna go?"

"Yeah, that's fine. Oh…, wait! The tournament is that weekend, and we play as long as we keep winning. The last game might not be over until eight or nine… What time did she want us to come over?"

"I'm not sure; I'll call her tomorrow and find out." I told him.

As it turned out dinner at Gail's was not the same night as the tournament. Deon's team played four games and won them all.

Since I had to call Gail back to confirm the dinner date, I took the liberty of inviting them out to see my 'Baby' play. Larry was very impressed with Deon's skill on the court and they acted as if they had been friends longer than Gail and I, at dinner. Men and sports……

We all talked about old times and how much fun is was growing up in D.C. Larry discovered that he had been to several games in the neighborhood where Deon had played. As I was helping Gail to clear away the dishes she smiled at me.

"What?" I asked.

"Jackie; he is so nice! I am so happy for you." Gail said.

"I know, right, and obviously he has passed Larry's approval." I said laughing.

"Girl, they act like they have been knowing each other for years." Gail said.

"I know."

We looked at Larry and Deon trying to out lie each other in the other room.

"Ok, now, tell me all about him." She said.

"Gail, I never thought I would meet someone that I am so compatible with. I mean he is so sweet, and he loves Ray-Ja." I said.

"I can tell that you're happy." She smiled for my happiness.

"I am, Gail, and you know what? Deon asked me to marry him.., I thought I was dreaming a few nights ago, but I couldn't have been…, but I'm afraid to ask him about it."

"Whoa...! What…? He proposed? Are you kidding?" Gail said excited.

"I'm not going to say anything, but…, I know that I wasn't dreaming.." I said, remembering…

"Jackie, are you really ready to take that step with Deon?"

"I think so. I really love him, Gail, and if he asked me, I mean… if he actually asked me…, when I'm really positive that it's a proposal… I'll say, yes, in a heartbeat."

"Ok…, Jackie, wait a minute, now, I just met this man, and, I must say that I am impressed with him, too…, but what's up with him. I mean, has he ever been married? Any kids? Any…, baby-momma drama?" Gail asked.

"No, he has never been married; he does have a son, Deonte', he's a little younger than Ray-Ja; He has an 'ex', but, she was only a girlfriend-- not a wife." I answered her concerns, in order.

"Uumm…, sometimes they can be worst that an ex-wife." Gail said.

"Well, I've met her and she is a piece of work; but not a threat."

"Look, we'd better get back in there. Deon will know that you're in here grilling me about him and, honestly, I know that he would rather you ask him anything you want to know. He's cool like that." I said.

"Trust. I'm sure Larry has already grilled him about you--and his intentions." Gail said, "You know how protective he is about you."

"I know he is and I really appreciate that. But Momma has already beat, him to the punch, and if Deon passed her test, he'll pass Larry's with flying colors," I said.

"I know you telling the truth, Ms. Garrett ain't no joke," Gail said leading me back into the den where Larry and Deon were bonding.

We spent the rest of the evening enjoying each others company and discussing Gail and Larry's wedding plans. They had decided on a June wedding and that didn't give us much time; June was less than six months away.

As we were saying our goodnights, Larry gave me a hug. "He's cool, Jackie, I think you got a winner this time."

I smiled and hugged Larry, again. He was so over-protective of me.

Larry and Gail were there for me when Reggie and I broke up. Since then, he has been like a big brother to me. I kissed Gail on the cheek and promised to call her next week so that we could finalize the wedding plans. Deon and I headed home.

In the car, Deon asked, "Well, did I pass?"

"Pass what?" I asked smiling.

"You know what?" Deon said, "*The, 'is he good enough for her test...'" test.*"

I started laughing.

"Don't tell me that you and Gail weren't talking about me in the kitchen." Deon said smiling.

"What?" Deon, I think you must be paranoid or something..., wasn't nobody talking about you." I said laughing.

"Uh, huh, ok, I'm paranoid...." Deon said.

"Honestly, I didn't think nothin' about you and Gail talking in the kitchen, until Larry said that Gail was in there grilling you about me." Deon laughed.

"What! Larry, said what? Just wait..., I'm gonna tell Gail that he threw us under the bus. But, yeah..., you passed, with flying colors Deon, they both like you." I said.

Chapter 40

The next few weeks were uneventful... Deon and I were settling back into a routine. He and Larry had become friends and talked almost as much as Gail and I did. I didn't think it could be accomplished in such a short amount of time, but the wedding plans were coming together nicely.

I had just hung up from speaking with Gail, and looked over at Deon.

"You really are happy for them, aren't you?" Deon asked smiling at me.

"Of course!" I replied, "Aren't you?"

"Yeah…, Gail is lucky to have you for a friend."

She and I have been friends for so long. And I am so happy for her and maybe one day she can help me to…uh… Uum…., we've always been there for one another." I said looking embarrassed.. at my almost slip of the tongue.

"She can help you… plan your wedding? Is that what you were going to say, Jackie?" Deon asked, softly.

"Look, Deon I know…, I know… this is not a comfortable subject for you…." I started saying....

"It seems to make you more uncomfortable than it makes me," He said.

"You know that's only because of what you told me, that your friend told you about me when we first started dating. I don't want you to think that I'm trying to trap or trick you, or anybody else into getting married." I said, hoping he understood my convoluted response.

"It seems a lot of folks are worrying about other folks tricking em' into getting married these days." Deon said, understanding me and answering in the same manner.

"You know what I mean."

"Yeah, I know what you mean...," Deon said, then, "Oh, I forgot to tell you that Leslie called when you were gone to the store."

"Ok, I'd better call her back." I said reaching for the phone.

Deon reached over, took the phone out of my hand, and kissed me, passionately.

"What was that for?"

"'Cause I love you..." Deon said.

"I love you, too, Deon." I said, "Now go away, so that I can call Leslie." Jackie said playfully.

"Leslie? Hi. It's me... You called? What's wrong?"

"I told him... I told Jamal." Leslie said.

"Did you find out..., for sure?"

"I took a home pregnancy test and it was positive, I called you but Deon said that you had gone to the store." Leslie said.

"Yeah I know, he just gave me the message. Leslie, what did he say?" I asked.

"Well, at first he just looked at me..., and then he smiled..., and then.... he hugged me. Jackie, I just knew that it was a goodbye hug, but when he let me go, he said that he had a feeling that I was pregnant, because he has been sick for the past week." Leslie said laughing.

"Sooo, is he ok with it?" I asked.

"Jackie, he's happy about it! He's trying to talk me into... keeping it. He is really excited about the idea of being a daddy." Leslie said.

"Sooo, what are you going to do?"

"Jackie..., he asked me to marry him!" Leslie said, sounding surprised.

"What? Oh, my God, Leslie. That's wonderful! I mean..., do you want to marry him?"

"I told him that I would think about it."

"Leslie what is there to think about...? You two love each other, and you're going to have a baby. What's to think about?" I asked.

"I'm just wondering if he would have asked me to marry him if I wasn't pregnant. I'll always wonder about that if I say yes. I don't want him to feel like I forced him into marrying me, because I was carrying his child," Leslie said.

"You're not going to believe this..., but Deon and I just had that very same conversation.... Look..., I'm not going to voice my opinion, one way or the other, Leslie, just know that what ever you decide that I will support you." I said.

"I know that, Jackie, and thanks for always... being there for me. I don't know what I'd do if I didn't have you to bounce things off of. I think Jamal and I will have to take this thing a day at a time, who knows...Maybe...I'll change my mind." Leslie said.

"I think he would have asked you to marry him, anyway Les..."

"You know Jackie, in my heart I think so, too. I really love him; but I'm so confused right now, I don't know which way is up. I really didn't expect any of this..."

"Well, like you said, take your time..., think it through..., and see what happens."

"Ok. Look. I'll see you Monday. Maybe we can talk about it some more over lunch or something," she said.

"Ok, Leslie, and look, if you need to talk again before then; call me, ok?"

"Ok, Jackie, goodnight... and tell Deon I said thanks."

"Ok, I will.... Goodnight." I said, a little confused.

I sat there thinking about Leslie's and my conversation. I then realized that Deon had gone to bed. When I went into the bedroom, he looked up at me.

"Leslie wanted me to tell you thanks." I said as I started to undress for bed. "What's she thanking you for?"

"Oh, when she called; she sounded upset, so I asked her what was wrong, and she told me what she was going through. I think that she and Jamal will work it out..." Deon said fluffing his pillow and yawning.

"You know, Deon, I think that it's pretty incredible that she was comfortable enough with you to talk about what's going on. Especially, since she swore me to secrecy."

"Yeah well, I have that effect on some people." He bragged.

"I know what effect you have on me…" I said sliding into bed beside Deon.

"I already know, but I love they way you show me." Deon said.

The next morning Deon and I got up and dressed, to go pick up Ray-Ja. Momma had insisted on keeping him Friday night.

"You know Ray-Ja has a million things on his Christmas list." I told Deon.

"Really, what does he want?" Deon asked.

"You name it, and he has it on his list." I said laughing.

"Well before we pick him up, I need to make a stop; it will only take a few minutes, is that ok?" Deon asked.

"Yeah, Sure…, where do you need to go?"

"You'll see." Deon said.

We drove for another twenty minutes or so, and stopped in front of a very nice house. Deon pulled into the driveway and left the engine running. He turned to me, "I'll be right back." He said, and got out of the car. I watched him walk up to the door and knock. One of my favorite songs came on the radio. I turned it up; when I looked back at the door Deon wasn't there.

I sat there listening to the radio until Deon returned. He got in and apologized for taking so long.

"That's ok, you were only gone for a few minutes," I said. "Who lives here? I really like the way this house. I always imagined a having a house like this."

Deon turned the engine off and turned to look at me.

"What's wrong?"

"Nothing is wrong…," Deon said.

"Why did you turn the car off? What's going on?"

Deon reached for my hand…"Baby, I've been thinking about what I could get you for Christmas, and I know it's a little early, but I hope you won't mind, getting your gift a little early.

"Deon, what are you talking about?"

Deon turned my hand over and placed a key in it.

"What is this? I asked.

"It's yours..." Deon said.

"Uhh...,What...? What's mine?" I asked him.

Deon smiled... and looked at the house.

I looked at Deon.... and then at the house.

"Deon! What are you saying?"

"The house, Jackie, it's yours." He said.

"What!.. Deon...! Oh My God! You bought a house!" I screamed.

"Well..., it's not completely paid for but...."

"Oh My God!" I said jumping out of the car. "You bought a house! OH, MY GOD!!"

"Merry Christmas, Baby! I hope you like it!" Deon said.

Just then, a very attractive lady exited the house and walked over to me.

"Ms Garrett..., finally, we meet. I'm Marva Hayes!" She introduced herrsself.

"Miss Hayes," I said hugging her. "How... How..., did you two do this?"

"Well, really it was Mr. Davis' idea. Miss Hayes explained, "He called me about three weeks ago and I told him about the property that I wanted to show you, based on what you were looking for, and well...you know the rest. Would you like to see your new home?"

"Yes! OH MY GOD!... I mean... Can I?!" I asked beaming.

Both, Miss Hayes and Deon laughed.

"It's everything I always wanted." Jackie said hugging Deon, with tears streaming down her face.

After viewing everything possible, in and around the house, Miss Hayes wished us well and said good bye.

Deon walked into the kitchen where I was standing--still in shock--and hugged me from behind.

"I hoped you would like it." Deon said, softly in my ear.

"I love it! I love it, and I love you. But how did you do this? I mean I know that you contacted Miss Hayes but, Deon this must have been very expensive." I said.

"Well…, the down payment wasn't so bad and the payments are within my means, but most importantly… you wanted it." Deon said.

" Oh, Deon.., I can't, I can't, let you buy me a house. I mean, I…I can't let you do this." Jackie said crying and turning to face him.

"Look, Jackie…, this house, is in your name…and your name…, only. I just did the grunt work for you, and took care of the down payment." He said.

I was crying so hard, I couldn't speak.

"Baby, it's what you wanted, isn't it?" Deon asked, tenderly.

"Yes, Yes…, Deon I could not have picked out anything better. I love it, I'm just…I don't know what to say."

"Well, maybe now you can answer my question…" Deon said.

I attempted to wipe away the tears that continued to flow.

"Wha…, what, question?"

"The one I asked you a few weeks ago." Deon said.

I just stood there…, trying to remember when Deon had asked me something that I had not answered…Deon just stood there waiting……

"Babe…, what did you ask me?"

"Ok…, maybe if I do it this way…," Deon said dropping down on one knee.

I looked down at Deon as he took my hand in his… "Jackie Garrett, will you marry me?"

I was crying so hard, I could hardly answer…"Yes…, Yes…, Yes, Deon, I will marry you!"

Deon stood up, walked over to the cabinet and picked up a small velvet box. He returned and handed it to me. I opened the box to reveal a two-carat diamond engagement ring. Deon removed it from the box…and placed it on my finger.

I was blinded by tears. "Deon, this is so beautiful…, I love you!"

Deon took me in his arms and kissed me, passionately.

'I thought it was a dream,' I said, under my breath, while looking at my hand.

The doorbell rang and snapped me out of my stupor.

"Is that the doorbell…? Is someone at 'our' door?" I asked wiping away tears.

"Sounds like it…, you wanna get the door?" Deon asked.

I tried, once again, to wipe away the tears as I opened the door.

Standing there…was Ray-Ja… and behind him…all of the rest of my family, including Gail, Larry, Leslie, and Jamal!

They were holding a banner that, simply, read…, "WE'RE IN IT FOR LIFE!"

CC/jad091600